The EOS

The End of Society

By Doyle Sinclair

Reality is plastic and the plastic is melting

Barcentor Books

THIS BOOK IS DEDICATED TO THOSE WHO WILL
NEVER GIVE UP ON THEIR DREAMS AND THOSE
WHO WILL NEVER BOW DOWN TO THE IRON
HEEL OF SOFT TYRANNY

CONTENTS

PART ONE - Normalcy Bias

What you don't know can hurt you.

We may never know what hit us

June 2017, in a Dallas Texas suburb -

Gerald King shook his head as Wendy told him about her

shopping experience at the grocery store. "So the shelves were actually

bare? That's hard to believe!"

"Well, they weren't completely bare, but here, look at this," she

pulled out her cell phone and handed it to him, "see, I took pictures." She

thumbed on the pictures application and handed it to him. Gerald flipped

through the seven or eight pictures she'd taken and then handed the phone

back to her.

"Well, that store has been going downhill for the past few months,

maybe it's just time to start going over to the Kroger or the Albertson's, I know it's a further drive, but hey, it's looks like that place is about to go under."

"Yeah," Wendy agreed, "I guess I'll have to do that, but both of those places have higher prices. Of course, if Pennington's is going under, I won't really have a choice."

Gerald sighed as they began their dinner, "I had a strange experience on the way home today too."

"Yeah, what happened?"

"Well, II stopped to get gas at the Racetrack, because this morning I'd seen that the gas gauge was getting low, and the price was one ninety-one, which is the lowest I've seen it in a month, so I pulled in there, and every pump had one of those yellow plastic shrouds on the pump handle, so I was about to go down the street but then I saw and employee pulling those shrouds off, and I pulled on in, and then I saw that electronic sign they have showing the price change, just as they were turning all the pumps back on, and the price had gone up over seventy-five cents a gallon!"

"Seventy-five cents in one jump? That's completely outrageous!"

"Yeah, tell me about it!" Gerald shook his head, "then I got to talking to the man in front of me, and he said that they'd shut down all the pumps just to change the price, and then turned them back on."

"That's the craziest thing I've ever heard. I know a few years ago it got up to three-sixty-five or whatever, but I've never heard of it jumping that fast in one day!"

"It's fucking OPEC, that's all. They're getting greedy."

Mid-August 2017 Dallas Texas -

"We've got to do something, we can't go one like this." Wendy said.

"I'm doing everything I can honey, the home office just won't let me work from home."

"And you've sent out how many resumes?"

Gerald shook his head, "Hundreds. You've seen how many responses I've gotten. Four, and every one of them want someone with a vehicle. But we can't afford the gas for me to do outside sales, travelling all over the state. Not with gas prices the way they are. Not at six-sixty a gallon. Jeez."

Wendy put her elbows on the table and put her head in her hands, "and the grocery store is getting worse by the day. I haven't seen any produce worth buying in two weeks now, and almost all the canned vegetables are gone. It's scary."

Gerald shook his head, "I wish I knew what the hell was going on. Grocery stores emptying out, gas stations out of gas and gas when it's available at almost five bucks a gallon. This is nuts!"

Wendy patted his hand. "You want another peanut butter sandwich?"

"No, I can't stomach another one of those. I hope I never see another peanut butter sandwich as long as I live, but the way things are going, I'll have to start liking them more, or prepare to become skinny again." He said ruefully.

"Yeah, I guess that's one upside to all this, we get free diet plans that actually work. I've lost sixteen pounds since all this started."

"I think I'm going to go take a walk around the neighborhood. If I see anyone I know, I'll ask them if they've heard anything about the gas and grocery stores situations. You want to tag along with me?"

She shook her head, "Nah, I think I'll watch some TV, see if any of the news stations are reporting anything new. You'd think that the government would at least tell us *what* is *really* going on."

"Yeah," Gerald smirked, "instead of the same old 'hang in there, things are getting better starting next week! Funny how next week never seems to roll around though."

"Yeah, I can't believe it. It's as if they made a video and play it over and over, same old thing every week."

"It is the same video, it's been proven. I saw that YouTube video showing how it was proven that's it's one video, with four different versions of it, and they change the view of the reporters in the room, to make it look different, but if you look at the slowed down video, you can see that the audio is incorrectly synced to their actual speech. And the newspapers too, running the same crap from the Department of Homeland Security, saying that the gas situation is OPEC and the food situation is due to El Nino and crops that were destroyed last year, blah blah blah. It's just moronic for anyone to believe all that garbage."

Wendy nodded, "But why would our own government lie to us? Why won't they tell us what the hell is really going on? Stephen, at the office, says he thinks the gasoline and food thing is all tied into some crazy terrorist act that the government is hiding from us!"

"But 9/11 wasn't hidden from us, and neither was twenty other terrorist acts over the past twenty years. Why would they hide something now? I'm sorry, but that just doesn't make sense."

"I know, I know, but what else could it be?" Wendy asked, "and why hasn't the media figured it out? The government may control a lot of things in this country, but they control the media, not all of them anyway. Maybe the big outlets, but not all of them. That's the part I just don't get."

"I know. I've never seen such a thing in my life."

"Well honey, enjoy your walk. I'm going to watch TV."

#   #   #   #   #

Gerald walked east from his house and made his way towards the old downtown area, a town square area that had been built up to look antiquated and give the appearance of a town square from the 1800's. The area was full of antique shops, specialty clothing stores, ice cream parlors and an old-fashioned movie house. Gerald could see that the area was full of people milling about and talking in groups. The square had been closed to auto traffic for years and the centerpiece of the square was a huge water fountain in the middle of the roundabout. He could smell barbecue and his mouth watered and his stomach growled.

He walked leisurely up near a group of men on the grassy area that surrounded the water fountain, hoping to be able to overhear some of what they were saying without appearing to be eavesdropping on them. Before he could turn his back to them and pretend to be standing idly nearby though, one of the men caught his eye and waved him into their group.

"Hey bud!" a man reached his hand out to shake, "Come on in and join us!" the man said. He was tall and solidly built, in his fifties and rugged looking, and Gerald guessed that the man worked outdoors. He looked like the outdoorsy, can-do type. "My name is Spencer, and this is Michael, Tim, Stephen and Charles." He said as he pointed out the men as he introduced them.

Gerald nodded at each man in turn, "I'm Gerald" he said, introducing himself to the group.

Spencer nodded, "We're all just discussing the general state of affairs. Guess that's the main topic of the day every day, nowadays."

Gerald nodded, "So what's the consensus? We going to make it out alive or what?"

The young black man named Michael answered, "According to Spencer here," he nodded at the older man, "things are about to get a lot worse."

Gerald looked at the group, they all seemed to be serious, and he looked at Spencer, "You really think so?"

"Oh yes, for sure," he nodded.

"How could you know that? And how could anyone know *anything* for that matter, seeing as how the government and the media aren't telling us anything to begin with?"

"Well," Spencer chuckled, "the media is useless in all this. They've been co-opted by the government. The government is no longer allowing them to say anything about this. Gone are the days when you could expect to get any real reporting from the newspapers and TV media. The government has clamped down on them and they aren't even allowed to say anything except for what they're instructed to say."

"That's hard to believe," Gerald argued, "what about freedom of the press? You're saying that the government is now controlling our media? That's too difficult to swallow, I don't care what anyone says."

"Yeah, well, you keep believing in fairy tales if you want to, but the Department of Homeland Security is now in charge of all media." Spencer said firmly.

"But why?"

"Because of *terrorism*. Terrorism is the great big, new and improved, re-branded *Communism* of this century. Ever since 9/11, the Department of Homeland Security has been amassing power and anytime they want something, or more power, they scream the bugaboo word, *terrorists*, and they're given whatever they want, *or demand*, on the pretext that whatever it is, they need it to *protect* us from terrorism, or from ourselves."

"So, this food and gas thing," Gerald reasoned, "all stems from terrorism?"

"No!" Spencer exclaimed forcefully.

"But you said that they-"

"No, the *government* says that it's terrorist-related. Well, they're not coming right out and *saying* that it is terrorist-related, but the fact that the gas pumps are being shut down and the food supply has dwindled and the Department of Homeland Security seems to be running things makes it pretty clear that it's terrorist related, or at least that's what they are wanting us to *think* anyway. Have you seen the DHS guys at your local supermarket today?"

"What?"

"Yeah," the man named Stephen nodded, "The Albertson's over on Royal Lane had two men stationed on each door this afternoon. Both standing there at the ready with an AR-15 at port arms, glaring at everyone who bothered to walk in there."

"Yep, I saw them over at the Krogers on Forest Ave." Tim nodded.

"What's the purpose of that?" Gerald asked.

"Why, to put down any rioters, or persons who might be considering a smash and grab." Spencer answered.

"Holy shit!" Gerald said, "things are getting that bad? I didn't think there was enough food left to bother trying to steal. Seems like they're probably guarding an empty store."

"They *are*," Spencer said, "for *now*. But if the store suddenly gets a shipment of food and the shelves are re-stocked, people are going to be rushing the stores to stock up, now that they've gone hungry and know what it's like to do without, they're going to freak out when they see enough to fill their pantries again. It'll be mass hysteria."

"We're all what you call Preppers," Tim explained to Gerald, "we all mostly just got started and have a few weeks of supplies and food, but Spencer here is the king of all Preppers."

Gerald asked what a 'prepper' was and Spencer explained, "a prepper is a person who believes a catastrophic disaster or emergency is likely to occur in the future and makes active preparations for it, typically by stockpiling food, ammunition, and other supplies."

Gerald looked skeptical,

"I just wish someone would explain why this is happening? What caused all these problems with fuel and groceries? Was it terrorism, or the Russians or OPEC, or a drought that affected crops? I mean, there's got to be a *reason* that all this is happening, right?

Spencer shook his head, "Son, you're not even asking the right questions. You're focusing on the exact *opposite* things you should be focusing on. You're not even looking in the right *direction*. You need to get your head right, or you'll be completely lost, alone and in the dark."

"Well, that doesn't sound right. Because if we knew what caused all this, we'd know what to do about it, right? If we knew what caused it, we could just fix it, right?"

Spencer shook his head. "No, no, no and no!"

"Why not?"

"Because, Gerald. Why is happened is not important at all. Oh, it may be in twenty, fifty or a hundred years when it's notated in the history books, but right now, you should care less about what caused it and why, and focus on the most important thing!"

"Which is what?"

"The most important thing is not to understand *why* it happened, or even *how* it happened . . . what is more important is to know is that it *did* happen, it *is happening now*, and you should be thinking about *how to survive it*. Nothing. Else. Matters. *Nothing.*"

Gerald looked puzzled.

"Look Gerald, the truth of the matter is that we may never know what caused it. You can't trust the government or media to tell you the truth, so why bother? You waste your energy of trying to figure it all out, you'll die pretty fast. Your one and only overriding goal should be to survive it. Whatever *IT* is, you want to survive it."

Gerald felt as if he were losing a purely theoretical argument, when all he wanted to know was why were they arguing in the first place.

"Look Gerald, it's like this," Spencer explained, "let's say that this region is suddenly hit by a prolonged temperature fluctuation. Let's say that this entire region is covered by snow and ice for twenty years. It hits us, and we're in the middle of it freezing our asses off. Right?"

Gerald nodded.

"Okay, so, you're freezing your ass off, and what do you do. . . start an investigation into weather patterns and start talking to hundreds and hundreds of individuals and gather reams and reams of information so you can figure out why it happened, or do you go looking for a nice warm cave and some cattle to kill and eat and some firewood to burn for heat and so on and so on?"

Gerald nodded, "I'd do the latter."

"Well," Spencer said, "You worrying about why this thing is happening now, is just like that guy in the ice and snow worrying about weather patterns and other nonsense. That guy will freeze to death long before he or anyone else figures it all out. What you want to do now, is not worry about why it happened, but how you are going to survive it! Get me?"

Gerald shrugged in agreement, mostly just to get the man and the others to think that he was as stupid about all this as he was feeling. But he still felt that this was all a temporary thing and all these guys, preppers and doomsayers, would be sitting there with egg on their face in a couple of weeks when this thing all faded away and everything got back to normal.

"Tell him," the man named Charles nodded at Spencer, "what you think will happen next."

Gerald looked at Spencer. All of the men in the group seemed deferential to the older man. Gerald wondered why they all looked up to him.

"Well, Gerald, I think that the next thing we'll see is rationing. Food cards of some sort, and there will definitely be a dollar limit on the amount of groceries one can buy."

"But how can the government arbitrarily decide to institute something like that?"

"Because the Department of Homeland Security can override any law under the guise of national security, and in order to prove it's a measure of national security, all they have to do is say it's terrorist related."

Gerald countered, "But wouldn't they have to prove that it is, actually, terrorist related?"

Spencer shrugged and shook his head, "Normally, but since it is terrorist-related, they can say that it's an issue of top secret security, so they don't have to prove anything. They simply say the word *terrorists* and no one can stop them from doing whatever they want to do. By *Executive Order.* The Department of Homeland Security has really gotten out of control since 9/11 and all they've done is get more and more powerful."

"The Department of Homeland Security doesn't sound like our government at all, it sounds more like Hitler's SS, or Communist Russia's KGB."

"Exactly!" Spencer chuckled and clapped Gerald on the back.

The man named Tim spoke, "So, Gerald, before you came over here, we were all wondering just what has happened to set all of this into motion."

"And?"

"Well," Spencer said, "That's where things get murky."

"No kidding," Charles said.

"You see, Gerald," Spencer explained, "the real kicker is this. We may never know. The government, whatever they're doing or not doing, may never tell us what started all of this."

"But why wouldn't they?"

"For many reasons. Number one, the government itself could be behind it. Or, the government themselves may not even know. Maybe it really is terrorist related. Maybe not. They may be keeping us in the dark because they're afraid that society may break down completely and there'd be chaos in the streets. Maybe they're afraid of being taken over by an angry populace. Maybe there is a solution that is being implemented as we speak and in a week all this will be behind us. There are as many theories are there are people, and the sorry fact of the matter may just be that we might never know what all this is about. We may wake up tomorrow and find that things are back to normal. Who knows?"

"Well, that's a comforting thought." Gerald said sarcastically.

Spencer laughed.

The aroma of wood smoke and barbecue drifted past him again and Gerald looked around to see where it was coming from. Charles saw him looking around for it.

Charles spoke up, "Hey, Spencer, could we give Gerald something to eat?"

Charles looked surprised, "Oh of course! I'm so sorry, Gerald, jeez, where are my manners? I completely forgot to offer you some dinner! Would you like some barbecue?"

Gerald's mouth dropped open in surprise, "Barbecue? Are you kidding?"

Spencer laughed and pointed past their group towards a large barbecue grill on rollers sitting next to two card tables next to a picnic table was piled high with aluminum pans full of food.

"There's our spread, just help yourself!"

Gerald looked at the older man as if he was being pranked, "Are you kidding? Where did all that food come from?"

Spencer laughed, and they walked over to the smoker and the group followed along.

He lifted the lid and pointed at the sausages, chicken breasts and meat patties and he gasped when he saw three large rib eyes. The tables next to the BBQ smoker has tins full of several types of potato salads, BBQ beans, butter rolls, corn on the cob, and cole slaws, and two large jugs of iced tea.

It was an amazing spread.

"Where did all this come from? Gerald asked as he looked at the group.

Spencer laughed, "you boys wait here while I go take a piss, and make sure he fills his plate up."

Spencer walked away and Michael picked up paper plate and handed it to Gerald, and instructed him to *'don't be shy. Just dig in.'*

Gerald started piling food on to his plate and looked up to see several of the guys doing the same, "But where did all this come from?"

Charles laughed, "Spencer is a Mormon."

Gerald gave him a quizzical look. He didn't get it. Maybe it was an inside joke of some sort in this group. Gerald didn't question the remark, he just dug in and ate. And ate and ate.

They chit chatted and made small talk, and ate, and after about 30 minutes Spencer made his way back to the group and they all gathered around the picnic table and several of the guys lit up cigarettes. By this time Gerald was so full he thought he would burst. The amount of food they had laid out was just incredible, and the fact that they just offered it up freely made him wonder what kind of group this was.

"I have some more news." Spencer announced as he sat down.

Everyone perked up.

"My buddy in Oklahoma says that things are no different there than they are here."

Stephen explained for Gerald, "In addition to being a prepper, Spencer is also a hamster."

"A hamster? I don't get it. A few minutes ago you called him a Mormon, and now you're calling him a hamster."

Spencer laughed, "well, first of all, a Hamster is a Ham operator group, we talk daily, and that's how I can get real news from all over the country, and not the filtered political spun bullshit that's on the TV and in the papers. Our network calls each other 'hamsters.'" He paused and took a drag from his cigarette which Gerald realized was a joint.

"The Mormon thing though, is true. I am in fact, a Mormon."

Gerald frowned, "But what does the fact that you're a Mormon have to do with all this food?"

Spencer laughed, "Good question." He winked at the other guys as if he was glad to be letting another person in on their joke, "You see Gerald, one of the tenets of being Mormon is that we have always been taught, hundreds of years now, that as a people, we should always plan for hard times, and one of the ways we are taught to do that is to always keep three to four months of food on hand, just in case. Many Mormons do as I have done, and have stockpiled *three to four years* of food. You see the Church and its members are commanded by the Lord *to be self-reliant and independent.* The twelfth prophet, taught us, *the responsibility for each person's social, emotional, spiritual, physical, or economic well-being rests first upon himself, second upon his family, and third upon the Church if he is a faithful member thereof.*

Also, to *acquire and store a reserve of food and supplies that will sustain life.* As long as I can remember, we've been taught to prepare for the future and to obtain a year's supply of necessities. With events in the world today, it must be considered to be a very serious conviction with which to live your life. We have a saying; *IF YOU ARE PREPARED YOU SHALL NOT FEAR.* "

Gerald replied, "I've never known that about Mormons."

Spencer shrugged, "Well, now you know. And this," he waved his hand towards the BBQ smoker and the tables full of food, "was just a way to give a few friends some respite from the past few weeks, and of course, we also made a new friend, that being yourself!"

Gerald felt his face turn red and he just nodded.

"Okay," Tim interrupted, "so what other news have you got from your buddies?"

Spencer explained more to Gerald, "my buddies that he's referring to are *hamsters*, ham operators across the U S, and the word is this," he paused dramatically and pulled out a regular cigarette, a Kool menthol, and lit it up, "the guys around the country are telling us that what is happening here is happening from shore to shore. The mainstream media has been shut down and the only info that is allowed out regarding the gas and food and any terrorist activity is the info that the government allows them to release. In other words, it is *pure propaganda*. The media outlets have been *encouraged* by the Department of Homeland Security to *comment freely* on Global Warming, El Nino, ISIS and *all things related to Kardashians* and other such ridiculous tripe. They have actually sent out guidelines for media outlets and one of the suggested topics, instead of the food and gas situation is, get this, *Hollywood lifestyles of the rich and famous*, and also articles such as, you'll love this boys, *Ten Ways to Tell if Your Neighbor is a Terrorist in Training*."

"That's the most absurd thing I've ever heard in my life!" Gerald said.

"Yeah, and the kicker is this," Spencer added, "The man who told me this works for one of the major news networks, TV, and if it got out that he released this information, he'd probably be thrown into prison for *terrorist activities*."

"That sounds insane! This is not Communist Russia in the fifties!" Gerald exclaimed.

"Well, it seems to me that it's pretty close to that, what with the D H S running loose like they are." Stephen added.

"True, very true." Tim nodded.

"I just can't believe these things." Gerald said, "how could things change so drastically in a few weeks? One day we're living in a comfortable democracy and then in less than a few weeks and we're living in Communist Russia? It's just not possible. Plus, if this is all true, and I'm not ready to admit that it is, then what is the end game? Why put the clamps on your own populace? That just doesn't make any sense."

"It's all for one thing. Power." Spencer answered.

"But that doesn't make sense either," Gerald argued, "the President of the United States is the most powerful man in the world, and he has that power without having to do these things to the American people."

"Ideology. Power. Money." Michael answered, "or some sort of combination of all three. Plus, you have to realize, that this power grab could be something that's being manipulated by another source. Someone pulling the President's strings."

"Now you're talking about some sort of global conspiracy or something equally as insane and paranoid. I swear, if you start talking about the evils of the Illuminati I'm going to get up and walk away."

Spencer laughed, "You're free to come and go as you please, we will not try to force our beliefs upon you. I personally don't believe in the Illuminati nonsense, and to answer your question, I have no clue who is behind all this, or why. That is the big question that the hamsters are all discussing, and millions of people across the country are wondering the same thing. Right now, all anybody knows is that certain things are happening, and all we can do is see them for the reality that they are happening, and hopefully, sooner rather than later, we'll find out the who, what and why of what it's all about. Maybe we will eventually find out what it's all about. Maybe we'll all die before we know the truth. The fact of the matter right now though, is that things are looking bad, and from what they're saying, things are about to go from bad to grim."

This pronouncement made everyone around the table sit up and lean forward to hear the rest of the news.

"Several things are expected to happen within the next ten days, none of them good I'm afraid." He paused and pulled out another joint and lit it up.

He took a deep hit, and blew it out and looked at Gerald, "I've got Arthritis and this stuff helps with the pain."

"Yeah," Charles laughed, "I've got arthritis too, give me a hit of that!"

Everyone laughed.

"Believe me son, you don't want this stuff bad enough to put up with Arthritis just to get high every now and then."

"So *you* say!"

They all laughed again.

"Okay, well here's the unofficial word. Sometime in the next few days a lot of things are expected to start happening. Number one, the government is probably going to pull the switch of mass communications."

Stephen whistled, "All communications?"

Spencer nodded, "The hamsters have several independent sources saying that the first thing to go is going to be social media. Facebook, Twitter, YouTube, any source on the internet, like Yahoo, MSN, whatever that isn't following the DHS guidelines on what is permissible to put out there for mass consumption is going to be shut down."

"Holy crap." Tim said, "that is some draconian shit!"

"Can that be done?" Gerald asked.

Several of the guys nodded, "Oh yeah, it can be done. Not a problem." Stephen said.

"You sure of that? Isn't the internet a free and open source?" Gerald asked.

"I'm an IT guy. I know how they could do it." Stephen nodded, "Believe me, there are back doors they can get in. They control the on off switch as it were."

"Next item is this, and it's a small ray of hope," Spencer continued, "and that's that the Anonymous collective has declared war upon our government and they are claiming that they will wage full out war on the powers that be if these *draconian measures* as Tim called them, are attempted."

Everyone smiled at that, and Gerald spoke up, "wait a minute, do you guys really believe that a bunch of random hacker kids around the country, who aren't even organized into an actual group that has never even met each other, is going to save the country? That's a load of ridiculous Hollywood movie crapola!"

"Not so fast there, Gerald," Stephen said, "they have always claimed to be a loose-knit organization with no real physical presence as a group, but I've always thought that was bullshit. I think they're far too organized to be as unorganized as they claimed to be. I never bought it. I think that they can make a real dent in things if they try to do so."

Gerald wasn't convinced, but he wasn't going to argue computers with an IT pro, but he wasn't going to believe fairy tales about a bunch of hacker kids either.

Spencer continued, "after they shut down the social media, they're going to start with the big media, and everything will be shut down except for state sponsored media content. The end game will be to shut down the internet for everyone except the government and those who are going to be wealthy enough to afford it."

"In other words," Tim added, "fuck all of us."

Spencer nodded, "Exactly."

Gerald shook his head, "I'm sorry guys, but I'm just not buying into all this. It's just too far-fetched and crazy. This all sounds like illuminati-conspiracy-theorist crap to me."

"And what was the price of a gallon of gas five weeks ago, Gerald?" Charles asked.

"Yeah," Stephen added, "and why are the grocery stores shelves empty?"

Gerald started to say something smart ass, but he drew his lips tight and said nothing, but shook his head.

Spencer continued his tale of woe, "within the next three days, we can expect to hear announcements from all of the utility companies announcing 'service cutbacks' in most major metropolitan areas. Water and electricity will be available in the evenings for a few hours only. Best stock up on candles and flashlight batteries."

"Major metropolitan areas *my ass*" Tim said, "it'll be nationwide. Why would they expect us to believe that if you're out in the boonies that things will be different?"

They all nodded at that logic. Gerald said nothing. He was beginning to believe that these guys were nothing more than a group of conspiracy buffs airing out their end of the world fantasies. All of these things couldn't possibly happen this fast and as they were saying. The country would collapse. The gas and food shortages were just aberrations, that's all. He just couldn't believe otherwise. This was the United States of America. This was the greatest country on the face of the earth. We have the best technology, the greatest education, and the strongest people in the world. We will not allow our own citizens to starve and be unable to move about freely and will *absofuckinglutely* will NOT take away our freedom of the press and freedom of speech. This country was founded on these principles, and the things these guys were talking about might could happen, in Russia, or North Korea, but never in the United States of America. Never. Not in a million years.

Spencer continued, "some sort of system will be instituted for allowing citizens to get their groceries and gasoline on certain days only, and here's another kicker, a nationwide system will be instituted to allow government officials to instantly identify citizens. A bar code of some sort is envisioned, like a tattoo or something on the back of the hand."

"Jesus Christ! Seriously?" Tim yelled.

"The hamsters say that this ID system is something that is being discussed, and as of yet, there are no plans to roll it out just yet. But there is something else that sounds very draconian, thank you Tim for what seems to be the word of the day."

Tim nodded and exchanged a high five with Charles.

"The D H S is expected to announce that there will be FEMA camps set up in all major cities to help citizens with *the crisis*. They neglect oddly enough though, to state just exactly what the crisis is."

"Dude," Tim interjected, "that's just like that movie Red Dawn."

Charles nodded and then laughed, *"Go Wolverines!"*

Now Gerald was sure that these were a bunch of guys who were like junior high school kids talking about the latest Michael Bay action movie, talking like it could really happen. He was really about to tell them that they were being immature and stupid, that none of the events they were discussing could actually happen. He held his tongue though, they'd just fed him the best meal he'd had in weeks, and that was something that he'd been unable to do for himself, so he would listen politely and after he walked away tonight he'd never have to see any of them again.

"The next thing on the list is that our wonderful government is expected to announce that there will be nighttime curfews enforced nationwide. This will be done under the guise that the government cannot spare the resources to protect citizens from ISIS and other terrorist organizations if we are just freely walking the streets. In other words, it's for our own good, because they are protecting us."

"They can kiss my ass with their fucking curfew bullshit." Tim said.

"Also, a nationwide program called 'Protect our Streets' or some such thing will be announced, and this program will offer all citizens a chance to legally hand over all privately owned firearms, and after a period of sixty days, anyone caught owning a firearm will be considered 'a domestic terrorist'."

"Wow. That's just amazing. They are really going full out, balls to the wall on this." Stephen said.

"Yeah," Michael added, "I guess the Constitution can just kiss my ass huh?"

"Yeah, congratulations people," Tim said, "it's now official, we live in a police state."

Spencer sighed, "hopefully boys, these things will be mollified or pulled back at the last minute, or maybe once they announce these things, people across the country will wake up and say hell no and rebel, but I'm kind of thinking that the American people will just go along with it like so many sheep."

"Of course!" Michael said as he shook his head sadly.

Spencer continued, "also there will eventually be a complete cessation of email and most, if not all internet services. The hamsters are also saying that cell phone towers across the country are being taken down. Basically, the government, boys, wants to control, as much as possible, our communications and interactions with each other."

"Big brother is here." Stephen announced. Then he added, "Before I forget this, I want to remind everyone of something. If you have one of those smart TV's, you know the ones that can access the internet, they have cameras in them just like your laptops do?"

Everyone nodded. This was something that Gerald definitely knew about because their flat-screen LG that they'd bought at Costco last year was hooked up. They watched Netflix stuff on it all the time.

"Soon as the shit hits the fan, you might want to unplug that thing. They can be used as listening devices and video cams to spy on people right there in their own living rooms."

"Nice. They want to spy on us, and we paid for the cameras and microphones they use to spy on us with!" Tim laughed.

Spencer took another puff on his cigarette and then spoke, "boys, back in 1908, one of the greatest authors of all time, I place him side by side to Mark Twain, Jack London, wrote a book called The Iron Heel. The Iron Heel was a book that George Orwell later used as a blueprint to pen his own novel, Nineteen-eighty-four. The Iron Heel chronicled the rise of an oligarchic tyranny in the United States. I say that, as of this year, his vision is well on its' way to becoming true. These may not be the end times, but they are indeed becoming the *bad times*."

Gerald shook his head slowly, "I just don't believe that all these things could, or will happen. It's just not possible in a country as advanced as ours, and as good as things have been for the past twenty years or so, that these draconian measures could come about. I am just very skeptical that this gas and food thing is anything more than a bizarre one-time event."

Stephen, the IT guy chuckled, "Spencer, what was it you said that kind of thinking is?"

"Normalcy bias," Spencer answered.

"What is that?" Gerald asked.

"Normalcy bias," Spencer explained, "is a mental state that some people revert to when facing a disaster or a new situation. It causes people to underestimate both the possibility of a disaster, or sudden dramatic change and its possible effects. This normalcy bias enables a person's denial to act and they fail to adequately prepare and make preparations for disaster scenarios.

The assumption that people who have a normalcy bias make is that since a disaster has never occurred, that it never *will* occur. This kind of thinking results in an inability of people to cope with a disaster once it does actually occur. People with a normalcy bias have difficulties reacting to something they have not experienced before. People, such as yourself, Gerald, tend to interpret warnings in the most optimistic way possible, seizing on any ambiguities to infer a less serious situation. So, when you say that you can't believe that this would never really happen, when in fact it is happening now, shows that you are reverting in your thinking process to a normalcy bias. This is a very dangerous way to think Gerald, because *your normalcy bias can kill you just as quickly as a rattlesnake.*

Now, the opposite of normalcy bias would be overreaction, or "worst-case thinking" bias, which means that small deviations from normality are dealt with as signaling an impending catastrophe. This worst-case thinking bias is more than likely what you are thinking that we are doing, but you would be wrong. The reason I say that is because we are not just freaking out an going off half-cocked. The things we are talking about are actually happening all around us. Your denial, and your normalcy bias could very well be a fatal mistake to you Gerald, you and your family, your wife and kids if you have any. I hope it doesn't come to that, but the fact remains that you don't have years, or even months to smarten up and do the right thing. In fact, you may not even have weeks or even days left before your normalcy bias kills you. You may have *hours*. Because if you don't do something smart, and quick, it may be too late to recover. I hope that's not the case, but I am a realist who does not suffer from normalcy bias. *Disaster is the new normal, and the quicker you come to terms with that, the better off you'll be.*"

Gerald shook his head, unconvinced. "So, because of your belief that things are about to get bad, and your Mormon beliefs in keeping a pantry of food and supplies ready for emergencies, that you have, did you say *years* of food and supplies stockpiled?"

Spencer nodded, "Yes, I do. Approximately three years of food, supplies, medicine and medical supplies, guns, ammo, gas generators etc. I am my own small city. My family and I are safe and will make it through whatever is coming."

"You must have a large house to be able to store that much stuff." As soon as the words left his mouth, Gerald noticed that Spencer stiffened a little.

"I do, but no one knows where I live."

"Why the big secret?" Gerald asked.

"Because, if the shit hits the fan, and half the people in town know where I live, then I'd have to fight off those who want to take it away from me. The people who didn't prepare, and in three days they're thirsty, starving, cold, and desperate and they come a knocking at my door? Sorry, but if a man didn't take the responsibility to prepare, them why should I suddenly become responsible for him? Any food I put into his mouth takes it out of mine and my wife's. I am generous," he waved over towards the BBQ grill and table full of food, "but I'm not stupid or careless. This little cookout tonight was just a get-together for friends. Most likely, after tonight, you boys won't be seeing much of me. I intend to keep a very low profile. I will be gray man from here on out."

"Gray man?"

"Invisible, inconspicuous, not standing out, unremarkable in appearance. If anyone sees me from this point on, if things get bad, I will be acting like the rest of the populace, appearing hungry and lost. But it will be an act. I will be sly like a fox. No attention will be drawn to me. It's a security precaution. Blend in, get lost, and stay wary."

"So that's just a way of saying that no one knows your address?" Gerald chuckled.

Spencer nodded, completely serious, "allowing someone to know my address at this point could get me killed. It would be like having a target painted on my forehead."

"That sounds very paranoid."

"Being paranoid in these times could be a life-saver, just as normalcy bias could be a death-wish. Remember, if I'm right, my consequences are that I have a couple years' worth of food to go through before it goes bad which is years, however, if you're wrong, it means a death of starvation or worse."

The meeting broke up shortly after that, and after a round of hand-shaking and good-to-met-you's Gerald headed home.

The meeting had brought about some conflicted feelings in Gerald. He was definitely worried about what was happening all around him, but he just could possibly give any reasonable credence to most, if not all, of what he'd heard tonight. It was all too far-fetched, and all those guys sounded like the type of people who call in to those middle of the night a m talk radio shows and talk about how jet contrails are a government conspiracy to poison us all. Conspiracy theorists of the worst sort. Sure, their ringleader, Spencer, may have stockpiled a few years' worth of food and been nice enough to feed everyone a very welcomed meal the likes of which they hadn't seen in weeks if not months, but that didn't mean that all of his crazy conspiracy theories had any credence whatsoever. He may be a nice guy, but underneath it all, he was still a crazy conspiracy-theorist at heart. *Hamsters!*

As he walked home, Gerald began feeling guilty for having eaten the wonderful meal while, at home, sitting on their couch, his wife was worried and hungry. He wished that he'd been ballsy enough to have asked if he could have taken a plate of food home for Wendy. He cursed himself for not having thought of that, and decided that while he would tell her about those guys and what they'd talked about, he wouldn't tell her about how he'd gorged himself on all that food.

#   #   #   #   #

Gerald told Wendy all about the guys and the conversation that they'd had about prepping, and he told her about the hamsters and all of the dire predictions they'd made. He expected her to be as skeptical as he was, but she surprised him.

"Maybe these guys are doing the right thing." She said.

"You really think so?"

She nodded and then stood up and took his hand and led him into the kitchen. She opened the pantry, she waved her hand towards it, "We have about two days of food left, and that's only if we are very careful."

"We'll make the rounds of all the grocery stores tomorrow. We won't stop until we have enough for a week, no matter what we find."

She nodded, took him by the hand and led him into the living room again, and turned on the TV, "Look at this."

The picture came on and Gerald frowned, the picture was of the old Indian Head test pattern that had been used back in the early days of television. He thought that it might have stopped being used in the sixties or maybe as late as the seventies. The picture was just the static test pattern, although he could hear music in the background.

"That's it? Just that old test pattern and that music? What is that song? Sounds familiar."

"That's the Scorpions, No One Like You." Wendy answered, "weird huh?"

Gerald was shocked, "Yeah, and it's just that old test pattern and the Scorpions?"

"No, give it a second, it'll change." She answered, "You'll see. It changes about every minute or ninety seconds or so."

"Changes to what?"

She shivered, "you'll see it in a sec. It's creepy too."

The test pattern went away, and was replaced with a blue screen, similar to the blue screen one would often see on a computer screen when there was a fatal error. The music changed to Neil Diamond's Cracklin Rosie.

"That's Neil Diamond?"

"Yeah, but you haven't seen anything yet, give it a sec and the list will pop up."

"The list?"

She nodded, "There! It's always a few seconds after the blue screen starts."

Gerald read the numbered list.

One - *Communications have temporarily interrupted, for more information please switch to Emergency Channel 2*

Two - *Emergency Curfews are now in effect. Citizens are required to stay in homes after six pm and up to seven am daily.*

Three - *Gasoline use should be monitored. No excess travel. Travel permits required for out of state travel.*

Four - *Internet and telephonic transmissions are reserved for official use only*

Gerald felt as if he'd been punched in the gut. This was real. The word Tim

had used, *draconian*, was right. His stomach clenched and he felt dizzy.

Five - *the Federal Reserve Banking System is currently experiencing higher than*

normal demands for withdrawals. Transactions are hereby suspended for an indefinite

period of time.

Gerald's mouth dropped open. He looked at Wendy, and she nodded.

"When I saw that, I immediately got online and checked our accounts,

and all of them have a big red warning that says, Accounts Frozen until

Further Notice by authority of Banking Regulation number something,

something, something. I don't remember what the actual number was, it

was like thirty digits long. I didn't even try to write it down. This is too

fucking scary, Gerald! What the hell is going on?"

Gerald blinked, he couldn't think of a thing to say. His mind was

spinning.

"As soon as I left the bank's web site, I got this weird page that

popped up on its' own and it read something like, Unauthorized Usage of

Digital Transmission - Service is now Temporarily Suspended by DHS order whatever, whatever and then it went off. The computer works, but there's no internet service."

Gerald shook his head slowly. This was just incomprehensible. How had Spencer and those guys known all this, and he was so totally clueless? He looked back at the blue screen and the list of ten items and kept reading.

Six - *FEMA outpost number six-eighty-one is located on the corner of Spring and Felton street at the site of the old Wal-Mart store. Any citizens needing food coupons must register and have photo taken for ID badges. Grocery purveyors will no longer allow purchases without food coupons.*

Gerald felt as if he were going to throw up.

Seven - *Utility savings services to begin within 48 hours. Utilities available eight hours per day during following hours. Eight AM until Noon and Four PM until Eight PM. Please contact your utility company to ensure that your payments are up to date. Payments hereafter will be your past month billing regardless of actual use.*

"So that means we will be paying the full amount of last month's bill from now on, but we will only get eight hours a day usage?" Gerald asked.

"Yep, that's it. Bullshit, huh? Gerald, *what the fuck is going on?*"

"I don't have a clue."

"And those guys you met at the square, they didn't know either?"

What's causing this?"

He shook his head, "No, they had no clue either. The head guy, their leader, the older man named Spencer, he said that these scenarios were called SHTF, *Shit Hits the Fan* scenarios. He said that it's entirely possible that we may never know or be told what caused these problems. We might just never know. We just have to deal with it and try to survive."

"But surely, the government will tell us what's going on!"

He shook his head, "Not necessarily. Looking at this, I'd say that they are correct, and that's it's highly probable that it is the government that is behind it all."

He looked back at the screen and finished reading the list.

Eight - *All citizens are required to surrender all firearms to local police department within 72 hours or risk immediate mandatory arrest and incarceration. All firearms of .22 caliber or larger are required to be surrendered. All concealed handgun licenses are hereby revoked and invalidated under Department of Homeland Security bill # 2A – X, Domestic Terrorist Act. All citizens are required to immediately comply with this DHS Executive Order. No exceptions.*

Nine - *Domestic terrorism is considered a* **Capital Offense to the Republic.** *The following acts are hereby considered* **acts of domestic terrorism;**

Owning, possessing or use of firearms.

Unauthorized public or private gatherings of four or more persons.

Unauthorized use of communications devices including short wave radio.

Discussion of laws of the Republic for purposes of fostering revolt, unlawfulness or any acts of civil disobedience.

Non-payment of utility bills, water, trash services, electrical etc.

Any and all attempts to construe laws as benefitting a citizen that is contrary to its' original purpose.

Unlawful travel.

Barter, hoarding or attempting to stockpile supplies including; foodstuffs, water, guns, ammunition, medical supplies, communications devices, books of law, written copies of the Constitution of the United States, and verbal declarations of intent to subvert the laws of the Republic, or fostering civil disobedience in any way, shape or form.

Gerald finished reading the list and the screen changed back to the Indian Head test pattern and the music changed to James Gang's Funk #49.

Then the lights went out and they were left in the darkness.

"Well," Gerald said dejectedly, "this sucks, but at least I can take a shower in the dark if I have to."

"Sorry honey, that was next on my list to tell you."

"What?"

"The water pressure is so low, the water just barely dribbles out of the faucets. It might as well be turned off. I checked it several times already. Carol, from across the street? She came by earlier and said that their water pressure was way down, so I checked it then. Apparently, it's the entire neighborhood."

Gerald shook his head in the darkness, "No, it's probably the whole city. Maybe even the entire country. Who knows?"

#   #   #   #   #

They went to bed and shivered in the dark, and finally got up and threw some blankets on the bed and snuggled together under the covers.

The next morning when they woke up the electricity was back on, but the only thing on TV was the Indian Head test pattern and the Nine Rules, and the Classics TV Channel which was showing reruns of The Andy Griffith show, I Dream of Jeannie, and The Honeymooners. Gerald sat at the kitchen table trying to think of something to do, but he didn't want to use any gasoline and there wasn't much to eat, so he sat there and turned everything over and over in his mind. Finally, he decided that he needed to burn off some energy and went out for a walk. He asked Wendy if she wanted to accompany him, but she said that she was going to go across the street and talk to Carol, and try to meet some other women on the street to see if they had any ideas about what was happening.

Gerald was about to set out walking, when he remembered that he and Wendy had bought bicycles two years ago, when they'd planned to start getting back into shape. They'd purchased expensive bicycles, and had ridden them a few times, and then they'd grown tired of them, and like most fads, their interests had been relegated to the attic. He pulled the bicycle down and checked the tires for air. He found a fanny pack that he'd used once when he'd gone camping and opened it. Inside was a small pair of ten power binoculars and two granola protein bars. He strapped the fanny pack around his waist, grabbed a bottle of water from the fridge and put it in the water bottle holder on the frame of the bike, and then set out on his ride.

He immediately headed for the town square, in hopes of seeing some of the guys form yesterday's group there, but was soon disappointed.

He made several laps around the town square area, and then decided to bike over to the FEMA site and see what that looked like. When he got within sight of it he stopped pedaling. He put the kickstand down and parked the bike next to a tree. He unzipped his fanny pack and pulled out the small binoculars and looked through the lenses. The old Wal-Mart was a hotbed of activity. There were perhaps two dozen semi's parked in the parking lot, and at least a hundred men in what looked like National Guard uniforms unloading supplies. The perimeter of the property was ringed by a ten foot tall chain link fence that was topped with circular strands of razor wire.

Gerald felt a sense of dread when he looked at the facility and he knew beyond a shadow of doubt that he would never step one foot on the other side of that fence. Not a chance in hell. He wouldn't allow Wendy anywhere near this place. Whatever they were planning, whoever *they* were, it didn't look friendly at all.

It dawned in him that if he could see them with his binoculars, then they were probably watching him watch them and they were using video cams that could capture his image and be run through simple facial recognition software and it would probably take just a few minutes to know his identity. He looked down at the ground, and then quickly got back on to the bicycle and pedaled away. Now he felt foolish, acting as paranoid as he'd ridiculed the guys in the group last night of being.

He pedaled for almost two hours, eventually finding himself on the outskirts of town on the far side of town opposite where the FEMA camp had been. There was nothing out here except for an old farmhouse that sat smack dab in the middle of a fifty acre parcel of land. He'd once heard that the owner had hit it big in the dot com expansion years ago, and had cashed out by selling his company for fifty million or so. Apparently he was an eccentric who raised sheep, ostriches and bees for hobbies and not much was known about the man other than he was *not a people person.*

Gerald was about to turn around and cycle back home when he saw movement in the tree line opposite the property from where he was sitting. He pulled out the binoculars and focused in on the movement. He turned the focus knob and got a surprise when he did so. The man was walking across the field towards the farmhouse in the center of the property, and he was carrying what appeared to be a large dog across his shoulders. Gerald watched the man making his way towards the house, which was actually a sprawling group of six or eight buildings. There were two houses, and several barns and what looked like detached garages that must be storage for farm equipment, Gerald guessed. He glassed the entire property, and then focused in again on the man carrying the big dog. He realized then that the man wasn't carrying a dog, but a deer.

Then, just before the man walked out of view next to a building,

Gerald realized that the man was Spencer. The old Hamster, the prepper, that he'd met the previous evening!

So, just like that, Gerald had stumbled across the man's hideout.

Gerald turned around and began cycling back towards town, wondering what he could do with this new information.

#   #   #   #   #

Two days later, Gerald and Wendy ate the last of their food. Gerald had done everything he could do to scare Wendy out of the idea that it would be a good idea to go to the FEMA site and register for food coupons. He told her that anyone who got into that place stood a good chance of never coming out again. He thought it was a prison that was carefully disguised to seem like a friendly place to go and get your handouts from the government. He recalled the movie Red Dawn and that scene where the boys saw their father penned inside a similar fence and he figured it might not be as dramatic as what the movie made it out to be, but he didn't really want to find out either. Just the idea of 'registering' for the basic necessities, like food and water made him angry. What the hell was going on in their country? There was no news being given as to what was happening and why, they were just told, *do this* and *do that*, and *don't do this* and *don't do that*. There were more *don'ts* than there were *do's*. Gerald and Wendy stayed out of sight, staying at home, although Wendy often went across the street to visit with Carol, the widower and another woman, Betty, who also lived on their street.

When they had eaten their last bowl of oatmeal, Gerald told Wendy that he was going out and that he planned to bring home some food tonight, one way or another.

She raised her eyebrows and smiled at him, clearly not believing him, but not saying so, instead she told him that if he got back and she wasn't around, she would be at Carol's house across the street. They kissed and Gerald got onto his bike and pedaled away.

As Gerald was riding down the street that passed by the Town Square he saw two men walking along together, and saw that it was Stephen and Charles from the Prepper group.

He pulled up alongside them and they chit chatted for a few minutes and commented that he was smart to have a bicycle. "It's a good form of transportation," Charles explained, "it takes no fuel and is quiet, which means it's tactically advantageous, so you can get around quietly without anyone knowing you're around."

"I'm surprised you guys don't have them!" Gerald laughed.

"We have motorcycles, but aren't going to use them until we need to bug out of town and go a long distance. Even then, they'll be dangerous because of the noise. Of course, they'll go fast and have the ability to go off road, but still, they're only going to be used to get out quickly and go far." Stephen said.

"What about your buddy Spencer? Does he use a bicycle or a motorcycle? I'd think he would have one or the other being that far out there on Makomis Road out in the middle of nowhere."

"No," Charles said, "as far as I know, he's strictly a walker, but heck, a guy like him, he may have a retrofitted jeep or something elaborate like that. More than likely though, he's going to just dig in and stay where he's at."

They chit-chatted for a few minutes and then Gerald took off riding again. Within two hours he was on the hillside looking down over Spencer's property through his binoculars.

The place was silent, no movement or sound whatsoever. He wondered if the man was inside, or traipsing around in the woods shooting deer.

After two hours of watching the property, Gerald decided that he was going to go down and knock on the door and say hello to Spencer.

He left the bicycle next to the tree and began walking down the long sloping hillside towards the long rambling farm house. He aimed for the middle building, figuring that it was the main domicile.

He reached the front porch, and no one had taken any pot shots at him or accosted him, so he grabbed the knocker and used it to rap on the huge steel door. The door was painted to look like wood, and Gerald wondered if a steel door that looked like wood was a security measure of some sort. Knowing that a guy like Spencer lived here, he figured that it probably was.

The door opened abruptly and Gerald was looking down the barrel of a shotgun.

"Whoa there, Spencer, it's me, Gerald, from the other night at the town square?"

Spencer nodded, "I remember you. How'd you find this place and what do you want?"

Gerald was somewhat taken aback by the level of hostility in Spencer's voice. The other night he had seemed so likeable and friendly.

I was out riding my bike yesterday and I just happened to see you when you were hauling that deer in. I had nothing better to do today, so I figured I might just ride out and say hello."

"Are you fucking stupid, or retarded or something Gerald? What the fuck would you do something like that for?"

"Just seemed like a friendly thing to do, you know, just drop by and say hello. Besides, I wanted to apologize for being so," he was about to say stupid, but changed his mind, "dismissive of your ideas the other night. I can see now that you and your, hamsters, were spot on with a lot of what you said the other night."

Spencer lowered the shotgun so that it was aiming at the floor.

"You do know that by coming here you've put my life in danger, right?"

"No, absolutely not. I mean, no one knows I'm here."

"Someone could have followed you out here, and now they'd know where I live, you asshole."

"No, I swear, there was no one who followed me, and no one knows I'm here. The streets are empty. I didn't see a soul in the past hour of pedaling. I apologize if I did something that I shouldn't have done. I guess I just wasn't thinking."

Spencer stepped forward and out on to the porch and looked left and right, and scanned the entire field of view for one hundred eighty degrees.

"Okay," his tone softened a bit, "I guess it's okay. Come on in for a cup of hot coffee."

They walked in to the room and Gerald was impressed. The place was immaculate and well stocked. They sat at the kitchen table, an island really, in an extravagant kitchen, and drank a cup of coffee. Gerald explained that he and Wendy had reached the end of their food stores and were afraid of what would happen next. He explained what he'd seen at the FEMA camp and Spencer had him describe, several times, exactly what he'd seen at the old Wal-Mart building, although Spencer immediately began calling it the Corrections Center. He told Gerald that if he stuck around town long enough, he'd soon see why he has dubbed it the Corrections Center.

Spencer acted brusque when Gerald told him that he and Wendy were out of food, and quipped, "If you came here to beg food then you've made a mistake son. You should know that."

Gerald shook his head and denied it, "No sir, I didn't come to beg food," although that was a lie, "I just came to ask if you think my best bet would be to get out of town, or stay around here. No matter what I do I'm not going anywhere near that FEMA camp, the Corrections Center," he said, making sure to use Spencer's name for the place, "and I told Wendy that I absolutely forbid her to go anywhere near there."

"Good boy, that's smart."

They talked for a while and Spencer gave him some tips about camping, and what types of plants he could eat in the area, and also how to do a few other things to live in the woods if needed, and finally he loosened up enough that he offered to show Gerald around.

He started with the panty and food stuffs, which took up a three thousand square foot cellar that he'd had dug out years earlier, and fitted with all the modern conveniences.

He showed off the gasoline powered electrical generators, and the cache of weapons which consisted of about eight handguns, four shotguns, two .22lr rifles, and four AR's. He also had a thousand rounds of ammo for each gun, and all the equipment to do reloading.

He showed off his woodworking and metalworking machine shop complete with welder, and also a ten thousand gallon water tank and a five thousand gallon gasoline tank and a gas pump.

He boasted that he could live here for years with just the foodstuffs he had stored, and that he could, if he wanted, build another house from scratch with the equipment he had on hand.

After the tour, they ended up back in the kitchen and as Gerald was getting ready to leave, Spencer walked him to the door, and then told him to wait a moment, and he disappeared back into the house. He came back with a small backpack, and handed it to Gerald.

"That's a small gift to you and Wendy." He said in explanation, "Just a couple days' worth of food. There's also a water filtration system in there. Just read the directions, it's pretty simple to use."

Gerald hefted the backpack on and figured it weight twenty-five pounds if it was an ounce. He figured that if there was mostly food in there, it was enough for a week.

"But listen here, Gerald," the old man said as he clasped his hand on Gerald's shoulder and squeezed the side of his neck, "This is the only help you're getting from me. There'll be no more handouts, and you need to never step foot on this property again, you understand that very clearly now, okay?"

Gerald nodded slowly.

"If I see you on my property again, I'll shoot you. Is that understood clearly?"

Gerald nodded again.

"If I find out that you led anyone here, or told anyone where I live, I'll still shoot you. Is that understood?"

Gerald nodded.

"This," he patted the backpack, "was a gift to you and your wife, but that is the only, and the last gift I will be giving out. You are now responsible for your own self. Understood?"

"Understood." Gerald's voice croaked, his throat having gone dry.

Spencer nodded his chin towards the hill, "Okay, you can go now, and remember, never ever come onto my property again. You do so at your own peril."

They shook hands and Gerald started trudging up the long sloping hill towards the tree and his bicycle. His legs were shaking in fear for some reason. He had no doubt whatsoever that Spencer would shoot him if he ever saw him again. The man was crazy.

#   #   #   #   #

David pedaled non-stop until he arrived home, anxious to show Wendy the food. He was excited to see for himself what Spencer had put into the back pack. When he walked into the kitchen, Wendy was sitting there and she had a pack of gum laying there on the table. She pointed at it, "Carol gave that to us. It's not much, but she says that the act of chewing will help make us forget about eating as much. Sad isn't it?"

David grinned broadly at her.

She gave him a look, "what? What's got you all smiley today? Did you have a good day out riding the range on your Schwinn?"

He slipped the back pack off his back and swung it around and dropped it onto the table with a loud thunk.

"What the hell have you been doing, collecting rocks?"

"Open it, Wendy, I don't know what's in there yet, I haven't peeked, but I think we're both going to like it!"

Wendy scrunched her nose up and spun the backpack around and grabbed the zipper and zipped it open. Then she picked up the bottom edge of the pack, picked it up and tilted the open top until the contents spilled out.

They both gasped.

"Oh my God! Gerald, where did all this come from? Did you rob the grocery store or something?"

They pawed through the contents together. A fully cooked five pound ham, and whole cooked brisket of beef, a water purifier, a small bottle of bleach with instructions on the side for how to use it to purify water. Four cans each of corn, baked beans, and green peas, and a pound of ground coffee, and a bag of sugar and creamer. A box of powdered mashed potato flakes, two packs of cigarettes and two small lighters, and twelve candles and a small handheld short wave radio with a crank handle, and a bottle of two hundred Advil. Last but not least, and small Glock pistol and a box of fifty rounds of 9mm ammo. Gerald knew just enough to be able to load the gun and chamber a round, but doubted that he'd ever be able to shoot a man with it, but figured that at short distances like fifteen feet or closer, he could probably hit what he aimed at.

They looked at each other grinning like idiots, and then Wendy jumped up, grabbed the can opener and opened a can of peas and a can of corn. She cut some of the brisket, heated it all up and feasted like kings. After they'd gorged themselves, they both lit up a cigarette even though they'd both stopped smoking years ago and Gerald regaled her with his descriptions of the layout that Spencer had out there on the edge of the county line.

She was duly impressed, and Gerald began talking to her about leaving town.

"If things get worse than they are now, staying in any urban areas will be very dangerous."

"Where would we go?"

"We'd have to go live in the woods."

"Live in the woods? You mean camp out and be homeless?"

"The cities will be very dangerous places to live, Wendy. There's going to be desperate people roaming the streets looking for food and shelter and if thigs devolve into lawlessness, women will be at a very high risk for kidnapping, rape . . .that type of thing."

They talked long into the night, long after the electricity was shut off and they lit a candle and smoked cigarettes and talked about their uncertain future.

#   #   #   #   #

They stretched the food out for as long as they could, but six days later they were back down to nothing. They'd barely left the house in all that time, and they began to notice that there were gangs of hoodlums roaming the streets after dark, so they never dared to venture out after dark. They also took the darkest blankets and sheets they owned and covered all the windows, hoping to give the impression that the house was shuttered and empty. Gerald kept the Glock on him at all times. Several times in the past few days there had been knocks at the door and they had stopped talking and waited silently for the knocking to stop and then when it did, they peeked to see who had been at the door. One time it was a couple who looked as if they been living in a gutter, and another time it had been a FEMA official, and twice it had been a small group of black kids who had been terrorizing the neighborhood. Every time the knocks were heard at the door, Gerald would position himself near the door but well inside the room, and he'd kept the Glock at ready fire position, just in case someone tried to come through the door and vandalize the house. He kept telling himself that he would definitely shoot anyone who crossed their threshold but he wondered if he'd be able to actually do so.

They were back in starving mode now, and they hadn't yet agreed on any plans of getting out of town. Neither of them had gone to work in so long that they didn't even think about it. The bills went unpaid, and yet for some reason, the utilities still came on daily albeit only for four hours a day now instead of eight. The water trickled out of the faucets and they finally gave up on water from the utility company. If they turned the tap on full, it would take almost an hour to get an eight ounce glass full of water. No one on the block had jobs anymore. It seemed like civilization had ground to a halt.

They were weak with fatigue. Both Wendy and Gerald were losing weight quickly as a result of their forced diets. Then Wendy fainted. Just dropped like a ton of bricks right there on the living room floor and Gerald scooped her up, his heart racing, and he was wondering if she'd had a heart attack, and his heart was racing so quickly that he feared that *he* might be having one.

When she came to, and he made her eat the last granola protein bar that he'd had in the fanny pack that he'd forgotten about, he made a decision. He was going to go back out to Spencer's farm, and if he was lucky enough and the old man wasn't there, he'd steal some food. If the old man was there, he'd beg and plead for some food, just for Wendy, not for him, and hope that the old man had heart enough to take pity on them.

#   #   #   #   #

He wrapped Wendy up in some blankets, put several of her favorite novels on the coffee table in front of her, and even turned the TV on for her to the Classics Channel where they were still showing reruns of old sitcoms from the sixties and seventies. He tried to leave the Glock with her, but she tried to refuse it. He insisted though, and showed her how to aim and pull the trigger. He unloaded it and made her practice dry-firing it a few times, and told her to shoot anyone that comes through that door, unless

you know them well enough to know they won't kill you. Anyone else, just

shoot them and then get the door closed and locked again, and if I have to

I'll bury the dead body in the back yard. She finally agreed, and he set out

on his bike ride.

He arrived at the old man's farm right at dusk, and he parked his bike

on the hill again, next to the tree.

He was halfway across the field to the farmhouse when he noticed

movement, two shadows, about forty yards away from him. Two bodies,

and they were approaching the farmhouse just as he was, but they were

being very stealthy. He'd only seen them because he registered a shadow

moving out of the corner of his eye.

He made it to the porch before they did and he knocked on the door

using the knocker. He turned around and looked back behind him

expecting to see them walking up to the porch, but he could see that they

were crouching down behind a small tractor. Whether they were having

second thoughts, or planning to rush the house when the door opened, he

didn't know, but it was too late now.

The door opened and once again he was staring down the barrel of a

shotgun.

"What the hell are you doing here again! I told you I'd shoot you. In case you don't believe it, I wasn't kidding. Gerald, boy, you just made a big mistake."

"Look Spencer, I know what you said, and I'm sorry, but I'm not here for myself. I'm here for Wendy, my wife. She's sick, she's probably going to die. I just want to help her that's all. Nothing for me, I swear. I'm only here for her. Please sir, I don't want her to die."

"I told you Gerald, you're on your own, now get out of here."

Gerald gave him a hangdog, pitiful look and slumped his shoulders down in dejection.

Spencer looked at the man. He knew that the man was harmless, but he also knew better than to start giving handouts, which he'd already done once before this very man. He was harmless, and it probably wouldn't hurt to help him one more time, at the least give the guys' wife a fighting chance. He wavered back and forth between remaining uncompromising and stolid, or being a good Christian and helping the man out one last time. He decided that it couldn't hurt to help him out one more time. It's not like things would go bad this time, it hadn't hurt to help him out again. He made a decision. He stepped back and was opening the door when something slammed into the door and shoved Gerald into Spencer face first and they both fell to the ground. Gerald landed on top of the him and his breath was knocked out of him. He pushed Gerald off of him and rolled to his hands and knees. Gerald scrambled backwards on his butt away from the fighting and then he saw what had happened. It was Stephen and Charles. They'd apparently figured out where Spencer lived after Gerald had inadvertently given up Spencer's location that day that Gerald had made his first trip out here and he'd seen them near the downtown area. He would have thought that all the preppers he'd met in the group that night had already known where the old man lived, but maybe the old man hadn't told anyone.

Gerald scrambled backwards until his back was against the wall and watched at Stephen and Charles beat Spencer and after a few minutes, it didn't take long, two on one, until the old man had the shotgun pried from his grasp.

Gerald scrambled to his feet, "Spencer, I swear I had nothing to do with this!"

Spencer held his hand to his head and scowled at Gerald, "Yeah, you did. You led them here!"

"No, I didn't!"

Stephen laughed, "Yes, Gerald, you did. We had no idea where he lived until you told us!"

Charles "Yeah, thanks for your help, buddy!"

Spencer glared at Gerald, "I should have shot you that day!" Then he realized that he was guilty of the very thing that he'd, just days earlier accused Gerald of; he'd fallen victim to his own sense of normalcy bias.

"Too late old man!" Stephen said, and the shotgun roared, knocking Spencer back to the floor, half his neck and shoulder and the side of his head gone in a cloud of blood splatter, pink mist and the smell of gunpowder.

Gerald yelped in surprise and horror, and then Stephen racked the slide on the shotgun and was turning it in his direction and Gerald ran as fast as he could through the kitchen and out the back door. Having had a recent tour of the place he knew the layout and he ran as fast as he could towards the nearest building, which was the communications shed and also where the firearms were stored. He ran into the building and locked the door just as he heard the shotgun roar again and he felt the pellets or slugs or whatever slam into the other side of the door. He knew that if Spencer hadn't been paranoid to install all steel doors throughout that that blast just now would have probably killed him.

He ran to the wire cage and the end of the room and grabbed the key off the desk where he'd seen it during the tour of the place with Spencer. His hands shook as he heard the shotgun roar again. That was Stephen trying to blast through the door. He had no idea whether or not a shotgun could breach a door like that, as his knowledge of firearms was rudimentary at best. He opened the cage and picked up a ugly gray Glock and saw that it had a magazine in it. He thumbed the mag release and the mag dropped out. He picked it up off the desk and looked at it. It was full, he slammed it back into the mag well of the Glock and them pulled the slide back to chamber a round. Now, he had no idea whether or not the gun had a safety or not but he was about to find out, as Stephen was blasting the door over and over and it was about to fall off its' hinges.

He got into a stance and held the gun pointed towards the door and just as he did there was one final shotgun blast and the door fell off its' upper hinge and Stephen shouldered his way through. He looked up to see Gerald and his face registered surprise to see that he was the one staring down the barrel of a gun. He began raising the end of the shotgun towards Gerald and Gerald aimed squarely at Stephen's chest and pulled the trigger. The Glock roared and Stephen took a step back and then lowered the shotgun. He looked down at his chest and then his knees dipped slightly. He dropped the shotgun and it clattered to the floor.

His mouth opened slightly, "What the hell dude, you shot me, you fucker."

Gerald nodded, "Yes, I did."

Stephen crumpled to the floor and Gerald wondered what he should do next. After a minute he felt his body trembling and he felt nauseous, and he bent over and vomited. After a few minutes, his shakes went away, and the rubbery-ness in his legs lessened and he straightened up. He grabbed a second Glock and made sure it had a full mag and then he picked the shotgun up off the floor and found a box of shells and he loaded it too.

He walked back to the main house, both Glocks tucked in his back belt, and the shotgun in his hands.

As he came around the corner of the kitchen and into the living room, he saw that Charles had his back to him. He was looking in a glass display case at some gold coins. He walked across the room and then Charles spoke, "I heard all the shooting! Was Gerald that much of a problem, or what?"

Gerald answered him, "I'd say it was *or what*."

Charles spun around and his eyes widened and he threw his hands up, "No!"

Gerald pulled the trigger and the shotgun roared and the blood splatter sprayed across the glass of the display case as the buckshot shattered it and Charles crashed into it and then fel dead to the floor.

Gerald tossed the shotgun to the couch and then walked into the kitchen, opened the big stainless steel doors of the fridge, found a beer and opened it and took a deep swig.

He finished the beer, and grabbed a second one and walked back into the living room. He had three bodies to bury, and a lot of scrubbing to do on the floors, but by tomorrow evening, he figured that he and Wendy should be safe and sound in their new home.

The End

The truth about Power Grid failure

An article in USA Today in 2015 stated that about once every four days, components of the nation's power grid is struck by a cyber or physical attack. A failure of the national power grid system could leave millions in the dark, instantly and without warning. The power grid failure could come about by man-made or natural means. Terrorism or the sun, either way, it could spell disaster for a nation of three hundred million whose lives depend upon electricity. As a society, we are ill-equipped to be instantly transported back to pre-industrial times. Millions upon millions would simply die, because we are almost completely unprepared to deal with the consequences of such an event. Rebuilding would take years, maybe decades. A generation or two may come and go before things would get back to what we now call *normal*.

PART TWO

Meet the new boss

Chuck Miller was reading the Monday morning newspaper while he ate his breakfast, which consisted of a heavily buttered whole-wheat muffin. He turned the page to the financials section and was shocked as he read the financial section. The front page had several financial stories that were taking center stage, the first one being the massive drop in the stock market three days before. It was the largest single day drop ever recorded and the story basically said that the financial losses would be many *billions*.

There was also an article discussing why citizens shouldn't panic and remove their money from banks. Chuck of course, already knew that, because the bank deposits were guaranteed by the federal reserve. He completely skipped an entire article that was talking about the U S to China debt ratio and how the U S maybe finally had working solution to pay off the debt. The Fed wasn't saying what the solution was, but that *measures were being enacted at this very moment.* Wilson wasn't worried about that, he had no money invested in foreign money markets, so the government's dealings with China meant nothing to him. Then he thumbed back to the stock listings and looked up his 401k fund. He looked at the listing, but there was no number, just some sort of a symbol that he'd never seen before. He looked down at the bottom of the page where the symbols legend explaining what they meant was located.

He had to put on his reading glasses to be able to read it, but found that the print was still too small to read. He got up and went to the junk drawer in the kitchen and pulled it open and took out a second, backup pair of reading glasses, and he sat back down and used both glasses together to see the symbol. The legend said that the symbol meant that the information was delayed to market reconfigurations. He'd never heard of such a thing in his life. Of course, in and of itself that meant nothing, he was a manufacturing plant floor manager, not a stock broker.

He fired up his laptop and pulled up the web page he'd saved that showed his company's stock symbol and he refreshed it. When he saw the figure, he knew something was wrong.

He had been invested in his company stock for almost twenty-seven years. Scranton Belsig was a company that produced small plastic fittings for coupling wiring harnesses to piping and tubing. Whenever anyone asked him what he made, instead of giving them a long drawn-out technical description that they wouldn't be able to understand anyway, he just explained that he made 'widgets' and that seemed to satisfy any curiosity and head off any further questions. Their products were boring, not sexy, and something that most people didn't even know existed. *Widgets* captured the gist of their company about as well as anything could.

He knew that the company fortunes had dipped recently because the economy was bad, but he wasn't worried because the company was in the process of being sold to foreign investors. Though the stock price had gone down over the past six months, the official word was that as soon as the sale went through, the stock would split, and his retirement fund would be complete. All he had to do after the merger was to wait six months for his vesting to be complete, and then he would cash out and begin his retirement. He had conservatively estimated that he would be able to retire with close to four million dollars, and for someone just a few years away from sixty, he figured he was in fair shape.

The stock symbol had changed, but the company page was definitely Scranton Belsig, but the new symbol wasn't the one that they been told to expect. The company that was merging them, swallowing them up, was a British company, Brigamond O & P Industries. The stock symbol he was seeing now though was something called ChinaToc NG. The stock symbol was CTNG and Chuck looked at the number, then pulled out his calculator and punched some numbers into it and checked the result. He figured that it must be figured in some other currency other than dollars. He knew it couldn't be dollars because it would mean that his four millions dollars was now somewhere in the range of sixteen thousand dollars, which was ridiculous. Not to mention the fact that he'd never even heard of ChinaToc. The sale to Brigamond O & P was all but a done deal. He frowned and closed the paper. He'd go to the CFO's office today and ask him about it. The info in the paper had to be a misprint. The online info wasn't even coming up. The page kept showing the page wasn't available. He figured that the sale had finally gone through and that there was just some web page, or internet screw up that was stopping the correct information from showing. Maybe the web page was being updated at that very moment. He felt a stirring of excitement in the pit of his stomach as he anticipated the idea of being a true millionaire.

He put away his plate, licked the butter off the butter knife, and used a paper towel to clear the crumbs off the little breakfast table, and then he got ready for work.

An hour later, he was driving through the large fenced area that was their employee parking lot. He noticed a long line of trucks at the back side of the plant. There was a strange symbol on the side of each truck. He shrugged, thinking that maybe the purchasing department had found a new source for plastics and they were making their first delivery. Lot of trucks though. Looked like a line of semi's about a mile long, maybe forty trucks or so.

He walked inside and walked back to his desk. As a supervisor, his desk was out on the floor, and it butted up against a wall. He didn't rate a real office, with walls and a door, but he didn't care, from his desk he could see the forty punch press machines that his group manned. He plopped down in his chair and was about to look at the production figures from the previous week when a group of about thirty men and women in white lab coats, and yellow hardhats began filing past him. Most were carrying clipboards and were scribbling on them, and some were punching in numbers on tablets. Every one of them was Chinese or Korean, or maybe Japanese, Chuck couldn't tell the difference, and he felt very un-PC at not knowing. He'd been stared at, and scolded many times for referring to all Asians as 'Orientals'.

The group filed past, ignoring him even though he stood as they filed past. If management was giving some sort of tour to a group of manufacturing reps to foreign visitors, they would definitely introduce the manager that oversaw production for an integral unit of the company.

He was ignored though, and as the last of them turned the corner, he sat down and picked up the phone to dial Barry Gordon's extension. Barry was another line manager for the production floor, but he was located on the far side of the factory floor, and calling him was easier than walking all the way over there.

"Barry."

"Hey Barry, this is Chuck."

"What's up, Bud?"

Chuck looked around to make sure that no one was listening to him. He had no reason to be paranoid but the incident with the Koreans, or

Chinese, or whatever they were had spooked him.

"Have you seen this big gaggle of foreigners doing a tour of the place?" he asked, "they just went by my line area."

"Yeah, they were here when I got here an hour ago. Weird, huh?"

"Yeah, no kidding. Any idea who they are?"

"No, Chuck, I have no idea, but I did notice one very odd thing."

"What's that?"

"Well, they didn't have any of our management people leading the group. I mean, how do they get a tour of our facility if there's none of our management people to conduct the tour and tell them what's what. You know? Explain to them just what the hell they're seeing?"

Chuck nodded, "Yeah, you're right. And now that I think about it there's something else odd about that group."

"Yeah, what?"

"Well, you know as well as I do that tour groups are not allowed to take notes, or take pictures or anything, and every one of those people in that bunch had note pads or tablets and I saw several taking pictures like it was no big deal. I mean, what the fuck? We suddenly don't care about our proprietary manufacturing processes anymore?"

"Yeah, that is odd to say the least." Barry agreed, "I just can't get over the fact that we're allowing them to just freely walk about without any management personnel to watch them."

"And," Chuck added, "the fact that no one bothered to let us know that this huge group would be poking around here all morning? You know how it usually is, the day before a group does a tour they send out a memo email telling everyone to clean up their area to give a good impression on our visitors yadda, yadda, yadda."

"Exactly!"

"Hey, wait a minute, here's an email just popped up. From the VP's office." Chuck said, "Let me open it up, I bet this is about this tour group."

"Okay," Barry said, "Looks like I haven't gotten it yet. What's it say?"

Chuck read it out to Barry, "From the office of Vice President Lou Stein, to all management staff and floor line managers, Monday morning meeting in main conference room, ten a.m., mandatory attendance required to all personnel. Subject: *reorientation seminar.*"

"What the hell is a *reorientation seminar?*" Barry laughed.

"Beats me." Chuck said, "I guess we'll find out in about an hour and a half."

Chuck piddled around for the next hour, reading an article in a magazine, and greeting members of his team as they made their way to their machines and began setting them up for the days production run.

A few minutes after nine he got up and began making his way towards the break room so that he could get a coffee and a donut to have during the meeting.

Sixty personnel, all production line managers and supervisors filed in and stood around in cliques making small talk until the upper management began filing in. The room smelled like cigarette smoke, as it was allowed to smoke inside the room, a concession that their union had to have fought bitterly for in this day and age of political correctness. There was also a smell of disinfectant as the cleaning crew had swabbed down the floors overnight. Chuck felt air blowing across the back of his neck as the air conditioners turned on and he wished he had brought his cotton windbreaker. He always forgot to bring it to meetings and the cold air on his neck always irritated him.

The front of the room had a dais set up, and winged out to either side of the dais were cafeteria tables, but no chairs for anyone to sit in.

Chuck thought that was odd, but figured it would be a short meeting. Just last year they'd all been called in to a meeting and had assembled, only to be told that the reason for the meeting was to announce that there would be a mandatory meeting that afternoon at four p.m. Chuck had written the incident off as typical American excess mismanagement bullshit, especially after four pm had arrived and the man who had called the meeting had forgotten completely about it and had to be summoned, *late to his own mandatory meeting.*

The upper management filed into the room. Eight of them, four standing in front of the tables on each side of the dais. The President and CEO, Marvin Rainwater, came in last and stood in front of the dais. He clutched a sheaf of paperwork. To Chuck's eye all of the upper management personnel had a dazed, almost deer-in-the-headlights look on their faces. Something big was going down. Chuck figured that this would be the meeting where they would announce that the company had finally been sold. Maybe some of the upper management were being cut loose? Maybe that was why they had the shocked look on their faces. Maybe they were dreaming of their sudden wealth. Chuck figured that if he was going to be cashing out for four million as a line manager, he could only imagine what some of the senior management staff were going to be able to cash out with. Some of them had small ownership stakes in the company. Small percentages of ownership maybe, but those small ownership stakes represented several times more than what he'd been able to salt away for years. Some of those people standing at the front of the room must be worth twenty or thirty million.

Barry leaned in next to Chuck and whispered in his ear, "Notice anything strange?"

Chuck shook his head and whispered back, "No. Like what?"

Barry used his elbow to nudge Chuck's arm, "Take a look around. There's not a single union rep in the room."

Chuck frowned, and looked around as Barry had suggested. "That's not right. Every meeting has to have a union rep present."

"Something strange is going on. Those execs up there look absolutely miserable. What with their golden parachutes and all, you'd think they'd be dancing in the aisles."

"No kidding."

The meeting began as Marvin Rainwater cleared his throat and raised his hands to caution the crowd to quiet down.

"First of all, I'd like to thank all of you for attending today's meeting"

A voice from the back of the room spoke up, "Wasn't it mandatory, so we didn't actually have a choice?"

Chuck turned around to see who had spoken like that to their CEO. It was Greg Kinn, a very outspoken man who'd only been with the company for a few years, but had been openly critical in the past, about management decisions.

Marvin Rainwater nodded towards the back of the room, "Excellent point Mister Kinn, now if I could continue, without interruption please, we'll get on to the reasons for today's meeting." He paused.

Chuck thought that the man appeared nervous and ill at ease, which wasn't like him at all. Marvin Rainwater was a charismatic force all his own. He always dominated any room he was in and was seemingly never timid, cautious, or at a loss for words. Today though, he seemed just that.

Their CEO continued, "as we all know, the company has been going through some unexpectedly tough times over the past three years, and while the ups and downs, the vagaries of the stock market and plastics industry has been healthy, our place in it has been slowly deteriorating. While we've attempted improvements and cost-cutting measures, these attempts were largely unsuccessful. So, as you know, last year we began courting suitors, hoping for a helping hand, which is just corporate-speak for an investor to give us a cash influx for a bailout. Unable to find any such entity, we began shopping the company for an outright sale, and as you all know, we have been in negotiations with the British company Brigamond Oil and Plastics."

"Excuse me!" a voice rose up from the far side of the room. All heads turned to that voice.

"Yes?" Marvin Rainwater answered the woman. Chuck saw that it was Julie London, who had been a union delegate for years.

"Sir? This meeting is out of order and will need to be brought to a close. Union rules state that no meetings between management and employees are allowed without some sort of union representation. For some reason there isn't a single union official in the room today, which is *against the law*, so to speak. Since you made this meeting *mandatory*, and there is no union representation present in the room, I'm afraid that we will have to shut this meeting down," she said, and then added, "*sir.*"

A loud murmur rumbled through the room, with several *that's rights* and *you tell em, girl,* and a loud *yeah, we're outta here!*

Marvin Rainwater held his hands up to shush the crowd and order was restored, though there was a low bass of under the breath mumblings in the room.

"I will explain that *in detail*, before we terminate this meeting, if you will all just bear with me for a few moments. *All* of your questions will be answered, trust me." He plead with the crowd, and then he took a sip of water from a water bottle on the dais. He continued, "As we speak, your Union Reps are meeting in the other conference room," he pointed towards the south end of the building, "Please, just let me explain what is happening." He looked around the room, attempting to make eye contact with as many as he could, to gain some trust.

"As you all know, we have been in negotiations with the British company, Brigamond Oil and Petroleum and we had expected the new corporate personnel to be moving into their positions in the next ninety days . . ." he paused again and used the back of his hand to wipe his brow.

Chuck thought that the man looked extremely uncomfortable, and it was strange to see, when you considered that the man was normally one of the more dynamic, likeable, charismatic individuals he'd ever met. Talking to a group of fifty or five thousand wouldn't normally matter, Marvin Rainwater, was easily charm the crowd, but this, this was unlike the Marvin Rainwater he'd known for years.

"Unfortunately, government regulators that monitor foreign investments in U.S. held corporations have scuttled the deal. They killed it dead in the water and I've been informed that there will be no appeals allowed."

"What the hell does that mean? No appeals *allowed?*" a voice from behind Chuck shouted.

"Well, this is fairly, uhm, *intricate*, but let me try to explain." CEO Rainwater said as he gave a weak smile, "what has happened is fairly *historic* in its' scope and complexity. He pointed to the wall behind him and someone dimmed the lights and a projected image turned on lighting up the wall. A PowerPoint presentation. The beginning image was a map of the United States. Just a standard map showing the states. No cities, just the image of the United States itself and the outlines of the states, and each state was labeled.

"Even for those of us who follow financial news, this may be hard to understand, but I will try to make it understandable, as much as I can. Please be patient, as this is all new to me too. Let me try to get through as much of this as I can before asking questions, okay?"

Chuck looked at Barry and Barry shook his head, as if to say, *I have no clue either.*

CEO Rainwater continued, "for many years, the Federal Government of the United States has been selling U S debt to Foreign governments, who now hold about 46 percent of all U.S. debt, or about four point five trillion dollars. The largest foreign holder of U.S. debt is China, which owns more about $3.2 trillion in bills, notes and bonds, according to the Treasury.

In total, China owns close to 11 percent of publicly held U.S. debt." He paused and took another sip of water.

Chuck looked at Barry, who shrugged. None of this meant anything to either one of them.

CEO Rainwater picked up his explanation, "ten days ago, unbeknownst to me and everyone on our board of directors, U S regulators scuttled our deal with Brigamond Oil and Plastics, a fact that I was unaware of until last Thursday. Since Thursday afternoon, I have been sitting in a room with several U S government regulators and other federal functionaries and trying to wrap my head around this, this new deal, that is now apparently in place. This new deal, let me just add, is one hundred percent against all my business sense, ethics, and sense of fair play, and I fought it bitterly and with the utmost amount of rancor and strength that I could muster. However, if you've ever heard the saying *you can't fight city hall*, then you can compound that to about the hundredth power, and say that *you can't fight the U S government.*"

"*What the fuck?*" a voice from the front row muttered. CEO Rainwater ignored the man and continued his explanation.

"This is going to be very difficult for you to hear, and harder even to understand, but please realize as I try to explain this to you, that this was against my wishes, and I fought it bitterly. This is not something that I would have ever done, not in a million years."

Now there were renewed mumblings throughout the gathering.

"As I mentioned, the sale of Scranton Belsig was shut down by government regulators last week, and I have been in a room with several government regulators and other government officials since that time, up until about eight hours ago. I have been without sleep, and am totally exhausted, but I felt it was my duty to come to you and explain this directly, rather than having you hear it from some specious government lackey." He paused nervously.

"As you see on the map behind me, the map of the United States, shows our proud state of Kansas, and also the states of Nebraska, and North and South Dakota. He clicked a mouse on the dais, and the map changed color. Now the states were all blue, except for Kansas, Nebraska, and North and South Dakota, which were now red. He explained, "These states in red are the states that are affected by this new governmental reorganization." He clicked again and a large yellow rectangle appeared in the states from Kansas up to North Dakota.

"This yellow rectangle that you see stretches from approximately southeast from fifty miles southeast of Wichita Kansas and then west to Liberal Kansas, and then up to just past Minot North Dakota to the west and then east to just northeast of Grand Forks North Dakota. This rectangle of land and everything inside this area is now considered a new state."

Chuck looked at Barry and Barry spoke, "they've formed a new state? That huge-ass chunk of land is a large part of the entire Midwest United States!"

Chuck nodded, "this is bizarre. Why hasn't anyone heard of this? I watch the news every day, there's been nothing about anything like this on CNN or any news channels."

CEO Rainwater continued, "as we all know from our childhood geography and politics, Puerto Rico is basically an unofficial state of the United States, and pretty much a de facto fifty-first state. Although it is not officially a state, just as Washington DC is not considered an actual state, both have been seen as candidates for officially becoming our fifty-first state in a legal sense. Neither has actually been ratified as such though. Now however, the government has brokered a deal with the Chinese government by which China will erase the debt they've bought from us over the past thirty five years in exchange for ownership in U S lands and businesses and tax-haven opportunities for a ten year span of time. This accord is hereby in full force, effective immediately as of this morning at seven a.m. central time. At that time, control of this company was ceded by Presidential authority to the Chinese government."

He clicked the mouse again and the large rectangle that covered the huge slice of the American Midwest stretching from just above the upper edge of Oklahoma and almost to the Canadian border, and containing east to west the middle third of the states Kansas, Nebraska and South and North Dakota not turned to a yellow color.

This area was designated on the map as 'Chi-Ter-OTUS' – The Chinese Territory of the United States.

Gasps and angry shouts erupted from the audience. *Bullshit!*

Fuck this!

I'm not a fucking Communist!

CEO Rainwater held his hands up in supplication, and patted the air, "Calm down people! Please let me explain!"

Catcalls and curses rose in crescendo and Chuck was beginning to fear a riot. Several pastries and crumpled coffee cups were hurled at the CEO and he looked around nervously.

That's when the doors behind him opened and what seemed like several hundred Chinese soldiers, all decked out in white uniforms, and carrying AR style rifles began flooding into the room and began working their way around the perimeter where they stood, rifles at port arms, staring at the room full of employees.

Chuck looked around the room, wide-eyed. The Chinese soldiers in their white uniforms with some sort of red and green symbol over the left top part of their tunics, which Chuck recognized as the company symbol that he'd seen on the stock page earlier that morning, stood at port arms, staring at the angry works, and Chuck realized with a lump in his throat that they wouldn't hesitate to shoot. The room quieted immediately and the door opened again and a group of Chinese men and women filed in. These, Chuck thought, had to be the Chinese management team, their new overlords. Well, *fuck this*, he thought, *I'm not working for the Chinese, no matter what kind of screwy deal our government has cooked up.*

The Chinese men and women were wearing the same white jump suits, but none were carrying weapons of any sort. Their uniforms were white, just like the soldiers, and they had the same green and red company symbol over their left breast, and each had a number on their right side, where a pocket would have been. They were numbered 1 through 9, and each number had a symbol next to it that Chuck figured was the Chinese symbol corresponding to that American number. These Chinese management personnel arraigned themselves at the tables on either side of the dais, and the American management personnel stepped back and stood against the wall, almost at attention.

Number nine walked to the dais and CEO Rainwater nervously hooked a finger under his collar and tugged on it, as if he'd tied his tie too tight that morning when getting dressed for work, and then he stepped back into the line with the rest of his executive staff. Now he looked scared.

Number nine spoke, "Good morning workers," he spoke with a Chinese accent but seemed to have a little trouble with English, "I introduce myself as Eason Chane and I am proud to be your new leader at your company." He paused.

Chuck wondered if the guy was expecting a round of applause or something, but Chuck knew his co-workers, and he knew they'd burn in hell before applauding this guy. Instead, when Eason Chane introduced himself, all of the Chinese management personnel standing at the tables on either side of him all rotated towards him and bowed to him. Eason Chane returned their bow and they all turned back to face their hostile audience.

He launched into his speech, "Workers, your government has been foolishly wasteful, and," he searched for the right word, "*profligate*. Your products have become vastly inferior, your work habits sloppy and filled with gross errors, and your managers have very few positive traits to distinguish them as leaders. Your executives in this country are ill-equipped to manage any business other than a child's . . ." he paused and leaned to his left where the woman wearing the number 8 whispered in his ear while she made a squeezing motion with her hand, "lee mon juice stand." He nodded at the woman for helping him find the word he had stumbled on, "Thank you, comrade Amei Maosu, number 8" the woman blushed and looked at the floor.

He continued his speech, and Chuck wondered if the man had such a poor grasp of American language, manners or nuance that he had no clue just how rudely he was being in speaking to them in such terms.

"Your American government has been like a spoiled child, wastefully spending money it did not have, and willfully compiling more and more debt with little or no regard to the idea of paying it back and having . . ." he leaned to the left again, and once again the woman, number 8 whispered in his ear, giving him the clue he needed to continue the speech. It was obvious that number 8 had the speech down cold. ". . . the ethical considerations to honor their obligations. Because of your governments almost unlawful willingness to betray their ethics, and act dishonorably in regards to their financial obligations, we have had no choice but to demand payment for this excess. When your government was faced with a decision to accept their responsibilities, they attempted to . . ." he leaned left again, and this time, number 8 had to consult a piece of paper and say the word in his ear. He frowned, and whispered it back to her and she shook her head and repeated it back to him. He frowned and then continued, ". . . they attempted to *bambaloozle* our government with more lies and empty promises. This time though," he frowned, and leaned forward and wagged his finger at the audience, "we were not content to be swayed by lies and," he paused, trying to conjure another word, "chicanery and falsehoods. We have been patient such as a parent with an unruly, spoiled child, but there is a time for teaching and admonitions, but when all else has failed, one must spank the child."

Chuck was looking around at his fellow employees and seeing all sorts of reactions, anger, disgust, bewilderment and confusion and some outright hostility. Whatever this was, Chuck was sure that it was a historic first and he wondered if it was even legal. They'd damn sure find out soon enough.

The man he knew as Number 9 kept speaking, "Your company was failing, and we are here to save it from ruin. One of the reasons your American companies fail so often and so spectacularly, is because of your parasitic relationship between the workers and your unions." He paused and leaned over to confer with his number 8 again, and after a few whispered words, he continued again, "your American reliance upon Unions has become a crutch by which ineffective work, and sloth is unduly rewarded. I am here to assure you today that your Union has no place in the Chinese culture of business. That is why your many union representatives are not present in the room today. Those persons were given an opportunity to renounce their affiliation with the union membership and failing that renunciation and promises to work without the protection of that organization they were terminated and escorted off the premises. Because they seem determined to demand unreasonable high wages for inferior work and sloppy products, they are deemed unemployable and as such they will be jobless until this agreement with your country allows them to work again in this geographical territory. They have, in effect, chosen to become homeless." He paused again and took a sip of water.

The person to his left, with the number 6 on his uniform, a large bruiser of a man who seemed ready to burst out of his uniform, and he was all muscle, Chuck noticed, whispered something to him.

"My colleague, Han Hoing number 6, who is now head of security for this facility, has asked me to remind you of a very important point." He cleared his throat, "Your union, the International Brotherhood of Electrical Workers, or I B E W as it is known to you, is not recognized by the nation of China, and is not allowed in this company. All of your union credentials, and benefits resulting from union membership is hereby rendered invalid. This company has no place for Union Membership or activities. Any activities, or attempts to enact or unionize, or organize any union will be terminated immediately. Persons electing to attempt to create, organize or engage in union activity will be summarily dealt with. Let me make this clear, ChinaToc NG, and the 'new' merged company, CHITOCUS, China Toc, U.S. will not ever recognize any union. You are hereby warned to refrain from any and all union activity. Do not even speak of these subversive and divisive activities on these premises. To do so will result in very harsh penalties for you. You must understand this very clearly and without fail."

"Fuck that!" a voice yelled from the back of the room, "We have the legal right to unionize, you can't just take that away from us! That's un-American! I don't care what you sorry-ass fucking Communists say, we can, and will have our union!"

Everyone turned to see who the outburst had come from. Chuck could see that it was from Gene Allison, a man whose job was to repair the machines when they needed repairing, and also to keep them all maintained. He'd been with the company for about nineteen, maybe even twenty years.

Eason Chane stared at the man from the front of the room. The room quieted down, in nervous anticipation of a confrontation.

Finally, number 9 spoke, "Sir, what is your name?"

"My name is Gene *fucking* Allison. I've been employed here almost twenty damn years, and I don't care who you are, or what you say, I am not going to work for a bunch of fucking Communists and I absolutely will, by God, be a part of the Union. You think you can stop me, go ahead and try, and while we're at it, *fuck you!*"

Eason Chane smiled and nodded, then spoke calmly, "Mister Allison," it came out as *Alley-sohrn*, "we will not permit this abrasive language in the company meetings. There is no place for it and it will not be tolerated. You will from this point on, speak with humble respect to your co-workers and your superiors. As for the union, we have stated the rules, and they will be obeyed to the letter."

Chuck expected Gene to sit down, after having had his say, his attempt at telling the new owners to go to hell, but Gene wasn't finished.

"Well, mister nine, or whatever your chink name is, I'll tell you this, I came to work for this company nineteen years ago, and I been a faithful dues-paying member of the union all that time too. I never agreed to work for you, or your fucking Communist government, and I damn sure won't work for you! You can take your sorry-ass Commie rules, and your company and shove them straight up your ass!" he ended his speech by grabbing his balls and giving them a shake and then raised his hand and gave the Chinese management team the middle finger.

Four members of the soldiers lined up on the interior perimeter wall stepped forward and grabbed him by the arms and he immediately began struggling against them and screaming curses at them and throwing punches. The four soldiers back away from him and one of them pulled a pistol-looking device that was yellow and red and aimed it at Gene. The man squeezed the trigger and Gene Allison was hit with the current and he immediately began shaking and jumping with the electrical current that was generated by the Taser. He went down in a heap on the floor where he began convulsing. There were several gasps from the assembled crowd and several women screamed. Instantly, the soldiers all stepped away from the wall, and many of them pointed their weapons at the crowd. Some of the soldiers pulled out handguns, and some pulled out the same yellow and red Taser devices and flicked switches on them, arming them, Chuck realized. They were obviously unwilling to put up with any and all dissent from the rank and file.

It was a scary display of power, and Chuck looked at Barry. They whispered, careful not to draw any attention to themselves.

"What the fuck is going on here?"

"You got me, Barry." Chuck answered him, "I wonder what they'd say if we just told them, *nicely*, that we no longer wanted to work for the company, that we resigned, and wanted to go work elsewhere. I mean, it's still a free country, is it not? You know, just take our 401k and retirement and try somewhere else?"

"I can't see how they'd stop us." Barry said, "At the end of this meeting, that's pretty much what I plan on doing, just give my resignation, and go home and hit the want ads first thing in the morning, you know?"

"No kidding. It's not like we're slaves or something."

The soldiers used plastic ties to cuff Gene Allison's arms behind his back and they also cuffed him around the ankles, and then they picked him up and took him out of the room.

Number nine, Eason Chane began speaking again, "You are our workers now, and this accord that our government has reached with your government gives us the power to nullify all previous contracts and agreements that may have been in place. You work for us now, and as such, you will model your behavior based upon our society's rules and modes of conduct, you will learn to act accordingly with how our workers behave. This is not only expected, but will be demanded of you. This trade accord between our governments will last for ten years. At the end of that time, you will be able to leave this company and attempt to obtain employment elsewhere."

The crowd began murmuring again and Barry and Chuck exchanged glances.

"That sounds suspiciously like slavery." Barry whispered.

Chuck nodded. "Let's ask."

He raised his hand to speak, and number nine nodded at him, "State your name and your question." He said.

Chuck stood up, "My name is Chuck, I'm one of the line production foreman here, "My question is this, 'what if we just decide, here today, that we no longer care to work for the company any longer? I have my retirement fund built up enough that I can just go ahead and retire, or seek employment elsewhere' . . ."

Number nine shook his head slowly, "I'm afraid that is impossible. Your government gave us full control. You may walk away , but your ability to work elsewhere is severely restricted. The names and social security numbers of every employee in this company is on a list. If you were to seek employment elsewhere you would be turned down. You are un-hirable for a period of three years. For a period of seven years after that three year period, you may be rehired outside of this company, but only at what your society calls minimum-wage level jobs."

A loud crescendo of angry voices rose up at that, and the soldiers around the perimeter of the room instantly assumed ready stances, in case they would be needed to put down a riot. The group of managers at the dais and the tables stepped back in order to give the soldiers room to operate if they were needed.

Number nine finally raised his hands and motioned for the crowd to quieten down, and after several minutes the crowd allowed him to speak again.

"I have heard many of you using the word, *slaves*, and I just want to assure you that this is not so. Our culture does not agree with the concept of slavery. We are a freedom-loving people and we rejoice in freedoms and liberty and happiness. Our people are hard-working, honest, and simple. We take comfort in many peaceful pleasures, and we honor our corporate masters by creating the most efficient working environments possible. Our products are above reproach and efficient and cost-worthy. Our attitudes toward work is quite different from the average American worker. Whereas the American worker produces products that are of value, they take too long to reach acceptable levels of production, and they pamper and spoil their workers to the point that the products themselves become inferior and worthless. We will train you on a more efficient working model, and we will educate you on how to maximize your workers in both work product quality, and in ethics and attitudes."

A hand rose from the audience, "What you are saying does sound like slavery to me, but the fact is, I have a lot of money in my retirement account. Surely, I can just go ahead and take my retirement, if I don't care to continue working, whether it be for this company, or any other company?"

Number nine shook his head, "Please, let me introduce Comrade Fayee Wong number 5, she is our equivalent to the position that you would refer to as Chief Financial Officer."

The woman, Comrade Fayee Wong (number 5) stepped forward to the dais and gave a deferential bow to Eason Chane (number 9), and then she turned to face the crowd.

"The accord of which Comrade Eason Chane, our illustrious number nine has spoken of, and was ratified by both governments last week, has been in planning for several years. The amount of money that your country was indebted to ours was many trillion U S dollars. This was unable to be satisfied by your country and our country, as well as many others, became more and more dissatisfied with empty promises of payments. Your country continued to print money which only served to devalue its' value even further. Finally, an agreement was reached by where our country would be granted tax-free status in this country and the authority to manage businesses and land ownership for this section of your country as indicated on the map behind us." She pointed to the map showing the elongated yellow section that ran up the Midwest part of the plains states.

"All of the land, farms, ranches, and all businesses in this area are now a part of what your government is referring to as the fifty-first state. Officially it is known as CHITOCUS, which stands for the China Territories of the Central United States. This accord does not give us, permanently, control of the U S land, but it cedes it to us to manage it and profit from as we wish, for a period of ten years. Because we knew that we might not, in some instances, be welcomed with, how is your expression, open arms, that we may have to put in place other measures in order to keep the companies and use them to profit from for this ten year period, to repay your countries debt to ours. So, in order to keep the businesses in this new territory, and to have the manpower to run these businesses effectively, we were given permission by your government, to have you, the workers, included as a part of this accord. So, we do, in effect have you as our employees for a period of ten years."

Chuck's mouth dropped open. He looked around the room. There was stunned silence.

She continued her explanation, "As to your question regarding your retirement funds, this may be a bit more complicated to explain. The employees of all businesses in the territory have had their 401k and all other retirement accounts frozen until the ten year accord is completed."

There were loud gasps in the audience, but the woman, Comrade Fayee Wong (number 5) ignored them and continued her explanation, "the accounts have also been modified and *corrected*. When your government ceded control of this company to China TOC NG, we looked at the value performance indicators for the past several years and we saw an alarming rate of poor performance, especially for the past three to six years. The value of the company has lessened considerably in that time. Because we felt that China TOC NG should not be obliged to start off poorly, we developed an algorithm to compensate for the losses you incurred before we took over. What that means is that we constructed a financial formula to allow us to compensate the new company and rescind your previous unearned bonuses and payment incentives in losing years. What that means is this, instead of being rewarded for your poor performance in the past six years, we have re-claimed that money paid to you into your retirement accounts and have used it to re-fund the new beginning of the company.

Because of that process, you may see that the figures in your retirement accounts is less than what you had previously seen. We, as a company, China TOC NG, do not, now will we ever, reward poor performance with incentives, bonuses and the like. We have also used the same algorithm to figure start-up costs for China TOC NG executives and management personnel to travel here and work to train you to be a more effective employee. That accounting also has served to lessen your retirement accounts. After the ten year accord agreement, when we cede ownership of the territory back to your government, you will have undoubtedly earned back a small portion of your retirement accounts, but we cannot absolve you of your losses as that would be a foolish waste of money. You must be willing to accept responsibility for these losses you have incurred upon yourself by your own laziness, ineptitude and shoddy work performances over the past six years, we are not responsible for these practices of mismanagement. The average Chinese worker would be ashamed to act as you American workers act when handling your work duties. You can walk away now and retire, if that is what you feel is best for you, but remember, if you do, you will be unemployable in the United States and your retirement accounts are frozen, as employees, for three years, and as non-employees, for the next ten years. When they are accessed, as I have explained, they will be minus the debits we have calculated for poor work performance and start-up costs that we have incurred in coming here to train you. Instead of complaining, you should be thankful, as our training regimen will mold you into much more efficient workers, and when you renter the American job force in several years, you will be a much more highly prized candidate."

The air seemed to deflate from the room all at once. Chuck turned to Barry, who was glassy-eyed, and dumbstruck. Someone down the row on Chuck's left raised her hand, and Comrade Fayee Wong (number 5) nodded at her to ask her question.

Chuck saw that it was Kay Thompson, who had worked for the company for fourteen years as an upper level administration assistant in sales.

"My retirement account had three hundred and ninety thousand dollars in it, how do I find out what's in it now?" she asked.

Chuck was flabbergasted at what she had socked away, especially as nothing more than a glorified secretary, but maybe she had been making a great salary, or she had poured every extra penny she had into her account. Whatever it was, he was surprised, because he thought that he was the highest in the company expect for the upper management level personnel.

Comrade Fayee Wong (number 5) nodded and turned to one of her cohorts, "I believe that Comrade Jolien Tsai, number 3, can help us with that computation, she is our accountant and human resources director.

Comrade Jolien Tsai, number 3 smiled and stepped forward to the dais and she bowed deeply to Comrade Fayee Wong (number 5) and then turned to address Kay Thompson. "I see that you have been with the company for sixteen years, and let me see," she began punching numbers into a calculator while consulting a list, which Chuck figured was a list of every employee and all their pertinent info.

"I see that your account is currently, in U S Dollars, in the amount of twelve hundred and forty-two dollars and ninety-three cents."

Several gasps and a few Gawd-almighty's erupted from the audience, and Chuck saw Kay Thompson's face go pale. Chuck figured that if Kays' three hundred and ninety thousand was only worth a tad more than twelve hundred bucks, then his four hundred plus thousand was probably in the neighborhood of fifteen hundred bucks or so. He said nothing, but looked at his co-workers. They were all glaring at the Chinese executives with murderous hate in their eyes. Not that he blamed them. The first thing he would do when this meeting ended would be to call an attorney and find out if any of this bullshit was legal. Surely it couldn't be. Their own government had basically sold them into ten years of slavery and given their life savings to the Chinese? How could such a thing possibly be legal? There was such a thing as basic human rights. He figured the company might indeed have been sold to China TOC NG, and that their corporate types just got over-eager and didn't understand U S laws. He also figured that their brutality would cost them. Having Gene Allison tasered would probably end up costing them a few hundred thousand too. They were not off to a great start.

The one thing that did worry him though, was the article that he had neglected to read in this morning's paper, about the solution that the government was working on, regarding the China - US debt. The article had hinted that there was some sort of fix in the works, and Chuck has disregarded it completely. He wished now that he had taken the time to read it. It was impossible that this ridiculous coup was legal in any sense of the word.

Chuck decided that five minutes after this meeting was finished, he would be on the phone with the Union, and then his attorney. Even though the man was a tax attorney, he should be able to weigh on something as strange as this. A Chinese corporation taking over a company, and basically telling them that they are now indentured servants? Ridiculous. Chuck had no doubt that after the meeting more than half of the employees would be walking out the door, maybe even ninety percent of the entire work force. There was always that ten percent of the people who would do anything that was demanded by anyone who claimed to be in authority.

The Eason Chane, number 9, continued, ". . . and we have," he paused, searching for the appropriate word, "concocted for you a list of acceptable and non-acceptable behaviors that will be upheld during your employment with China TOC NG and I will request now that our Director of Human Relations to present them to you. I introduce to you, Elvae Hsiao number 7." He gave a slight bow and the woman walked to the dais and looked out at the group assembled before her.

Chuck noticed that the woman, Elvae, was a thin, severe-looking woman. To him, she appeared as a gray-haired grandmotherly type. Grim, with a lined face and her hair in a librarians bun, pursed lips as if she just sucked on a lemon, with horn-rimmed glasses. She had an old-fashioned severe gaze of fastidious and humorless sourness that any and all friendliness was completely foreign to. Chuck figured the woman had probably last laughed maybe forty years ago, and that the laugh had only been prompted by someone else's pain. She was a dry twig of stern and over-disciplined values that pre-empted all gaiety out of hand. Chuck shuddered, imagining a school child returning an overdue book to this shrew.

She nodded curtly and began speaking, "Welcome new employees of China Toc. You will begin by understanding that we will not suffer any slackness, idleness or lack of proper appreciation for the leaders of this company. The nine leaders you see before you today will be appreciated with reverence and respect and the utmost admiration."

She paused and took a sip of water. Chuck noticed that the water bottles they all had were not Dasani, Fiji, Auquafina or the Wal-Mart brands. It was some sort of Chinese brand. He realized that the trucks he'd seen lined up outside earlier were probably trucking in all sorts of Chinese products for this bunch. He wondered if this nine person leadership team had also been packed in by semi too.

" . . . we understand that none of you is competent at this point in our beautiful language to correctly pronounce our names, but you must attempt to learn them, out of respect, and until that time you may refer to us by our ranking numbers. Number one, two, three, four and so forth."

Chuck frowned. What they were saying is that they demanded respect. He guessed that the American value system of earning respect was not their way of doing things.

". . . we will naturally, allow you some," she paused to remember the word she needed. Chuck could tell that none of them were anywhere near fluent in English, sure they spoke English, but their word choices often seemed odd and off-base.

". . . we will allow you some *leeway* in coming to terms with the circumstances and changes in the company, but we will expect all workers to conform to the standards we set forth. Three day should be ample time for all workers to adjust to the new conditions and begin production rates at the new levels. These levels are considerably higher that what you have been achieving previously, and that is because your work ethic has been sloppy and inefficient. The levels that you have reached in the past have been woefully inadequate. Your best month in the past three years is hardly admirable, and our new monthly levels of minimum production will be approximately one hundred and seventy-five per cent higher than that. These levels will be reached, of that there will be absolutely no doubt and we will maintain these levels on a consistent basis."

Chuck laughed. Those production levels were absurdly over estimated. This plant was unable to reach such levels unless more and newer equipment was brought in.

"We will also begin daily re-education classes in which we will allow you to be instilled with pride and excellence and admiration for our new and improved way of working. You will become prideful, yet supplicant in your admiration of the new way of managing your work and career."

Barry leaned in close to Chuck and whispered, "Is this bunch Chinese or North Korean?" and giggled under his breath, "whoever the fuck they are, I'll give them this, they've got balls!"

Chuck whispered, "This is all bullshit is what it is. I'm about to walk out of this mickey-mouse meeting and call an attorney. This can't possibly be legal."

"True that. And check it out, every one of them is wearing one of those phone headsets so that they can talk amongst each other all the time. Creepy."

"Yeah, very creepy, very totalitarian if you ask me. Like North Korea, but with less bumbling idiocy."

". . . the new workdays will be twelve hours and you may enjoy three full breaks during the day of fifteen minutes each, during which time you may enjoy a leisurely lunch, or stroll around the exercise track around the inside perimeter of the campus . . . this track will be finished later today . . .and you may also use the time to spend with your co-workers in lively discussions regarding how best to improve your work, or you may simply choose to meditate or exercise your body in a refreshing session of tai chi movement. Those of you who wish to further enrich your mind may choose to consult with your team leader and allow that leader to benefit you with their wisdom so that you may become a better worker."

Barry snorted at that and was rewarded with a glare from one of the men at the front of the room, one of the ones that hadn't yet spoken. Chuck noticed that three of the white-suited soldiers stepped away from the wall and lowered their weapons from port arms as if they were about to attack. They received a shake of the head from one of the men at the front of the room, and the three soldiers relaxed slightly and stepped back against the wall.

Chuck wondered what would happen if someone said *fuck this* and attempted to leave the meeting. He'd already seen a co-worker tasered and couldn't imagine what would happen if someone were to more overtly challenge them. It was highly illegal, holding them all in this room, by force, it was illegal detention, and maybe even kidnapping, but whatever the legal distinction was, he planned on having his attorney hear about it damned soon. There was no way he would work for these Communistic clowns. The whole thing was a farce.

"Leaving the campus during your workday is prohibited. Smoking on the premises is prohibited, the designated smoking areas are, at this time, being converted into Tai Chi exercise areas, and all soda and snack food machines will be replaced with bottled water machines and also vending machines that will dispense Lettuce, bananas and boiled eggs and rice. You will come to love these tasty treats as much as you now enjoy the Doritos and Cheese Poofs . . ."

Chuck rolled his eyes, thinking he surely must be dreaming or in an episode of the Twilight Zone.

"Three new buildings will be in place on the campus by tomorrow. These dormitories will have beds and toilet facilities and will allow workers to live on the campus so that they may always be near their work. This will allow dedicated workers to always be on time, and volunteer for extra work, so that they may be exemplary workers and over-achieve their production quotas. These workers will be among the most highly valued workers and will be a shining light and example to others to follow. These dormitories will, of course, be segregated into both male and female buildings, as there will be no sexual fraternization allowed between co-workers. "

Chuck leaned back and crossed his arms across his chest. He knew that the dorms would be empty. There is no way any self-respecting American worker would agree to such working conditions. In fact, he half-expected a riot to break out any moment. The mood in the room was alternating between murderous outrage and stunned disbelief. Like himself, most employees in the room were almost in shock, the disbelief so palpable it was as if they'd been punched in the gut . He knew that most workers in the room would be calling union reps and attorneys as soon as this meeting let out. Most would already have left if not for the fact that there about forty armed guards lining the perimeter of the room. Armed guards in an

American business making sure that no employee left the room? The legal consequences of that action alone was going to make worldwide fucking news within twenty-four hours, Chuck reasoned.

He tucked his head down on his chest and tuned them out. It all sounded like some sort of slightly updated Communistic propaganda spiel that had been crudely adapted to an American company, and there was nothing in it of value to anyone working or living in the U.S.

He listened as the woman, known as Elvae Hsiao number 7 continued, "talking to co-workers is prohibited during your work shift unless your discussion involves work related matter, but we encourage you to instead, talk to your group leader in order to avoid miscommunication between leaders and workers and also to avoid wasting your valuable work time. Coming to work late is inexcusable and will be met with punishment and fines. No reading materials, books, magazines, newspapers or other such items will be allowed on the factory work floor. All music devices and cell phones will be locked away during your work day. Sunglasses will not be worn anywhere on the campus and no jewelry will be allowed to be worn on the body where it can be seen. All tattoos must be covered completely, and if any tattoos are visible and unable to be covered up by clothing or makeup we will offer tattoo removal services that may be scheduled through the medical office. Costs of tattoo removal will be deducted from the workers' paychecks. Workers are encouraged to maintain a plain and unremarkable appearance at all times. If any workers need instruction upon these matters you are encouraged to present yourself to the medical office at first opportunity. Women will not be allowed to wear clothing which shows any part of the breasts, and blouses must be buttoned up to the neckline. Men will no longer be allowed to wear blue jeans and must adopt a style corresponding to the garments that you see your leadership group wearing, which means that men will be required to wear the official pants of the company. All shirts must be buttoned of to the throat area, and no necklaces, rings, or other jewelry is allowed. No metal studs, earrings, or other adornments will be allowed on faces, lips, noses, ears or hands."

Chuck noticed that the official pants of the company were the loose fitting slacks that were pretty much gray, shapeless, formless things they were wearing. Chuck had heard them called the Mao suit. There was no way they'd get all these people to wear those hideous things.

He was getting to the point where he was seriously considering getting up and walking out of this place. Surely they wouldn't shoot him. On the other hand, they'd already shown no compunction whatsoever about using a Taser on an employee, and even though Chuck knew it wouldn't kill him, he knew that his heart may not be able to handle it. Those things *could* kill.

He wondered how many people would follow him out if he decided to get up and exhort everyone to walk out. There were about eighty or ninety people in the room, and he figured that maybe twenty five or thirty would actually have the balls to stage a walk out. The problem was though, that they had almost twenty men with AR's standing at the ready, and if each rifle held twenty or more rounds, which they probably did, then if the Chinese were serious about stopping any rebellious employees, then they had plenty of firepower with which to do so.

Chuck didn't want to be shot, tasered, or even punched, so he stayed put. The attorneys and the Union guys could take care of this bullshit later.

" . . . all workers must be careful to maintain a placid appearance on their face at all times, China TOC leadership will not tolerate looks of negativity or dissatisfaction. Shoes must be black and have tied laces at all times, no sneakers or boots will be allowed in the building. If workers are unable to provide their own shoes at this time, they may purchase shoes from the commissary and the costs will be deducted from their paycheck. No chewing of gum, or breath mints, cough drops, or tobacco products will be allowed. Any workers appearing for work that have odors of cigarettes, or other body odors about them or on their clothes will be encouraged to use the company showers in the dormitories and then re-present themselves to their floor manager for inspection before their shift is to begin. Personal hygiene is the worker's responsibility and must be done before reporting for work; failure to do so will result in administrative penalties and fines."

Chuck gave up on trying to follow the exhaustingly long list of rules and just tuned her out; instead looking around the room to study the looks on his co-workers faces. Most looked extremely upset, and several men were red in the face and seemed as if they were about to attack the *leadership group*. Many of the women, especially the older women, were crying, and most, like Chuck and Barry, were looking around as if to say *what the fuck is this?*

Eason Chane, number 9 eventually retook his place at the dais and began formally introducing the leadership group and explain who would be in charge of what groups on the factory floor. Chuck ignored them and began plotting his calls. First, he'd call the factory Union rep and lodge an official complaint, and then he'd call his attorney, and then his CPA. There was no way he would allow his retirement nest egg to be compromised by these Communist lunatics. He could care less what deal the friggin president had made with the Chinese. It was simply unlawful to do what they claimed that they were doing.

The meeting ended with all of the leadership group applauding themselves and bowing to each other, and Chuck noticed that most of them also glared out at the American workers as if they were expecting the Americans to also bow to them and applaud them, and they seemed offended by not getting these ceremonial acts of homage. Chuck wanted to give them all the double bird, but he tempered his anger by the fact that this group was ringed by soldiers carrying AK-47's. What was the admonish from that old song? *You don't tug on superman's cape?*

Chuck and Barry and several others immediately headed for the break room where they all began to pull out their cell phones to make calls to Union reps and attorneys, but they were stopped when they discovered that there was no cell phone service.

"No problem," Barry said, "I'll just go get in the car and drive to the nearest spot to pick up a signal and make my calls. I'm not working for this batch of Commies." He began walking towards the exit. Chuck followed, and watched as Barry grabbed his timecard and punched out and then walked towards the door. He was stopped by the new floor manager, Cui Jiane number 4, and questioned.

Chuck wasn't close enough to hear the words, but from the animated body language and histrionics, he could see that the woman, Cui Jiane was not going to allow him to leave. He wondered how it was possible that these people could think that they could keep them imprisoned and force them to work? He watched as Barry became more and more agitated, and soon he was red-faced and screaming at Cui Jiane number 4, and within seconds four of the white-suited armed guards were surrounding Barry and

Cui Jiane number 4.

The men moved in to an arm's length of the two argued and suddenly Barry stopped and backed up. He blinked his eyes and looked at the guards. He said something to one of them and it must have been some sort of epithet or provocation, because the guard pushed Barry. Barry fell back on his heels and into the arms of the guard behind him who grabbed him by the backs of his arms. He then held Barry's hands together behind his back by his wrists, and the third guard stepped in and slipped a pre-looped band of zip cord over his wrists and then jerked on the free end quickly tightening it so that Barry was cuffed from behind. Then, from behind him, the guard pulled out another zip tie and squatted down and looped it around Barry's ankles and then quickly drew it tight. Barry must have felt it because he looked down at his feet and then yelled, "Let me go! You can't do this!" The guard behind Barry then pushed his forward so that he was falling face down, and before he could hit the floor face first, the two guards on either side of him grabbed the zip tie at his wrists, preventing him from hitting the floor, and the two guards behind him grabbed the zip tie between his ankles. Now they had him face down, horizontally and they began marching him away from the door and across the production floor. It was like carrying a short length of telephone pole. All Barry could do was wriggle from the waist, but the guards were too strong and in great physical shape that Barry's struggling was no problem for them to control.

The whole maneuver had taken less than five seconds. It was a slick move and had obviously been rehearsed and used many times.

Chuck was shocked at the sight of a co-worker being physically restrained right in front of a hundred co-workers. There were gasps and shouts throughout the production floor by those who'd watched the confrontation. Without any further word, the guards carried Barry off the floor and down a hallway and Chuck saw the door slam behind them, and he could hear Barry yelling for someone to call the Police, or the Union, or an attorney.

Unfortunately, their cell phones were unusable, and Chuck heard someone say that the pay phones in the break room were out of order. He walked over to his desk and picked up his phone. It was a land line and he was relieved to get a dial tone. He dialed 911 and waited for the emergency operator to answer. He was shocked when he heard a Chinese voice speak.

"China Toc USA, can I help you?"

Chuck held the phone away from his face and looked at it, as if it was a foreign object. What the hell?

The heavily-accented voice repeated, "China Toc USA, can I help you?"

"I need an outside line. I need to call out. Now."

"Yes sir, thank you , sir." She answered.

Chuck breathed a sigh of relief. Finally, he was getting some assistance.

"Provide me, sir, if you please, with the number you wish to call and I will assist in dialing it for you."

Chuck frowned, and the exhaled in frustration, "Nine-one-one, please. I need to dial nine, one, one!"

"Is there an emergency sir? That is an emergency number."

"Yes there's an emergency, *that's* why I'm trying to dial nine-one-one!"

"Thank you sir," the young girl's voice was exceedingly polite, "What type of emergency is it that you require assistance with? I will happily alerts China Toc security to assist you in your troubles."

Chuck wanted to scream, "I don't need China Toc security, because China Toc security *is the fucking* problem! Now *get me a god-damned outside line, right fucking now!*" Chuck was so angry now his hands were shaking.

"Sir, I must admonish you that China Toc policies prohibit the type of language that you are using. You may refer to the policy in section two of the personnel handbook of policies and regulations stating *that foul and cursing language will be prohibited and unacceptable for any reasons-*"

"Look lady, I don't give a flying fuck about the policies and regulations. I just watched a man cuffed and taken away, and I want the police here, and I want them called right now!"

"Sir, I see that you are located in section eight, row seven of the production floor, I will send assistance immediately. Please have a seat and wait for them to arrive at your station to assist you."

Chuck sighed, "I am sitting, now will you please give me an outside line?"

"Sir, you will need to speak with your manager for authorization to obtain an outside line, and I can see sir, that you are not seated. Will you please comply and have a seat and wait for assistance?"

Chuck slammed the phone down onto its' base unit and looked up. He knew there were video cameras mounted all through the place, but as far as he knew, they hadn't worked in over three years. There was no need for them though. There was no pilferage because no one would any use whatsoever for the plastic pieces they produced. It would take several truckloads of the pieces to be worthwhile, and even if you could steal them, you'd have to sell them to their current customers, and that would be discovered rather quickly. Plus, Scranton Belsig would never have considered spying on their own employees. The cameras were there to allow supervisors to watch the production lines in operation and see if there were any slowdowns or glitches. He supposed though, that it would be just like the commies to have them up and going again.

Within minutes his desk was surrounded by four of the white-suited guards, with rifles of course, and a man who's badge identified him as Leon Laiex number 1. Chuck could see from his stern face that Leon was a no-nonsense kind of guy. Probably took his job way too seriously, but for that matter, all these commies did.

Leon Laiex number 1 was talking softly on his headset as he approached Chuck's desk.

"Is there a problem?"

Chuck heard a shout from behind him, it must have come from the far side of the production floor. Another skirmish was break out apparently. He fully expected that most, if not all of the employees would not be showing up for work tomorrow. This was too outrageous to be believed. In the United States of America in the year 2019, it just seemed inconceivable that these things could happen. This was a free country after all. Slavery no longer existed, and slavery where a foreign country came in and took over American businesses and employees? It was unreal. He knew too, that it was illegal. There was no way that the American government would allow this to stand. Again he thought, China Toc may have bought the company, but they couldn't treat employees like this. No way.

"Sir, what is the problem?" Leon Laiex number 1 said as he stepped up face to face with Chuck, squaring off with him. Chuck looked slightly down at Leon Laiex number 1. The man was just a tad shorter than him, and Chuck outweighed the man by a good ninety pounds. The man looked adequately fit, but in a fight Chuck figured he could easily best the man. He wasn't menacing in the least. Other than his voice and his cocksure attitude. He seemed to have confidence to spare.

"Yes, *number one*," Chuck said, using the numeric as sarcastically as possible, "there is a fucking problem. I just saw a co-worker brutally attacked and taken away and I intend to call the police and file a complaint for assault and-"

"First of all, *sir*," Leon Laiex number 1 leaned in close enough to Chuck that he could smell his stale breath, and said in a menacing tone, "you will *immediately* refrain from using vulgar language with me. I will not, under any circumstances, tolerate it."

Chuck noticed that Leon Laiex number 1 seemed to have a more accurate grasp of the English language than his cohorts.

"And what the *fuck* are you going to do about it if I don't? You know there is such a thing is this country as the First Amendment, also known as freedom of speech? Are you and your goons going to beat me up too? Maybe after that you'll be promoted to number one and a half!"

Leon Laiex number 1 leaned in so close to Chuck's face that Chuck could have bitten his nose.

"*Worker*, if you continue to disrespect me with your language I will force you to show respect, and trust me, sir, I will need no help whatsoever from my *goons*, as you choose to call them."

Chuck laughed in the man's face.

"*You're* going to force me? *Without* your goon squad and rifles and tasers? Not very likely. Just how would you plan on doing this?"

Leon Laiex number 1 smiled and stepped back a step away from Chuck. He turned to his four man squad and muttered something to them. They seemed to relax and a couple of them broke out in smiles.

Chuck watched as Leon Laiex number 1 reached into his tunic and pulled out a small wooden stick that had a tiny chain attached to it and a key ring loop at one end. He held it up and put his finger through the metal loop at the end and twirled it around so that the piece of wood twirled round and round.

"Worker, do you know what this is?"

Chuck shrugged, "A broken, dirty chopstick?"

Someone behind them giggled, it seems that they now had an audience.

Leon Laiex number 1 smiled as if he too got the joke, and took a step closer to Chuck but in a non-threatening manner.

"Worker, this little piece of wood is called a Kubaton, or a *come-along*. We also call it a *Tootsie-Roll*, because apparently it resembles your American piece of candy?"

Chuck nodded. The piece of wood did indeed look like a Tootsie Roll. Same thickness, maybe an inch or two longer. Same dark brown color with the same four sections that the Tootsie Rolls had that he remembered from his childhood. He couldn't imagine such a thing being useful as any sort of weapon, unless he was slow enough to allow someone to jab it into his eye. He had absolutely no intention of allowing that, so, in his opinion the object was a joke.

"Oh, I get it *number one*," he grinned, "you're going to *shove that tootsie-roll up your ass* and I'll fall on the floor because I'm laughing so hard!"

Leon Laiex number 1 smiled again, and twirled the keychain loop so that the little wooden stick circled round and round his finger. He walked slowly around Chuck in a circle and then stopped behind him and leaned in close to his ear and whispered,

"No, what I am going to do though, is this"

Chuck felt his head jerked violently back by the hand full of hair that Leon Laiex number 1 had grabbed and he was pulled off balance so that he was rocked back on his heels. He could feel Leon Laiex number 1's arm supporting his back and then he felt Leon Laiex number 1's right hand with the tip tootsie-roll come-along shoved up under his jawline where it angled down just below the ear. Leon Laiex number 1 pressed in, ever so slightly on the bundle of nerves there and Chuck felt as if his body has received a jolt of electricity. His back arched even further and his heels began dancing on the ground. He felt as if his entire body was being electrocuted. The pain was fiercely intense and unlike anything he'd ever felt before. He immediately understood why they called the device a come-along. He couldn't image resisting this slight pressure that was causing so much intense pain more than one more second that he had too.

Leon Laiex number 1 removed the come along and quickly shoved Chuck back to his feet and Chuck reached up to feel his neck. The pain had subsided immediately. He was grateful for Leon stopping the demonstration of pain, and then repulsed at having felt anything but pure hatred for the man.

"You see Chuck," Leon Laiex number 1 said amiably as he stood, calmly relaxed before him, there is no need to be antagonistic. Those feelings are detrimental to your career and your health. Anger causes cancer you know. Can we not be professional co-workers, even be friends and *get along?*"

Chuck glared at the cocky little man, "you can threaten me physically, and you can threaten my job all you want, but I will never, ever, be friends or co-workers to a bunch of Commie assholes like you people. Never. I quit. I'm leaving this shit hole of a place. Right now."

Leon Laiex number 1 nodded, "Fair enough. We will allow you to leave, and I will offer my hand in friendship and respect," He said cordially as he put his hand out for a handshake. Like all Americans who've been programmed throughout their lives by the simple act of a handshake,

Chuck automatically responded by putting his hand out without thinking.

Leon Laiex number 1 grasped his hand to shake it and then placed his other hand on top of Chucks' and then Chuck felt Leon Laiex number 1 bending his palm downward at the wrist and his fingers upwards with his left hand and in his right hand the end of the *tootsie roll* began pushing into the back of his hand. The nerves in his hand exploded in pain and Chuck immediately dropped to his knees and yowled in pain. His hand felt as if it was being torn from his body while it was also being run over by a car. Tears sprang immediately to his eyes and his knees hurt from having dropped onto the concrete factory floor so heavily. He writhed in pain and squeezed his eyes shut so tightly he felt his head might explode.

Leon Laiex number 1 relaxed the tootsie-roll slightly to lessen the pain, but kept the pressure on just enough so that Chuck didn't dare try to stand up or even move slightly. Leon Laiex number 1 leaned down and whispered in Chuck's ear.

"Despite your willful ignorance and insistence upon slanderous epithets I will do you one more favor before I escort you from the premises and terminate your employment with China Toc." He leaned in closer, but spoke louder this time, no doubt to allow the other workers to get a preview of what was headed their way if they resisted in the ways that Chuck had done.

"You have repeatedly cursed me and the other leaders with your profane slurs. I have the authority, and I should, but I won't this time, allow the goons, as you call them, take you out back and beat you until you pledge your everlasting allegiance to the mighty corporation that is China Toc. I will give you leniency simply because you are too stupid to understand just how spoiled and ridiculous your pathetic American worker ways are. You are practically useless as a member of meaningful society." He lessened his grip on Chuck's hand and helped him to his feet. Chuck felt sweat on his forehead. He was trembling with anger and fear. He'd never felt such incredible pain so quickly and efficiently applied, and yet when it was over, it was simply gone. Like it was never there. But he'd never forget it, that's for sure.

Leon Laiex number 1 helped him to his feet, and then started walking him to the exit. Chuck knew that within minutes he would be on the phone to the police to have this man arrested for assault, and then he'd be calling his Union rep, and then he'd call an attorney.

Leon Laiex number 1 stopped at the door, and opened it for Chuck. The sunlight streamed in and made Chuck blink.

"What happened to Barry? I saw you guys cuff him and haul him off. I want him walking out of here with me. If that doesn't happen there will be a hundred cops here within the hour to arrest you people."

Leon Laiex number 1 smiled condescendingly at Chuck,

"You have no rights to demand anything ex-worker. This is not United States of America. This territory belongs to China. Did you not pay attention in the meeting?"

"That's bullshit. This is not a Commie fucking country. This is the United States. You'll be in jail within an hour my friend. You just watch and see. I'll be back."

Leon Laiex number 1 smiled and shook his head, "The American authorities has no legal right to do anything on this property. You can call them. It makes no difference. They will simply explain to you that they have no authority to come onto this property. Only the laws of China are enforceable on these premises. You will see."

"Fuck you, you Commie bastard. You go straight to hell."

Leon Laiex number 1 reached forward and placed his right hand on Chuck's wrist, and at first Chuck thought that the man was going to shake his hand again. Then he felt the man pushing his hand down and then he felt the other hand at the back of his elbow and suddenly the tootsie-roll was pushing into the back of the nerves there and his arm was going numb. He screamed, but Leon Laiex number 1 held the wrist in one hand and the Kubaton against the back of the elbow and the pain forced Chuck to go up

135

onto his toes to lessen the angle of upward force and his arm just got number and number and shots of electric painshot back and forth from his elbow to his fingertips and back again. He moaned in pain as Leon Laiex number 1 held him, dancing in that awkward position of pain and he leaned forward and whispered in Chuck's ear, "We are not *Communists* you thick-headed moronic simpleton. What we are is, your leaders. When you come back here, and you will come back, crawling on your knees begging for a job, you will be brought to heel. You will be subservient and humble and meek and you will give us the respect we deserve. We are saving you from yourselves. Now, I am going to let you go. I have work to do and no more time to waste on your foolishness. You are hereby terminated from your employment with China Toc."

He shoved Chuck out the door and Chuck stumbled forward and heard the door shut behind him. He fished his keys out of his pocket and began walking to his car. Two of the white-suited guards walked behind him and he wanted to give them a good cursing, but he knew that if he started a confrontation there was a good chance that he could get seriously hurt, so he swallowed his pride and said nothing to them. He could hear them softly chattering on their headsets, no doubt offering an ongoing progress report to number one. Chuck could just imagine the dialogue. *Yes, he's in the car.*

Yes, he is driving away. No, he did not cause any more trouble.

Of course, we will watch to make sure he leaves the premises and causes no more problems.

No, he is not turning around and coming back.

#   #   #   #   #

Chuck drove to a fast-food restaurant and pulled through the drive through, ordering a burger and fries, and then ate it while he sat in the parking lot. When he finished, he called his family attorney, Richard Little and told him what had happened that morning.

"That's quite a story Chuck," Richard explained to him after he'd heard the story, "but I've just found out about this myself. In fact, the firm had a long meeting about the situation just this morning. I just got out of the meeting a few minutes ago."

"And?"

"Well, Chuck, the fact of the matter is this; the U S government did make this deal with China. We are all astounded by the scope and depth of this thing, and it affects all businesses in the section of the country that they showed you. A big rectangle stretching from the Kansas-Oklahoma state line all the way up to just under the Canadian border. All this land is now officially a Chinese province, or in strictly American terms, the 51st state. The 52nd state if you want to consider that Puerto Rico has been a state for the past fifty years or so. Either way, they weren't lying to you."

Chuck was stunned, "Okay, so let's say that this is true, and that all this land, the American fucking Midwest, is basically China. . . they can't really force us to work for them, can they? That would mean that we are basically slaves!"

"No. They are *not* able to force you to work for them. If they said that, then they are incorrect, however, if you quit, or are fired within that ten year period of time, you will be unemployable anywhere in the U S, Canada, and Mexico, except at fast food restaurants, or any other minimum wage jobs, and you will forfeit all your 401k and company stock, savings accounts etcetera."

"You're shitting me! So, now I'm a minimum wage worker?"

"Well, my advice would be not to quit or be fired, and I say that because you will never get hired anywhere. The reason you won't is because there will be so many people who are making just slightly more than minimum wage who *will* quit and go back to working in fast food places and other minimum wage jobs because they won't be losing much, and they will be able to avoid working for the Commies. These min wage jobs will fill up rather quickly, and you'll never find a job."

"This is horseshit!"

"I know, I know. The other thing is this . . . if you think you can quit working there and then just move out of the U S – China territory and start over in the so-called free world, think again. You're on a list. It's a criminal offense for any business to hire you outside of the China territory for the next ten years."

"This is absurd! How can the U S government literally sell its' land and it's human workers to the Chinese? You're telling me that the U S government has *sold me as a slave* to China!"

"Yes, that's what it amounts to. But, there is good news, it's only for ten years."

"Jesus fucking Christ Richard, if I were over there right now I'd punch you in the face for that fucking remark! Only *ten fucking years?*"

"What can I say buddy? It's out of my hands. It's not like I'll make any money off of it. We're not allowed to litigate anything from any claims made by workers against the Chinese government. It's hands off. No attorney can help you."

Chuck said nothing. His mind was reeling.

"They've also taken all of our money?"

"Yes, I'm afraid so. There's no recourse for it either. The light at the end of the tunnel for that is that, in ten years, when the territory and all the businesses inside the territory has reverted back to U S ownership, your funds will be returned, just as long as the company has proven to be profitable in that ten year period. If it is profitable, which it probably will be. . . I mean, they're not even going to make the Chinese pay ANY taxes. . . so, they're already ahead of the curve compared with American companies. Anyway, then your money will be returned in full. If it isn't, everyone's funds will be docked an appropriate amount to make up the difference and you'll receive the rest of it. Then things will go back to normal."

"Except that I'll have lost ten years of being able to increase my retirement fund!"

"True, but I believe that it's a moot point."

"Why is that?"

"Because, I believe that in ten years, our government will look back at the past decade and they'll think that this experiment was a success and they'll allow the Chinese government to retain control, and I believe that they'll also sell off other problematic and poorly producing industries. One of the partners here has already came up with a name for it, 'In-Place-Outsourcing,' and I believe he's right. Imagine the Chinese taking over the cable companies and whipping them into shape, or the airlines industries. The mind boggles, doesn't it?"

Chuck sighed, "I'm fucked then."

"Why is that?"

"Because I got into a huge fight with one of the Chinese managers and the bastard even physically assaulted me. I plan on calling the police and filing a report. I want that Commie bastard arrested! Before it was over with, I quit, was fired, whatever. They walked me out the door."

"Oh my God, Chuck, you didn't!"

"Yeah, I did."

"Well, the police will not help you. Calling them is a waste of time. You have no legal recourse. This thing was put in place by the President himself. The media will be calling it the great sellout, or something equally as bad. But, it's a done deal. The U S is now officially co-opted by a foreign government. China actually, physically owns a huge chunk of the U S. My advice to you is to go back there and beg them, get you job back if it's at all possible. Apologize to them. Tell them you are sorry. Whatever it takes. Unless of course, you would rather take your chances on a minimum wage job, competing with kids a third your age."

"Well, I can't live on minimum wage, and my 401k that they now own has almost half a million bucks in it. I don't want to throw that away, even if I do have to wait another ten years to collect it. But I sure as hell don't want to work for those bastards again. They were tasereing and beating people!"

"Yeah, unfortunately, they have a right to do those things since they are not bound by U S laws."

"What are you guys going to do?"

"Well, we aren't affected, other than being unable to give legal help to any Chinese workers, which is what you are now. The treaty only permitted them to take over labor intensive industries, manufacturing and farming and those types of industries. Mom and pop companies with less than a hundred employees are exempt, as are educational and legal institutions and military and entertainment. It was mostly manufacturing companies."

"Is there any thought that the American people, as a whole, will object so strongly to this that the President will nullify the treaty and call it a failed experiment?"

"Not that I can see. This is a done deal, and the money experts, taking all of the emotion out of the equation, are saying that the companies, the industries affected will actually show a lot more profit, and in ten years will be much improved. Which is why I said, that in ten years when this so-called experiment is over, that our government will look at it and say, let's do it again with other industries. In other words, I think that this, in-place outsourcing, is the wave of the future. I don't like it, and Nancy and I have been talking for years about moving to Belize, and I think we're going to sell out my partnership stake in the firm and go ahead and pull the trigger on a shorefront villa we've been looking at."

"No shit?" Chuck paused, then swallowed his pride, "Can I hitch a ride with you down there? I'll work as your pool boy, errand runner, anything you want until I'm able to get myself set up and self-sufficient. I swear I'll be out of your hair inside of six weeks."

"I'm sorry, Chuck, can't do it. They've already flagged all China-US workers passports. You'll never get out of the country, and if I got caught helping you, it's a third degree felony and I'd end up doing twenty years in a federal pen. That's not exactly hard time, but it's a helluva lot worse than sitting on the beach in Belize sipping a Mojito."

"Crap. Well, I've got to decide what I'm going to do."

"Good luck buddy, and hey, at least remember one thing."

"Yeah, what's that?"

"If you do go back, at least you won't have to worry about having a job for ten years, that's security, and it's not like they can lay you off and find a horde of resumes from people begging to be hired, you know?"

#   #   #   #   #

Chuck sat at home for three weeks, making phone calls to friends, begging for jobs with anyone who had a family owned business with less than a hundred employees, but no one was hiring. The two that were hiring explained to him that they literally couldn't hire him, not legally anyway, and they were unwilling to do such a thing illegally because of the severe consequences they'd face if caught. He considered starting his own small business, mowing yards or something equally as menial, but he didn't have the financial resources to attempt such a thing, and besides, he had no skills that would allow him to make a decent living. He spent some time looking in the want ads online, but got zero replies to his resumes, and the few calls that he made were met with less than warm responses.

After almost a month of unemployment, his checking account was almost empty, as was his pantry. His car payment would be late, and so would his utility bills. He cancelled his auto insurance and also his cable TV, but he was losing ground too fast to be proud. He finally came to the decision that he could get out of the China territory and take a big chance on being able to get a new identity and start over, or he could go back to China Toc and ask for his job back.

The lure of starting over was strong. It would be a wild and exciting adventure, but he also knew that it could just as well be a cruel and miserable nightmare. He was the wrong side of middle age, and he was out of shape physically and he was not very confident about his chances. If he had been ten or fifteen years younger he would have taken the chance. After long and tortured thought, he came to the conclusion that government-imposed slavery was more prudent than self-imposed misery and death. He would go back to Eason Chane and China Toc and ask to be reinstated.

#   #   #   #   #

He was made to park in a parking lot almost a half mile from the building, and then when he made it to the gate leading into the employee parking area where he'd have to cross before he made it to the main building, he was forced to speak into the speaker and computer screen mounted on the gate. They made him wait for almost forty-five minutes while they located Eason Chane to come meet him at the gate and escort him inside. While he was waiting, Chuck noticed about ten new modular buildings that had been added to the campus. Several large trucks drove past as he waited and he could see that the company was buying many new production machines. They were apparently very serious about hitting those absurd numbers that they'd bragged about on the first day. He guessed that with their slave-driving mentality that they'd probably hit those absurd numbers too.

Eason Chane approached the gate and stopped without opening it. Chuck looked at him through the metal links. He took a deep breath, and tamped down his distaste and spoke in as cheerful a voice as he could muster,

"Hello Eason Chane number 9, how are you this fine day, leader?" Chuck hoped he wasn't laying it on too thick.

Eason Chane stared at him through the chain link fence for a long time.

"You are Chuck, the line production manager who left on day one, correct?"

He nodded, "Yes, Eason Chane, you know that I am."

"If I remember correctly, and I do, you calling me commie bastard and many other names on that day? You are not wishing to repeat those names today?"

"No sir, I am not. I offer my apologies to you for my poor behavior. I have learned, and I wish to speak with you about coming back to the company. I believe that as a fair and respectful leader of men that you will allow me to learn, under your direction, to become a profitable and thankful member of your team." Chuck was making up his speech as the words came out of his mouth. He knew that these people were egotistical in that they believed their way was the best way, the only way, and he was literally under the rock and the hard place. It was up to him to choose between subservience or misery. Subservience would at least put food on the table. Misery was nothing more than a quick spiral downward. He would play Eason Chane's game and he would chew his own tongue off before he screwed it up. He was proud, but he wasn't a fool.

"Good enough, worker Chuck, you may follow me."

He unlocked the gate and allowed Chuck inside, and they walked into the building. Chuck was astonished to see dozens more machines and three complete new production lines. He was also surprised to see almost every one of his old co-workers. None of them had dared to leave? That seemed impossible. Then he saw Barry, working at a machine, instead of managing a line of workers. Barry turned to watch them as they passed by, and Chuck could see that one of Barry's arms was in a sling, and that he had a patch over one eye. He looked as if he'd been beaten to within an inch of his life. Every inch of flesh on his body that Chuck could see was bruised. The look in his face, in his one eye was that of total and utter defeat. He looked like a dead man standing.

They passed by his machine and then Eason Chane stopped and began talking on his headset. Chuck, not knowing Chinese had no way of knowing what they were saying, just waited. After a moment, Chane turned to him, "Wait here, I must go solve a problem, I will return in five minutes."

Chuck agreed, and Eason Chane stalked off to solve his crisis. As soon as he turned the corner, Chuck walked the few feet back to Barry's machine.

"Barry? Buddy, what the hell happened to you? You get in a car accident or something?"

Barry shook his head, "No man, don't talk to me directly, they're always watching. Just stand there and listen up as I work."

Chuck answered, "Okay" as well as he could without appearing to be talking to his friend.

"Chuck, that first day?" he coughed, "they took me into a back room and beat the fuck out of me. I fought them. Hell, I fought for two full days. I wasn't the only one back there either. Tony Perkins, Russ Hamilton, and Joy Layne, and Joan Weber? They killed Tony Perkins, and put Joan Weber into a fucking coma. The rest of us, we gave up fighting. They beat the rebellion plumb out of us. Whatever you do, don't cross them, don't resist, don't sass them in any way. Learn their names, their fucking Chinese names, not their numbers. Play along. Stay calm and stay alive. Being alive is better than being dead."

"Jesus Christ, Barry!"

"Trust me Chuck, just do whatever it takes to get along."

"But Barry, I know you. You're not the type to give up, and put up with this kind of crap! You're saying give up? Just let them stomp on you like a bug?"

Barry glanced at him, "Yep, that's exactly what I'm saying."

Chuck felt a shudder of fear go through his body. He saw Eason Chane across the room, heading back in their direction.

"Chuck?"

"Yeah Barry?" he looked back at his friend and saw a spark in his face, like he'd suddenly come back alive.

"In ten years?"

"Yeah?"

"I'll get out of here a free man once again. A true U S citizen, and I'm going to come back and pay Eason Chane *number fucking nine* and his eight friends a little visit. And when I do? God help their miserable fucking worthless souls."

"Worker Chuck," Eason Chane said as he came back around the corner, "follow me."

Chuck followed him and glanced back for another look at Barry who was working as fast as he could, as if he was a machine himself.

Eason Chane led him to a room that had a plastic chair facing a blank white wall. A pull down projector screen was on the wall, and there was a projector mounted overhead.

"Worker Chuck, before you will be allowed to re-take your original position, you will be required to participate in a three day reorientation which will hopefully instill in you some productive values and a sense of duty to leadership."

Chuck had to fight to keep the look of distaste off his face, "Okay,

Eason Chane. I agree."

Eason Chane turned the lights down, "You are required to sit through the entire production. Do not leave the room. A bathroom break will be allowed later. I will return in four hours. Watch every minute of the presentation. Do not sleep, do not be bored, and do not lose your concentration. I will return in four hours to give you a bathroom break, and we will have tea. Then you will be given a test, if you fail this test, you will be escorted out of the building and you will be right back where you were yesterday, with no job and no hope of ever being allowed back to employment with China Toc. Is that clear?"

Chuck nodded.

Eason Chane turned on the projector and left the room. The video came to life on the screen and it began with a group of children singing a patriotic song, and as they sang, the words scrolled across the screen in English. Chuck knew immediately what this was. It was a piece of government propaganda that was tilted towards Chinese life and values, and the 'virtues' of China Toc as a career and lifestyle. The music was loud, overbearing and the lights flashed hypnotically and rhythmically. Words flashed on and off the screen in flashing blurs. Pride! Then the scene would change and show a group of factory workers and the word Teamwork would flash at the same time that flashing lights flickered. This was basic mind control. Brainwashing. Heavy-handed and blunt and unceasing. He figured that the leadership at China Toc knew that men like Barry responded to physical stimuli and so they beat him. He also figured that Barry may not know it yet, but the beating he'd been given would not be the last one. Chuck figured that they'd beat on Barry many more times before it was all over with, and in ten years Barry would be as docile as a baby lamb.

In his own case, he guessed that they figured his key was mental. He tried to concentrate on the video, knowing that he dare not fail the upcoming test in four hours. He would do everything he could to please them. But he also knew that he had to divide his mind. One half was theirs, and the other half was his. He would remain rebellious but he would pretend, in their presence to be subservient and thankful to them, and all the while, he would plot the same revenge he knew that Barry was plotting.

It would be tough, mentally, to keep his wits. He would need to appear brainwashed, but at the same time, resist it and keep his sanity, keep the core of himself complete and intact. He tried to remember the novel by George Orwell, Nineteen-eighty-four. Had Winston been able to stay himself and defeat the state? He couldn't remember.

The End

The truth about U S debt owned by foreign countries.

Every American should be concerned by the huge amounts of debt that the U.S. government owes Chinese lenders. The Chinese own $1.25 trillion of U.S. debt. In fact, foreign governments own almost 50% of all U.S. debt. Meanwhile, Japan is increasing its holdings of U.S. debt to over $1.23 trillion, challenging the top spot among foreign creditors.

In 2016, the total amount of official debt owed by the federal, state and local governments is $21.6 trillion.

Some experts predict more than $120 trillion of unfunded future liabilities on the federal government balance sheet. More than $6 trillion is actually owned by the federal government in accounts dedicated to Social Security, Medicare and other entitlements. Some of the debt is owned by investors and corporations, including individuals who purchase individual U.S. Treasury's to the Chinese government and Japanese governments.

One of these days, the bubble will burst. Something will have to be done about it if our economy is to survive.

PART THREE

Batteries Not Included

Ray Chandler woke up and looked over at the alarm clock. He used a

battery powered alarm clock, because it had several features that he liked.

First of all, it had a loud beep-beep-beep that gradually increased the longer

he let it go off without shutting it off or hitting snooze. The snooze bar

itself was a wide plastic button that covered the full top curve or the clock,

so it was easy to roll over with a hand out and just tap down on the space

bar and reset it for ten minutes, so it was operationally easier to manage

than one of the flat, square radio/alarm clocks that most people used. Plus,

it had a dial face like an actual clock face and it glowed neon green in the

night. The clock face was about as big around as the palm of his hand, so

gave a lot of brightness in the room. It was like having a night light and

alarm clock in one. It was so bright in fact, that he could pick it up and use

the damn thing as a flash light in a dark room. He'd had several girlfriends

that had been reluctant to sleep over because the glowing clock face was so

bright at night. The glowing face of it was like one of those uranium

glowing fancy watches, but on this clock, the full face glowed instead of each individual number or the tip of the clock hands. He'd solved the problem with any sleepovers by leaving the alarm set and turned on, but he put the clock in the drawer of the nightstand.

He saw that it was two-forty-five am and he wondered what sound had awoken him from his sleep. He was usually a deep sleeper, and if he woke up, it was usually because his subconscious had registered some sort of noise that was unusual.

Then he realized that there were no other lights on in the apartment. No amber glow from the numerals of the dvd player, and no amber light from the lower edge of the TV to show that it was plugged in but turned off. He sat up and walked into the living room. No light from the TV or DVD player in there either. He looked towards the land line phone. No faint green glow from the handset, and not red light from the base. He looked into the kitchen and saw that the clock on the stove was out too.

He looked towards the windows and saw no lights bleeding in through the blinds from the parking lot lights. He walked to the window and put a finger in between one of the thin metal blades and raised it. No lights outside and the street lights and traffic lights at the intersection were out too. In fact there was no light anywhere, not even a pair of car headlights, and that was unusual because the intersection he was near was a busy one.

Odd. Years earlier he'd seen a blackout for an entire neighborhood when he'd lived closer to downtown Dallas, but that had been a transformer that had blown. You could tell it was something like a blown transformer because across the highway from that house he'd seen lights on everywhere. But his entire neighborhood had been completely dark. This though, was all four corners of the intersection and he was fairly certain that if it was a blown transformer, that it would affect all four sections. At least one of them would be on a different power station. The Dallas suburb that he was in was certainly big enough to have more than one transformer station, but still, he decided to go outside and get closer to the intersection so that he could look further in all four directions to see where the power outage stopped.

He went back to the bedroom, but stopped in the kitchen to rummage around in the junk drawer to find a flashlight. He had a Fenix FX Flashlight that was extremely powerful. It was just six inches long, but would put out 1000 lumens. You point it at someone's face and turn it on and it would be like having them stare into your car's high beam headlights for about twenty seconds. It also had five power settings, plus a strobe function.

He thumbed it on and went back into the bedroom and threw on his jeans and a t-shirt and slipped his on New Balance Trainers. He grabbed a light zip up hoodie and walked outside and down the steps from his apartment. He went through the parking lot to the sidewalk and made his way to the end of the block and looked up and down the intersection in all four directions. Strange.

There were cars all up and down the street in the north and south directions, but they were sitting in the street as if they'd all run out of gas. He looked up and down the cross street to the east and west, but there were no cars. Not surprising since it was a minor street. Preston Road though, running North and South was a major street, and there was constant traffic at any hour of the day, granted that at this time of early morning the traffic was light, but it was rare for him to loom out his window towards the intersection and not see several cars within thirty to forty seconds. Not exactly rush hour traffic, but it was never empty as it was now. He saw that every stalled car's owner was standing outside their vehicles, some had their hoods lifted and some were gathered in groups talking. None of the cars had their headlights on either. It was extremely dark. The intersection back to the South and the next intersection to the North both had shopping centers, strip centers, filled with restaurants, fast food joints, grocery stores, and the usual clutter of cell phone stores and bookstores, furniture stores and whatnot. These intersections were always lit up from the stores signage, even at night, plus the parking lot lights that were always on at night. Now though, there was no light whatsoever. To the north, Ray could see that there were a couple more people like himself that had flashlights, and he could see one person back south that also had a flashlight, but otherwise it was lights out everywhere. Ray figured that whatever electrical outage this was, it must be a big one.

Then he realized that a power grid electrical outage wouldn't affect automobiles, so what could it be? It was quiet too. The electrical hum of the city, that one that you never knew was so pervasive until it was silenced, was gone. It was eerily quiet. Ray could swear that he could hear the voices of the people standing in the road outside their cars, even though they were at least two hundred yards away. He stilled his breathing for a second and turned his ear towards them. Yes. He could hear the murmur of the voices. He couldn't make out what they were saying, but he could hear the sound of voices. He heard a dog barking in a neighborhood behind him.

He did another three-sixty from where he stood, and then he saw that there was an orange glow coming due east from where he stood. He heard a muffled explosion and then the area next to the orange glow seemed to flower in orange over the tops of the houses that was in between him and the orange glow. Must be a fire of some sort, something had definitely exploded over there. He figured he'd probably be hearing the wail of fire trucks and EMT sirens any moment now. He waited a minute. Nothing.

Ray decided to walk down the street and talk to some of the people whose cars had died, and see if they had any idea about what was going on, but before he did he went back upstairs and rummaged around in the bedside table and pulled out the Glock. It had been there for almost two years. It was his minimum gesture towards home protection. He'd taken it to the range a few times, just enough to ensure that he could shoot it accurately, and he knew how to field strip it and clean it. He wasn't a marksman of any sort, but he could hit what he aimed at within fifty feet, which was good enough for self-defense purposes. He knew that he should train more with it, and had even considered taking a more advanced gun course to be trained more efficiently, but he'd never followed up on it. Even though he could easily go and get a carry permit, it was easy enough to do in Texas, he'd never followed through on that either. He had two boxes of nine millimeter ammo for it, and he carried the gun with a full mag and a round chambered. He slipped it into his pocket and walked back down the stairs and headed towards the biggest cluster of cars in the street to the North.

He walked up on three men sitting on the hoods of their cars, all parked side by side, just as they'd been traveling in traffic when they'd given out. A tall black man with cornrows and wearing a Cowboys jersey, a young teen-ager with a faux hawk, and an older man with a light windbreaker and a Golden Retriever on a leash.

They nodded at him.

"Hey guys!"

"What's up dude?" the tall black guy asked.

"I live back there, and woke up, saw the power was out, looked out the window and decided to check it out. What seems to be going on?"

"We have no idea," the old man shrugged.

"Everything just stopped." The kid said as he waved his hand around to encompass their surroundings.

"Well, the electricity is out in all the apartments," Ray used his thumb to indicate the apartments he'd just walked from, "and it appears that it's the same for all the houses in the neighborhoods." He said as he looked around. The neighborhood across the street from his apartments, which was the neighborhood just next to where they were currently sitting, was a high end neighborhood with homes that ranged anywhere from two or three million to over seven million. They were huge estates, but they were also, almost zero lot lines. Homes made not for the fabulously wealthy, the billionaires, but definitely for the millionaires.

"What the fuck is this all about? Electric out," the black man said, "cars won't work, this is some sort of twilight zone shit going down."

"Don't ask me," the older man answered, as he reached out to give his dog a scratch behind his ears, "but I need to get home and get Buck fed. He's getting grouchy."

"By the way, I'm Ray Chandler," Ray said, introducing himself to the guys.

The older man nodded, "Art Miller, and like I said, this here," he nodded at his dog, "is Buck. He's a softie, but if you mess with him, 'specially when he's hungry, he might nip at you. No need to be scared, just warning you."

The black man lifted his chin at Ray, "Eddie Poe."

The young kid with the haircut gave a little wave of his hand, "Nate Hawthorne. I live down there past Belt Line. If this shit don't clear up soon, I gotta a helluva walk to make just to get home."

"Then you better get walking," a voice spoke up from behind them, "because these cars ain't going anywhere. They've just become junk."

They all turned towards the voice to see a man, in his late thirties, maybe forties, wearing black cargo pants, laced up combat boots and dark green t-shirt with a long sleeved plaid checked flannel shirt over it. He had an army green backpack slung over his shoulders. Ray thought that the guy looked like an outdoorsy type of guy but he also looked as if he could fit into the corporate world. If a car had a flight, this guy wouldn't waste time worrying about calling triple-A, he'd have it changed in a matter of minutes. He gave off the aura of a take-charge guy, and Ray felt like the guy's voice resonated with authority. He had no reason to think these things, just first impressions, that's all.

"Why do you say that? What do you know that we don't know?" the black guy, Eddie Poe challenged him.

"What's your name?" Ray asked. "I'm Ray Chandler." He stuck his hand out for a shake. The man took his hand, nodded and shook, and then introduced himself,

"I'm James Henry. Call me Jim, or James."

The other guys gave their names one by one, and when they finished, the newcomer, James Henry looked at Eddie Poe, "I know enough to know that these cars will never run again, that's for sure. I know *what* happened, but not how or why, not that that even matters at this point."

The guys all looked at the newcomer, James Henry.

"So?" the old man asked, "what happened? Why has everything quit running?"

The newcomer, James Henry pointed to the East,

"You guys see that?"

They all looked towards the East, where Ray had heard the explosion coming from earlier. The orange glow on the horizon seemed to be in two areas now.

"That explosion, was more than likely from a downed airliner, coming in from the East, probably headed towards Love Field or DFW airport. Could have been a small aircraft headed for a small private airport, although that glow, from the fire, looks a bit too large to be from a small plane. Of course, it could be a small plane that hit a gas station or something like that. "

"Why though," Art asked, while he used his hands to rub Buck under his chin, "would a small plane, or a large one for that matter knock out electricity, and our cars. Doesn't make any sense."

"It wouldn't," James answered, "the plane, if that's is what's on fire over there, went down because of the same thing that knocked out all the electric here, and stopped all of our cars."

Nate spoke up, "And what's that, mister smart guy?"

"Electromagnetic pulse."

"What the hell is that?" Ray asked.

"what causes it?" Eddie Poe asked, " and how long before everything gets switched back on?"

James scoffed, "what causes it is a bomb, or a sunspot." He explained, "and as for when it gets *switched back on*," he laughed, "maybe a year, maybe five years, maybe twenty or more. No cars for a long while gents. They're all dead weight. Useless as a squared bowling ball."

Their discussion was interrupted by a noise. They all turned to the North, and saw a car, headlights on, picking its' way through the stalled vehicles in a zig zag pattern. It was slowly coming towards them.

"Well, mister smart guy," Eddie Poe sneered, "I guess that blows your theory right out of the water."

"Actually, gentlemen," James answered, "when that car gets closer, I believe you'll see that it was made before seventy-six, definitely before the eighties anyway."

The car was still several hundred yards away, so Ray figured there'd be no way that this guy, James, could know the year and make or model that far away.

"What year would matter, a car's a car, right?" Nate said.

"Not exactly." James turned his back to the car and faced them, "See, any car made in the eighties is going to have all sorts of computer shit, electronics and such in it. The cars, trucks and motorcycles made before we started adding all that shit to them will not have been effected by the EMP, the electromagnetic pulse. So, if you see a car, it's an old one. Or, it's a newer one that someone has altered so that it wouldn't be affected by EMP."

They watched as the car finally pulled up onto a sidewalk and began coming faster now that it wasn't being slowed down by having to maneuver through so many disabled vehicles. They could also see that dozens of people that had been waiting outside their own stranded vehicles were trying to flag the driver down, but the driver ignored them all, and drove resolutely onwards towards them.

No one spoke for a moment, and then the car bounced off the sidewalk curbing and shot across the intersection and up onto the sidewalk closest to them and then sped up. As it passed by they all looked at the car. The car was an old sixty or seventies model Plymouth. Ray couldn't tell what model, because the man gassed it as it passed them, probably to avoid having them accost him for a ride. Within a minute the car had travelled as far south as they could see. Past the intersection south of them. When it was out of sight, they all looked back to James Henry.

"Told you so. *Old car.* Completely *unaffected* by the EMP."

"Bullshit, I say." Eddie Poe challenged him. He slid off the hood of his car and opened the door and sat down in the driver's seat. He put the key into the ignition and turned it. Nothing. Not a click, nothing.

He stepped back out of the car and closed the door. He put the keys into his pocket and raised his hands, "Now what mister smart guy?"

"Yeah," Ray asked, "What is this EMP thing you said that caused this?"

"Should we at least try to push them out of the middle of the street?" Nate asked, "You know, just in case emergency vehicles come along and need to get through? And, I don't want my car to get towed, I can't afford that shit. Seems wrong to just leave it here in the middle of the street."

James Henry laughed, "No. Just leave it here. Trust me. This thing isn't worth wasting another minute on. All of these cars are dead and gone. You'd be just as likely to catch a ride on an actual dinosaur as you will to get these things running again. And, there won't be any emergency vehicles coming through here to save the day either."

"How do you know that?" Art challenged him.

James pointed towards the east where the orange glow from the supposed aircraft fire was still lighting up the horizon, "You see any red and blue flashing emergency lights from cop cars, ambulances and whatever over there?"

"No, so what does that mean?"

"It means that there are no emergency vehicles running, because their electrics all got fried just like these." He pointed to the southwest, "right down that street, about three quarters of a mile from this spot is a fire station. We could jog over there in about six minutes. You see *any* flashing lights from that direction? Hear *any* sirens?"

They shook their heads and looked at each other.

Ray spoke up, "I live in those apartments right there," he pointed at the apartments on the corner, "when they do a fire run, I can hear the sirens from my bedroom, and if I look at that intersection there, I can see the reflections of their emergency lights. I can usually see the reflections of the red and blue flashing lights from my couch through the window blinds. So, you're right. If there was an emergency they could respond to, we'd be seeing their lights and hearing their sirens by now."

"So, what is this EMP bullshit you're talking about?" Eddie Poe asked.

James Henry leaned back against the hood of Nate's car, and pulled out a pack of cigarettes and held it up. "Anybody mind if I light up?"

Art shrugged and Eddie Poe and Nate nodded. Ray motioned for him to go ahead.

He lit the cigarette and took a drag.

"Boys," he began, and then he reached down and gave Buck a rub on his ear, "nice pup!"

Nate slid backwards up on the hood of his car and leaned back against the windshield. Ray lifted his foot and rested it on the bumper and leaned his forearms down on his knee. Buck moaned, and looked west, and everyone looked to see what it was that had alerted the dog, but whatever it was, it wasn't making itself known to them.

"The electromagnetic pulse is something that we've known about for years, but no one has bothered to pay much attention to it. The government sticks it's head in the sand and tries to ignore it. They see no way, no cheap way, to protect us from it, and it's not exactly a political hot button that will get them votes if they talk about it, so they pretend like it's extremely unlikely to happen."

"What caused it?" Eddie Poe asked.

"There's no way to tell."

"If there's no way to tell what caused it," Ray theorized, "then how do you know that the EMP is truly what caused all this?" he lifted his hands and waved them outwards.

"Well, now that's a decent question," James answered, "but, I *know for a fact* that EMP caused this, because there's nothing else, no other causative factor that could have caused exactly what we're seeing here."

"Doesn't seem possible," Art said, "to be that sure that this EMP thing caused this thing, and know that nothing else could have caused it."

"No true," James said, "let me explain just what does cause Electromagnetic Pulse, and also, something called Coronal Mass Ejection and once you understand that, you'll get my point more clearly." He paused took another drag from the cigarette, which was just about down to its butt. He flicked it away and the butt sparked as it landed on the street, and glowed for a few seconds before going dark.

Nate chided him, "Litterbug!"

James laughed and shrugged, "Within a week, these streets will be filled with garbage, fires, and roving bands of thugs, killing and looting and terrorizing everybody and everything in their path. So, I'm not too worried about a cigarette butt."

The guys all frowned at his pronouncements.

"I'll explain later why that will happen, first I want to explain EMP to you."

"Yeah," Art said as he ran his hand down Bucks' back and petted the dog affectionately.

"For explanation simplicity," James continued, "I'll use the terms EMP to describe both man-made EMP and Coronal Mass Ejection as the same, even though they are technically different. One is made by man and the other is a natural phenomenon coming from the sun. They both cause the same damages and will produce the same consequences for us afterwards. An electromagnetic pulse, or E M P is just a short burst of electromagnetic energy. This burst occurs in the form of a radiated electric or magnetic field and it can be natural or man-made. The EMP creates devastating and irreversible damage to electronic equipment such as computer chips, and electrical wiring. A really powerful EMP event, such as lightning strikes, can cause damage to physical objects such as buildings and aircraft." He paused and took out another cigarette and lit it up.

"Man-made nuclear and non-nuclear devices can be used to create EMP weapons. A nuclear burst high above the earth at an orbit of

100 miles or more would set off an EMP burst. A weapon of this sort set off above the Midwestern U S could damage all electrical systems and computers across the U.S. in an instant. Now, a natural EMP burst which is what occurs from a Coronal Mass Ejection from the sun would cause the same damage as a man-made EMP.

A geomagnetic storm is a disturbance of the Earth's magnetosphere caused by a solar shock wave and/or cloud of magnetic field which interacts with the Earth's magnetic field. This solar flare from the sun causes a huge increase in the solar wind pressure and initially compresses the magnetosphere and the solar wind's magnetic field interacts with the Earth's magnetic field and transfers increased energy into the magnetosphere. This increased magnetic current overloads all computer chips, burning them out, fusing or melting them into useless bits of plastic. In other words, when this happens, everything electrical, and computer driven becomes worthless. So, gentlemen" he paused dramatically and spread his arms to indicate everything around them, "look around you and what do you see?"

"Holy shit," Eddie Poe exclaimed, "are you kidding me?"

"This could be an example of a natural EMP caused by the sun, or it could be that someone, such as China, North or South Korea, or some other country decided to fuck us. That's why I say that there's no way for us to know why it happened. We may find out eventually of course, or we may never ever really know who did it, or why, or if it was natural. The whole point though is this . . .it doesn't matter why it happened, or who caused it. What you guys need to realize is that surviving it is the only concern you need to have."

"Can't we just replace all the computer chips affected by it?" Nate asked.

James shook his head, "I'll get to that in a minute, first, let me explain a few more things about this type of problem."

"Have at it." Ray said.

"See, if it is the sun, then there's no way for us to have avoided it. Our electrical infrastructure and computers could have been protected by taking protective measures. Our government knew about the dangers our society faces if we are hit by a massive Coronal Mass Ejection, or a man-made EMP. For the most part though, they ignored the problem, because it was too big a problem to tackle, and scaring the shit out of the populace would never get them any votes. It was far easier for the politicians to constant reassure the voters that the U S is the strongest country in the world and every is, and always will be all right, as long as they get elected. Talking about CME and EMP was something that they shied away from, partly because they themselves had no answers that wouldn't cost a fortune. Then too, there are millions upon millions of people who simply would never believe that something like that could ever happen. The people in this country have, for years, been affected with an intractable complacency, also known as a normalcy bias. A normalcy bias is an error in thinking. It simply means that a person insists in believing that just because something has never happened to them, that it never will. It can also be termed as a 'complacency bias.'"

"Keep your head stuck in the sand, like a good ostrich." Art said.

"Exactly."

"So, I still don't understand why we can't just replace the fuses in the electrical cabinets, and put new computer chips in the cars and computers." Nate said, "you know? Just do that and turn everything back on and get going again."

James shook his head slowly, "because, Nate, all the computer chips sitting on the shelves, in the packages in the warehouses, they're all worthless chunks of plastic right now. So naturally, the next thing you'll ask is, why not just make more?"

Nate nodded.

"Well, we can't just make more, because the factories operate by machinery, and all that machinery has fuses, circuits and computer chips in them to make them run, and they're burnt out too."

"Holy fuck." Eddie Poe said, "what you're saying is, we're screwed to the max."

"In a word, yes."

Nate shook his head, "I still don't get it. Somebody somewhere has to have electricity. I mean, it can't just go away like it never existed, can it?"

"Well, there may be some good news."

"Damn," Art said, "I'd sure like to hear that!"

"Well," James explained, "depending upon whether or not this EMP was caused naturally, which would be the worse-case scenario for us, or if it was the man-made kind, which would be better for us, it could be a better-case scenario, depending upon how the man-made version was set off."

"What do you mean? I thought you said that all EMP's were deadly."

"They are," James nodded, "however, let's just say that this one," he raised his hands to encompass the area around them, "was caused by some nut-job terrorist who set off a nuke in Dallas, or within a few miles of here . . . in that case, the affected area would be small, relatively speaking. Like maybe the Dallas and Fort Worth area, and not much outside that area. In that case, we'd be back up and running in a matter of months or maybe a year or two. Because everything would have to be repaired, all the computers, all the electrical lines. . .an EMP event can cause the copper in electrical lines to fuse together and they can't be just turned back on. Every inch of electrical wiring in every electrical line in every building, on the electrical lines," he pointed to the electric lines strung from the telephone poles alongside the road, "and even the lines in the ground, would have to be replaced. You can imagine how long that would take."

"That's crazy. I just can't believe that things are that bad!" Nate said.

"You're allowing yourself to be ruled by," Art interjected, "what he said earlier. . ."

"Normalcy or, complacency bias." James nodded.

"If it has never happened before, it probably won't happen in the future. Everything is okay, and always will be." Ray said.

"Now, the really bad case scenario is that the EMP was caused by a terrorist, or another government that wanted to send us back to the preindustrial age and they exploded a nuclear warhead over Kansas."

"But, Kansas is several hundred miles away from us, how could that affect us here?" Eddie Poe asked.

"Because," James said, "if someone exploded a nuke a hundred miles up in space over Kansas, that electromagnetic wave would create an air wave that would spread outwards in all directions, and because the air is thinner up there, there'd be nothing to slow it down and it would go from mid-America towards each coast with nothing to slow it down. The best-case scenario for an antagonistic government to do that to us to shut us down, would be too detonate three nukes each a hundred miles up, one over Kansas, and then one over the East coast and another over the West coast. That would effectively shut the country down for good."

"Jesus, kid," Art said, "you're scaring the shit out of me now."

James nodded, "Scared is good. We can't afford to be lulled into inaction by normalcy bias, and we can't afford to sit around thinking the government will just 'fix it' for us next week."

Nate shook his head, "I hate to be dense, but I still don't understand how this thing, this invisible thing, can just kill all the electricity, and then make it where we can't use it anymore!"

James smiled, "Let me see if I can explain it a little more in depth."

"Please do."

"You've heard of the Northern Lights? The Aurora Borealis?"

Nate nodded, "Yeah we learned about them in high school. We even saw a video showing them. The sky at night was all green and sparkly. It was like, up in Alaska somewhere. Our science teacher said you can't see them much further south than that."

"Exactly," James said, "Well, there was a solar storm, which causes CME's to happen, back in 1859. Obviously it wasn't a nuclear warhead, and that also was before computers and houses were wired for electricity, but there were some crude electrical devices, such as the telegraph. You know how the telegraph worked, right?"

"Yeah, we also saw a video about that in science class. The teacher even had one set up in the room so we could try it out. Pretty neat, but nothing compared to email." He laughed.

"On September 1–2, 1859, one of the largest recorded geomagnetic storms occurred. This coronal mass ejection in 1859 was the largest CME ever to hit earth was recorded, and is now known as 'The Carrington

Event"'"

"Never heard of it, but okay."

James continued, "Studies have shown that a solar storm of this magnitude occurring today would likely cause widespread devastating problems for all of modern civilization. The Carrington solar flare was a major coronal mass ejection (CME) that travelled directly toward Earth, taking less than 2 days to make the 93 million mile journey. Scientists believe that the high speed of this CME was made possible by a prior CME. These CMEs will typically take several days to arrive at Earth. Aurora Borealis was seen around the world, those in the northern hemisphere even as far south as the Caribbean; Aurorae seen over the Rocky Mountains were so bright that their glow awoke gold miners who began preparing breakfast because they thought it was morning. People in the northeastern US could read a newspaper by the aurora's light. The aurora was visible as far from the poles as Cuba and Hawaii."

"Son of a bitch!" Art exclaimed and let out a whistle.

"Yeah, scary huh?" James added.

"Okay, continue," Nate said, now that you've scared me shitless.

"Telegraph systems throughout Europe and North America failed, they were even giving the telegraph operators electric shocks. Telegraph pylons were showering sparks. Some telegraph operators said bursts of fire were shooting out from their Morse keys.

Baltimore newspapers reported that, "The light was greater than that of a full moon."

"Wow," Ray said, trying to imagine what those people were thinking. He figured that, with electricity being new to them, they probably had all sorts of crazy ideas, and nowadays, people who knew nothing about CME and EMP must be just as confused. Something that had always worked and they took it for granted, and now it wouldn't work no matter what they did. Some people would stupidly go to their phone to call the electric company, and then they'd get an even ruder shock.

James continued his explanation for them.

"So guys, here's what would happen to America after a major EMP event.

Instantly, there would be no cell phones, computers, gas stations, no natural gas or water service, cold storage would be a thing of the past, food processing plants, useless. No trucking, no railroads, no airplanes, no ATMs, no inter-bank transfers. Americans would revert to eating whatever food they could hunt, fish or forage within walking distance of their homes.

City-dwellers would flee en-masse, or face starvation. Gangs of 'zombies', and I don't mean the kind you see on TV shows. Not the walking dead bullshit you see. I'm talking about dangerous, frightened, hungry groups of people who would stop at nothing to procure food and supplies, roaming the urban areas . . . that's what I meant earlier about this street in a week will be looking like a war zone. That's why I'm not worried about a cigarette butt or two. This," he waved his arm to indicate their surroundings, "will look like the end of the world, IF, this event is major, and by major I mean bigger than Dallas. If this thing is state-wide or God forbid nationwide or world-wide, then you're looking at millions upon millions of deaths, *very quickly*."

"No way." Nate said. Ray thought that Nate was beginning to get panicky.

"Such an event that is so catastrophic in nature you would think that our government would have planned for how to handle it long ago. They haven't. When it happens, you will be on your own. Everything will revert to, literally, kill or be killed. Staying in any urban area is pretty much a fucking death sentence."

He paused and lit another cigarette, "As I have already mentioned, there are two main sources of electromagnetic pulse (EMP) that potentially could take down the national electric grid: a major geomagnetic solar flare, and scientists say the chances are great for another large one to hit earth very soon. Or an attack by a hostile nation-state using a nuclear weapon detonated at high altitude over the US mainland. Iran and North Korea have long understood that the US power grid is vulnerable to attack by an EMP weapon, and they've tasked their scientists and military planners to consider and perhaps plan an EMP event.

North Korea has successfully tested an EMP weapon during its 2006 and 2009 nuclear weapons tests, and Iran has tested detonating ballistic missiles at high altitude and they've made it known that those tests were successful. So, we are definitely vulnerable."

"But what would any of those countries stand to gain by sending our whole nation back into the preindustrial age?" Art asked, "wouldn't that render our country useless to them too?"

James shook his head, "who knows? It could make it easier for them to come in and take over. But, as I said earlier, wondering the why is a waste of your time. Every second of your day now needs to be geared towards one thing and one thing only; survival."

"But, is an EMP attack on America really likely?" Ray asked, "I mean, I know we need to think about survival, but just from a theoretical or intellectual viewpoint, is this thing more likely man-made or a CME from the sun?"

"It's hard to say if it was man-made or natural. We may never know. But, as I've said, our nation without power would instantly revert to the early 1800s, when a pre-industrial America was unable to sustain a population of more than 100 million persons. Such a catastrophe would cause a kill-off of more than 75 to 90% of our population. When an EMP hits us, your currency, if you could even get to it, is worthless. Water may come out of your pipes for a little as a few hours or may last around three days. Most U S citizens do not keep more than three to five days of food on hand, and when all electric is shut off there will be quick usage due to spoilage."

"Yeah, I've got about two days of food in my pantry and refrigerator right now." Art said.

"Yeah, and your fridge is dead right now. I'd say you have a day or two, maybe three before it's useless." James added.

"The time required to get a replacement for any one of the 370 or so largest electrical transformers in the United States is currently at a minimum of 3 years. If an EMP event affects the entire world, delivery times would be much, much longer. The United States has no capability to manufacture those transformers. Manufacturing transformers requires a lot of electrical power and that capability cannot be developed after an electromagnetic catastrophe. The transformers need to be made before there is an actual need. Because of the inevitability of an EMP or CME event we need to accept the fact that the current power grid upon which our lives depend is only a flawed infrastructure. The electrical grid infrastructure has served us well, and we've been able to entrust our lives to it. The fact is that the electric power grid began as a convenience, but if it goes away, we will start dying very quickly. In fact, and this is going to blow your minds, boys," he paused as if to underscore the gravity of what he was about to say, "We do know that if an EMP event knocks out the current power grid hundreds of millions of people will die. This is not scaremongering, this is an absolute fact."

"The government has known about this possibility for years? Art asked.

James nodded, "And there are some government computer systems that are protected, but not nearly enough of them. We are pretty much sitting ducks."

Eddie Poe shook his head and, resting his arms on his thighs, looked down at the ground and exhaled, as if he was fatigued.

"Again, we may not ever even know what caused it, because

widespread communication systems are knocked out, leaving ninety-nine point nine percent of the world population to just guess as to why, but as I'm trying to explain to you guys, that knowing what caused it means almost next to nothing. Instead of wasting time trying to figure out why we are in this position right now, we need to use our resources just to survive. If a thug attempts to car-jack you as you sit at an intersection waiting for the red light to change, you don't waste time trying to understand what led the thug to a life of crime. No, what you do is try to survive the attack. You can try to understand it later, when you're not dead."

"I just realized something," Art said.

They all turned towards him.

"My grandmother. She's in her nineties, has Alzheimer's, she's in a nursing home. She spends several hours a day on a breathing machine."

James shook his head, "I'm sorry man."

Ray asked the obvious question, "If this thing is widespread, like all of North Texas, or the whole state, or God forbid, the entire country . . . all those people in the hospitals, they're as good as dead aren't they?"

As soon as he said it he realized how insensitive the remark had been and he saw Art blanche at the reality of what had just dawned on him.

James nodded somberly, "all the elderly, sick and infirmed in the hospitals, cancer patients, and those types . . . they're as good as dead. Diabetics are in trouble. Anyone with a pacemaker . . ." his voice trailed off.

"Shit!" Nate mumbled.

"The grisly fact is that the hospitals are about to become death factories. Without electricity, all those people will be the first to die. The sheer numbers of deaths in the hospitals will become unmanageable. Hospitals will be forced to become triage centers and they will be forced to conduct mercy deaths in order to stave off suffering. The deaths will become problematic too because with electricity the bodies of those who've passed will begin rotting and there will be too few people to handle proper disposal of the corpses. The corpses will begin rotting and diseases stemming from unsanitary conditions will spread quickly. When every man, woman and child in the country being forced to spend every moment of their day trying to stay alive and just eke out a day's survival, only to have to wake up and do it again the next day, will eventually force the doctors and nurses and caregivers to completely abandon the hospitals. The hospitals will be little cells of death. Get near one and you'll risk almost certain death." He paused and took a deep breath, "guys, if this thing is nation-wide, or world-wide, we can expect to see a die-off of ninety to ninety-five percent of the entire population. Sorry to be so grim, but those are facts, not speculation."

No one spoke for almost two full minutes.

Finally, Eddie Poe spoke, "Jesus Christ, James, that kind of prognosis makes me want to go home and hang myself."

"That's another thing I was going to explain."

"Jeez," Ray said, "let me guess. There's more bad news?"

"Well, guys, it's no secret that a lot of people out there, will be unable to believe that things are really as bad as they actually are-"

"That's the normalcy bias thing you were talking about?" Nate asked.

"Exactly!" James answered, "so another consequence of this, is that as soon as people begin realizing that the government is not going to be able to step in and just fix things. . .they will begin to get despondent, and there will be *a lot* of suicides."

"Oh jesus. This just gets worse and worse doesn't it?" Art said, "Wholesale death and dying, and on top of that, suicides?"

"Well yeah," James said, "think about the people you all know, the people you all work with . . . how many of them have their lives, their egos, their very existence tied up in their belongings and their things, and their hedonistic activities. Their X boxes, their BMW's and their constant ego-gratification systems. Their six-figure salaries, and their ego fortifying titles and their social lives, drinking, partying and never-ending cycles of superficialities. All these social constructs are blown away and meaningless in the snap of a finger." He raised both arms and looked left and right, "just like that, it's all gone, and it's highly unlikely to return in their lifetimes. A CEO who made well over five hundred grand a year, is now homeless and helpless and the man who was mowing his lawn last week for a paltry fifty bucks and had less than a couple hundred bucks in his bank account, now has a better hold on life than that CEO. The tables have turned and they've turned in a big way."

"Everything is upside down now. If this thing is big, or well, bigger than small."

Nate spoke up, "Earlier you said that that fire over there," he pointed East towards the orange glow on the horizon, "was probably an airplane going down. Don't all the major airlines have something in place to protect airplanes in flight? I mean, if they didn't, and it's just hard to imagine that they wouldn't, because if they didn't that would mean that every airplane in flight, which is thousands all across the U S every day . . ."

James nodded, "Yeah, that's right. If you're on an airliner when this thing hit, then your plane is going down. No ifs ands or butts about it.

Every plane in flight will go down. There will be thousands upon thousands just from airline flight deaths."

"Damnation!" Art spat out.

"What will happen to all the nuclear facilities around the country? Will there be nuclear meltdowns?" Ray asked.

James shrugged, "I'm afraid that my knowledge in that aspect of all this is inadequate enough to even hazard a guess about that. I seem to recall reading something to the gist of those facilities having the ability to shut down safely if the electrical grid went down, but I am not sure if those systems were actually in place, or were just being planned. So, I have no idea."

"So, we've heard all the bad news, unless there's more. . ." Ray said.

"Yeah, now that we know what might be happening, or actually what is probably happening," Eddie Poe said, "what do we do next?"

"Well, here's the thing guys," James started slowly.

Ray thought it was almost as if the man didn't want to share any more information.

"My plan is this, and you should do the same . . . well, actually, let me just say this . . . I am going to tell you the smartest thing you could and should do, but make no mistake about this, I am NOT offering to take any of you with me. I am on my own form this point on out. I have taught myself what to do in this situation, and if you didn't well, that's on you. I will not help any of you guys escape, and I am not going to stick around to teach everyone about survival skills and all of that. You guys understand that?"

Everyone nodded.

"Okay, with that understood, let me say this; the safest thing you can do, if this thing is widespread, and not just a local thing . . is to get the hell out the big urban city areas. This area here will be a hotbed of crime in about seventy-two hours, and you do not want to be here when the shit hits the fan."

"How can you know that?" Nate challenged him.

"Because the stores will run out of food within forty-eight to seventy-two hours. Because the water from your faucets will stop running within the next few hours. No one will have access to their money, and they'll be too stupid to realize that their money is now meaningless. There is no heat, no air conditioning, no TV, no nothing. Because every asshole out there, every thug with a bad thought in his head will realize that no matter what they do, the cops will not come for them because they will be unable to communicate with the people. Nine one, one calls are a waste of time. Some asshole wants to rape his neighbor, who's going to stop him? Rape and murder will be commonplace. Some guy wants to go get revenge on his ex-wife's new lover, who's going to stop him? Some dude wants to go punch his boss for years of bullshit that he's endured, who will stop him? Moving around through the city during a *loss of civility* which is government-speak for a severe societal breakdown can be extremely dangerous, even life-threatening. There will be thousands of predator-types who will take advantage of this occasion to prey upon those whom they perceive as weak. Let's call them opportunivores. These *opportunivores* will not obey laws because they will have no fear of punishment. People are not going to just keep on acting as they always have. To expect that is just ludicrous. When all law enforcement is removed from the society, these so-called opportunivores will become lawless and they'll run amok. The level of violence is about point five right now, and within a week it will be at fifteen. The needle of the violence meter will be pegged over to the right in the red, and it won't let up. It will be like the wild, wild west out there. Murder, rape, robbery, and every depredation known to man will be sport for these crazed thugs. No more law to bother them, so they will run amok. These urban areas are about to become nightmares."

"How the hell will we protect ourselves?" Art asked.

"If you have a gun, that's a start." He looked at Ray, "I know you do."

"How'd you know that?"

"I've seen you unconsciously touch it. Make sure it's still tucked into your waistband. Typical rookie giveaway for a novice or new carrier. I try to be observant. Being observant can keep you alive nowadays."

"So, you're saying to just abandon your house? And go where? Plus, if I abandon my house, when I get back, the bank will have repossessed it for nonpayment of my mortgage." Nate said.

"Your house will be unlivable in a few days." James explained, "no sewer services, so the toilet won't work, no water, no electric, no heat or AC and your food will be gone in two to three days, and when roving gangs of violent thugs start beating the door down to get inside and loot what they can from the place, if you're there they'll kill you. If you have a wife, girlfriend, or daughter, they'll rape her. If you have a dog, or cat, set it free immediately unless you have the fortitude to eat it. Most people don't. Do it a favor, set it free, it will probably live longer than you, as long as it can keep from being caught and eaten."

"Okay, so, get out of your house and go where exactly?" Eddie Poe asked.

"Get as far away from the population centers as possible. If you have camping skills, get out to the woods and set up shelter. If you have camping supplies, then you will be able to make yourself comfortable at least."

"How far away should one want to get to?" Art asked.

"I would say a minimum of fifty miles."

"Fifty miles?" Ray asked, he'd expected the man to say five miles or maybe even ten, but fifty? That seemed excessive.

"Yeah, at the very least. Realize that the populace of the Dallas, Fort Worth area totals almost seven million. These people all start leaving the area, which they will, there will eventually be a mass exodus from every heavily populated area. My advice would be to get out, and to get very far away, very quickly. Find a wooded area near a lake to set up camp. Stay hidden. Do not tell people where you are going and most importantly, and this next piece of advice may be harsh and very hard to take, but it is pure truth . . . from this point on, you need to *treat everyone you meet as a direct threat to your life*. Because they will be."

"That sounds extremely harsh." Nate said.

"Look, you may not believe it right now, but if this things goes more than a week, you're going to see random violence in the streets. People will be attacking each other for scraps of food and a bottle of drinkable water. Law enforcement will be spotty at best, but more than likely it will be nonexistent."

"How are we supposed to defend ourselves in all this random senseless violence that you're predicting?" Art asked.

"Well, I don't know about you guys, but I carry a gun, and I have the skills and attitude necessary to use it if needed. I will not hesitate to put down anyone that is threatening to me."

"Well, that's all fine and dandy, if you happen to have a gun, but what about if you don't have one?" Ray asked.

"That's an odd question coming from a man who has a gun in his pocket now."

Ray felt his face flush in embarrassment, "How'd you know that?"

"Like I said, I'm observant. You've touched it several times, readjusted it, it's a newbie thing. You don't carry often and it makes you slightly uncomfortable. That's okay though, you carry it for a week and you'll stop advertising that you're carrying. You let people know you're carrying in the days to come, and someone will take it away from you and kill you with your own gun."

"You're kidding." Nate said, "now you make it sound like it's going to be the wild-ass west out there from now on."

"Oh, it will be."

"Kill or be killed, huh?" Nate answered sarcastically.

"Absolutely."

"I don't think I could ever be comfortable carrying a gun." Nate said.

"Carrying a gun is not supposed to be *comfortable*, it's supposed to be *comforting*."

"And if you're not lucky enough to be a gun owner and you don't want to be at the mercy of the lawless in this upcoming version of hell that you've laid out for us?"

"Law of the jungle," James replied, "find someone weaker than yourself, and take theirs from them. Steal one. Barter for one, if you have something worth bartering and can find someone foolish enough to give you a gun. Or, at last resort, bash someone over the head and take their gun by force."

"You've got to be kidding." Art said.

"Look guys, if things get bad, and I really suspect they will, then your chances of surviving *without* a gun, for self-protection and for hunting meat, go down tremendously. That's why I say that if you can get a gun, and a lot of ammo, the better off you'll be. Your chances of surviving without one, is almost nil."

"I gotta gun. What else do I need?" Eddie Poe asked.

"I'd get home asap, and find as many containers as possible to store water into. Get a cigarette lighter, you'll need to make fire when you get to the woods and set up camp. Canned foods, and a can opener. These are a lot of your standard 'bug-out' items. Toilet paper, toothpaste, soap, medicinal supplies, sleeping bag, as many socks and comfortable shoes as you can bring. A tarp or tent, several knives, several belts if you have more than one. Rolls of duct tape, a compass, binoculars, flashlights, batteries, magnifying glass, bleach-"

"Bleach?"

"Yes, Nate, *bleach*. To purify the water you'll need to drink."

"also, a pot or pan of some sort to boil water in . . . and a Bible, cigarettes, booze-"

"Now you're talking, cigarettes and booze!" Eddie Poe laughed.

"Not to drink for yourself, but to have for barter. That stuff will be valuable."

"A Bible?" asked Art, "how is that survival related?"

James shook his head, "It's not, in the classic sense of helping you eat, drink or stay warm or alive, but, we're talking about a lawless society where people will be confused, afraid, and always on the edge, extremely stressed and on the verge of losing their minds. You have a Bible, and come across someone like that, you may be able to trade it for something good for yourself. Some people need, and even crave, their spiritual comfort and there's no telling what they'll give up to get it. You ask me, books will only be good for kindling to get fires started, but a Bible might be worthwhile as a barter object. Now, that said, I wouldn't go carrying the entire works of Mark Twain around with me, but a Bible, yeah sure."

"You can't drink lake water?" Nate asked.

"You can," James said, "but you'd get sick as a dog, maybe die. No, don't drink anything that hasn't been purified."

"I have a question,"

"Yeah Ray?"

"Even if I had everything listed there, which I don't, how the hell would I carry it all? No backpack can handle all that stuff, and my car is a new one, so it's not going anywhere. If I'm going to *bug out*, as you call it, where will I put all this stuff? I can't carry much stuff on my back if I'm hiking fifty plus miles into the wilderness. Water is especially heavy, and tents, sleeping bags and bleach and pots and pans and all that kind of stuff?"

"Well, some of us, preppers, people who have believed for years that something like this could, and would, eventually happen, have prepared for that eventuality. Some of us bought old cars and made them off-road ready and EMP-proof. Cars, trucks, motorcycles, vans, things of that nature. We planned ahead. This scenario," he spread his hands out at shoulder level,"is called a *S H T F* scenario. That stands for '*Shit Hits the Fan*'. There is also another acronym, which is *T-E-O-T-W-A-W-K-I*. Some guys say it as teotwawki," he pronounced it as a nonsensical-sounding word, and then explained it, "The End Of The World As We Know It.'"

"And just what will be your mode of transport out of here?" Eddie Poe asked.

"That, is something I will not be discussing with you boys."

"Fair enough!" Art nodded.

"And another thing," James continued, "you boys make it out of the city, and get settled in to the woods, be very careful about walking up on another cabin or camp in the woods. You stumble into someone's hideout without being invited or at the very least without making it known and shown that you are unarmed and not a threat, you may just get shot. I know you would in my camp. I would shoot you down without a seconds' hesitation."

"That makes sense, if this scenario becomes what you say it will." Art remarked.

"My advice to each of you, if you don't have an EMP-proofed vehicle to get you away from the city, is to head over there" he pointed South, towards a large intersection about a mile and a half from where they were sitting, "and you grab you one or two shopping carts. Get two, because you can use a belt or something to strap them together, in line, one in front and one in back to put your bug out supplies into. It's not the optimal way to carry a ton of shit, and it'll tire your ass out pulling or pushing it, but it beats two back packs or rolling luggage. Rolling luggage would be the worst. Those things wheels will crap out on you after about five miles of road travel, and then you'd be carrying it. Not a good plan. A two-wheeler, like a warehouse loader is not bad, as long as you can strap everything on it. They have better tires than the shopping carts."

"Wow, dude," Eddie Poe said, "you really have though it all out haven't you?"

"Well, I've believed for years that this was going to eventually happen."

"What's the most important item you can have?" ray asked.

"Gun, ammo, water, cigarette lighters, toilet paper." He listed them out, "Oh I almost forgot. IF you have money in the form of gold and silver, bring it. It may be worthless, but there will be people who think that this whole thing will be 'fixed' next week, and they'll still be blinded by the idea of keeping and adding to their wealth so they'll be foolish enough to get rid of items they think are worthless for some gold or silver. If you have paper money, it's light enough to carry it, and it will make good kindling for fires. Can't hurt to bring it."

"So," Ray asked again, "you're saying that having a gun, along with ammo is pretty high on the priority list?"

"Most definitely. It could, and probably will, save your life. You don't have a gun, and be ready, willing and able to use it, I very highly doubt you'll live another month if this thing goes that long. Learn how to purify water, be ready to lose some weight due to eating less, and keep your gun loaded and ready at all times and you just might survive this."

"And if you don't have a gun," Nate repeated, "you're pretty much dead meat."

"That's right boys, and I can see that two of you do have a gun. Ray here does, because I know it's in his pocket, and Eddie Poe, you've got one too, now don't you?"

"Why you assume I do? Because I'm black?"

James laughed, "No man, not because of that. I can just tell. You don't seem to be bothered by the idea of not having one, and a couple of times I've mentioned a gun, you've glanced at your car. If I was you I'd go get it out of the glove compartment and keep it close at all times."

Ray's eyes widened in surprise as Eddie Poe grinned and then stood up and walked around to the passenger side of his car and reached in. They all heard a clunk as the glove compartment fell open, and then he slammed it shut and walked back to the group, the handle of the Glock sticking out of his waistband.

"Glock 19 huh?" James nodded, "Nice piece to have. You got ammo at home?"

"Yeah, I got about five hundred rounds."

"Good for you, sir."

"Any words of wisdom," Art said to James as he nodded towards Nate, "for us guys who don't have a gun or an old car to bug out in?"

"Yeah, actually, I do." James said.

Nate and Art leaned forward.

"I would never do this, because I plan to travel fast, and alone, but . . . you could travel together. The more people in your party, the harder it will be to attack. A lone traveler, such as either of you boys, are likely to get picked off real quick."

Art nodded, and looked at the younger kid, Nate.

"Sounds good to me, whadda you say kid? Two's better'n one?"

The kid nodded his assent, but Ray could see that the kid still didn't believe that things were really going to be bad. He just wasn't buying into the entire scenario. Ray was almost certain that if Nate was questioned away from the group, that he'd say he expected life to be back to normal within a week.

Ray looked up at the stars. The guys, seeing him do so, looked up too.

James spoke, "Your hesitation could prove deadly to you. You want to act, and you want to do it now. Don't make a fatal mistake."

Ray nodded. The fear inside him threatened to overtake him like dizziness from too much liquor. Like being drunk, he also felt as if he wanted to throw up. If he took this stranger's word for what was happening and he got out of town, and things went back to normal in a few days or weeks, it could prove to be devastating damage in his life. He could lose his apartment, his car, his job and if he came back to start over he'd be in the hole for God knows how long. On the other hand, if he got out of town and what this man was saying was true, then he'd have a leg up on those who didn't prepare, although he hadn't prepared either, and he was barely knowledgeable about camping and he could still screw that up enough to risk his life.

Still though, he had the gut feeling that this guy James wasn't just some nut case prepper from the back woods. He seemed to know what he was talking about. He looked at the ground and thought about his immediate future. Walking out of the city and into the wilderness was no small thing. A million different things could kill you. Minor things that you wouldn't give a few seconds thought about in your regular, normal life. Living off the land was no easy feat. A small scratch could kill you. Step on a cottonmouth or a rattler. Eat the wrong berries from a tree. Sleep outdoors without the proper clothing and get too cold. Overheat yourself and get a sunstroke. Not to mention the other people as a danger. Ray knew that if James was right and the inner city people began leaving the population centers, then there would definitely be encounters that would be problematic. He had one hundred rounds of ammo, one gun and two magazines for it, and not nearly enough training. He had eight or ten knives, good sharp folding knives, and some steak knives and one brand new K-Bar knife in a leather sheath. He had a sleeping bag and a small tent that he'd had for years, and he knew just enough about outdoor survival to be halfway safe. He wished he knew more, but if this thing was, what had James called it, a Shit Hits the Fan situation? Then he knew that his time to learn was over. It was do or die. It was a grim decision to make. Stay and put your life at risk through inaction, or take action and put your life at risk through attempting to do something you've never done before, where the smallest mistake can kill?

Ray didn't even want to have to make the decision. He wanted to go home and sleep and think about it, plan it all out and get more knowledge about what had happened, or on the flip side, get more knowledge about how to survive. Unfortunately, the luxury of casual introspection was receding in his rear-view mirror. He need to make his decision to act, or to dig in and hope for a miracle.

He looked at the guys, "Fuck it. I'm getting out of Dodge. I think James is right, the shit has hit the fan." As soon as he said the words he felt as if his life had forever changed, but then, maybe his life had changed when he was peacefully sleeping a few hours earlier when this thing had happened without a whisper.

"Okay James," Art spoke up, "you seem to be the expert on these things, and I respect your decision to go it alone, it's your right, obviously. . ." he trailed off, as if he wasn't sure that he really wanted to ask the question.

James nodded somberly at him, "Go ahead."

"Well, I know I can live out in the sticks, in the woods and survive and all that, my question to you though, is . . .what should we do, or what could we do, to give ourselves an edge out there? I'm an old Army guy. I don't believe in relying on luck. That shit's for amateurs."

"Yeah, you got that right. Luck is for people who forgot to make a plan. Strictly amateur hour."

Ray's mind was immediately swirling with a list of questions he wished he could ask James. It would take days though, and like James said, they didn't have time to waste.

"The biggest caveat I can possibly give you is to watch out for the most dangerous animal you're likely to encounter out there."

"Bear?" Nate asked.

"No. *Man.*" James answered.

"I will also stress this, over and over and over. Get a gun. Don't have one, find one. Can't find one, *steal* one. Don't be queasy about it. Forget about ethics and fairness until this thing, society, gets back on track. The gun, and that attitude will keep you alive just as surely as water and food."

"I'm just not sure I can just kill someone." Nate said.

"Well, you *will*, unless the person you *should* be killing, kills *you* while you waste time worrying about sin and whatnot. Trust me guys, things are going to deteriorate *very* rapidly now that this thing has finally happened. *Get your gear, make a plan, get the hell out of Dodge as fast as you can.* The more space you put between yourself and the horde of citizens that's out there right now wallowing in complacency and normalcy bias, the better."

"So you are actually proposing that those of us without guns, use force and take, or steal, rob, someone of theirs? Just on the off chance that we may need it someday? Sounds barbaric to me." Art said.

"Yes, you're right. It is barbaric, but if things go to hell in a bad way, and I'm betting they will, you'll be seeing quite a few barbaric acts by what we call normal people. I'm telling you guys, what happened hours ago changed the world in a big, big way. You're going to see horrific things. People going crazy because of hunger, fear, anger, and just plain old general craziness. When the veneer of civility is stripped away, when our creature comforts and what we've come to think of as our basic necessities, the things we've taken for granted, electricity, food, shelter and water are denied us, then we'll become animals. Trust me, it is going to happen."

"Isn't harming someone else, theft of someone else's property, and what you're suggesting, which is to harm someone if we have to, like using force to take a gun away from someone, isn't that becoming the bad thing you're describing?" Art countered, "turning us into animals?"

"Yes, in a way it is. It is also survival." James reasoned, "but, if you see a man with a gun and that man has no desire to use it, no knowledge of how to use it, or no plan of how to use it for protection, then you might as well take it. If you don't some really bad guy will not only take it from him and then kill him with his own weapon, but then he will use it to prey on other innocents. I'm just suggesting that you try to find a gun and keep it for your own survival. If you can do so without harming anyone, then that's great."

Ray interrupted them, "let's drop the gun thing for a minute. Let me ask you this James,"

James turned to him, "Fire away."

Ray continued, "well, forgetting about using a gun, or knife or whatever for personal survival, when we get out of Dodge, what's the best direction to head to? Strictly from a survival standpoint. And, I'm not asking you to reveal any details about *your* plan, I'm just asking about geography, climate and accessibility. *Where* should we go?"

James nodded, and then stood up and began pacing back and forth in the area in front of them as he thought about what he was going to say. He finally stopped and turned on his heel, "Guys, I'll tell you this . . ." he pointed towards the North, "you could head straight north towards Oklahoma and when you get to the Texas Oklahoma border you go East and eventually you'll be at the Arbuckle Mountains. There's a lot of wildlife in that area, and it would be a great place to make a camp. Of course, when it gets cold you'll freeze your ass off, but that could happen in Dallas too."

"I didn't know Oklahoma had mountains." Nate said.

Art shook his head, "They're not mountains like you'd see in Colorado. These are just hills mostly, but yeah," he nodded at James, "I know exactly the area you're talking about. Arbuckle Mountains, Turner Falls area. Yeah, I been there. Can't miss it, if you follow the highway straight up."

James nodded, "Also, you go that way," he turned and pointed directly west, "and head on over to Grapevine, just past the Grapevine Mills Mall, that huge-ass thing out there just North of the DFW airport, and you'll get to Lake Grapevine. Lots of trees, big ass lake, lots of game and sources for food. It would be an okay place. The problem with it is, it's too damn close to Dallas and Fort Worth. Could be crowded."

Ray nodded, "Yeah, that would be really close to here."

"Now, you go south," he swiveled and pointed south, "there's not much until you get to Houston, Austin, or San Antonio and the Texas Hill Country. Going south, it would be warmer, obviously, but you'll be running smack dab into the middle of all that population that'll be spilling out of those areas. Between Houston, San Antone, and Austin, you're talking about a shitload of people. Millions and millions of people from those areas, not to mention the hordes of people from Dallas who'd be on your tail with the same idea, and that's millions upon millions of people . . . *all of whom you want to avoid.* Of course, you get past all of them and make it to Galveston, or, you strap on your walking shoes and make it all the way down to Corpus Christi, then you're sitting pretty. But, that's a long ass tough haul to make and lots of people to get in your way the entire trip."

He paused and lit up another cigarette, "By the way guys, these things here?" he held out his cigarette in front of him, "these little beauties are about to get real scarce and extremely valuable. I'm glad I stocked up. Got twenty cartons." He laughed, "Gonna use them as currency. These Bic lighters? You see any on the ground, pick them up. They could save your life. The ability to have fire is absolutely crucial. I have a bag of a hundred of these. Great for survival, and if I have to I can reap big rewards with them as barter item."

"Then that means you're literally burning money right now." Art chuckled.

James nodded, "true that. Okay," he continued and turned and pointe East, "in that direction you got Louisiana. The piney woods East of Dallas that starts around Longview and goes all the way into Louisiana. Lots of timber, game, and many lakes to fish from. You ever drive from here to Shreveport to go gambling, you probably have seen deer at the edges of the woods all the time. If you haven't seen them there, then you've probably seen their carcasses from where they tried to cross the roadway and got clipped by a car. Every trip I ever took out there I bet I saw twenty or thirty carcasses on the side of the road or two or three live deer at the edges of the woods. That area is just chock full of deer, rabbits, black bear, and all sorts of wildlife. It's a bonanza area and it's big enough to hide in. You find one of those East Texas lakes, make you a camp, and you'd be set up good. You be lucky enough to have a rifle or bow and arrow for hunting and you could live like a king."

"And you're absolutely certain," Art asked, "that this is *it*, that the *shit*, as you say, has *hit the fan?*"

James nodded, "Yes, I am. Because there is nothing else that could have caused all the electricity, and every single computerized item, cars, signs, street lights, etc., to have all shut down at the same exact moment. Think about it. If the electrical grid goes down, all your houses and apartments and street lights and all those interconnected things will stop working, but the cars too, at the exact same moment? No. It was EMP, and the only two questions are whether it was caused by man or nature, and also, how widespread it is. If it is just Dallas, then it's not that big a deal, I mean, it's a disaster, but could be repaired within months or a few years. But, if it's nationwide, or world-wide, then we've just been sent back to the 1800's before electricity, and obviously since all of our societal infrastructure is based upon electricity, then this becomes a disaster unlike anything mankind has ever experienced before. Like I said, if this thing is world-wide, forget that, if it's nation-wide, then you can expect to see a die-off of seventy percent or more of our population."

Art nodded somberly.

"Within the next seventy-two hours, maybe a little longer, but damned soon, you'll be seeing chaos and rampant unchecked crime in the streets. That's why I say that any tiny shreds of complacency bias will kill you surely as a bullet. The time to act is now, gentlemen. Within seventy-two hours I plan to be far away from here. I highly suggest that you do the same. Save yourself. Also, if you head for the hills so to speak, try to find some fishing line and hooks. Guns and ammo obviously. A pot to boil water in. A way to make fire. A tarp or tent. Medical supplies. Socks and shoes. Belts, rope, wire, or anything that can be used to tie things. Zip ties for sure if you have them. Binoculars. Barter items such as gold or silver coins, cigarettes, booze. Any and all drugs, illegal or not. Flashlights and batteries, and sharp knives, can openers, gloves. Put as many clothes on as you can walk with, keeps you warm, and saves you space in whatever you use to transport your camp. Find a place where there's wood, water, game, and few people. Hide yourself, and learn how to barter. Be tough with people. From here on out *every human being you meet is a potential threat to your survival.* And when I say *survival*, I don't just mean your campsite and bedroll. I mean that every person you mean is a direct threat to you living another hour. You best learn that and get used to the idea, because that cautiousness, or paranoia will eventually save you from getting killed. This is no game, and it's no TV show. Don't expect happy endings."

"Sounds brutal." Nate said.

"Kid, you ain't seen nothing yet."

"I have another question, James." Art said.

"Okay."

"What's the point of bugging out if this thing is just local? Because, if it's local, shouldn't we just hang in here and suffer for a couple weeks or whatever until the fix is made? I mean, how are we supposed to know? If communications are down, how do we know if things are okay in Houston, and the affected areas is just Dallas, or if it's the entire country that has been blasted back to the eighteen hundreds?"

James nodded, "Good question, Art, and I'll tell you."

"Yeah," Eddie said, "I don't want to bug out and lose everything I got. I was just getting to the point where I was ahead for the first time in my life. Savings account and all that jazz, you know?"

"Well," James said, "there's a couple ways we'll know. One you can see for yourself, and another that you'd have to be in the loop too know. You'd have to be a guy like myself, a prepper, in other words."

He paused and lit up another cigarette, and the group watched as a group of men and women, all outfitted in jogging clothes, ran by them. Ray thought that the group looked hypnotized. They didn't seem to notice the chaos all around them. They seemed unaware that the world had stopped, that there were no electric lights and all the cars were dead on the road. All they seemed to be aware of was the road before them, and their rhythmic jogging. Like a gaggle of geese flying south, they were all in formation.

The group ran out of earshot and James continued, "In the next few hours, if this thing is local only, then we should be seeing planes flying overhead, or helicopters, or functioning cars coming into the area. Also, emergency vehicles such as ambulances and cop cars and whatnot. Because if this thing is local, then it will be big news and there are people who need help, people in hospitals and older citizens. BUT, if you don't start seeing these vehicles, then it's highly likely that the EMP or CME took out the whole state or, most likely, the entire country. If there ever is any sort of official announcement it's going to be along the lines of *Authorities say domestic terrorist attacks imminent – Martial Law may be in effect soon.*"

"This still sounds too much like science-fiction to me," Nate said, "it just doesn't seem possible. I still think the government wouldn't let this happen."

"Denial!" Eddie Poe said sternly as he pointed his finger at the young man, "normalcy bias!"

James nodded, "Exactly!"

Nate looked around, as if he was expecting someone from outside their group to roll up and bolster his point, but nothing happened.

"There is a form of communication though, that has not been affected by the EMP, or CME, or whatever it was that caused this." He paused and looked at the guys, "Ham radio. See, there are groups of guys like myself all over the country. *Preppers*, as I told you earlier, is what we're called. And there are many of us who invested in Ham radio systems, and we learned how to protect the vulnerable components in storage containers called Faraday Cages. Now that this has happened, the first thing I'm going to do when I get home," he looked at his watch, and Ray saw as he did that James wore an older watch with a radial dial. Ray was pretty sure that the watch was a wind-up type too. No electronics to mess up in it. ". . . probably within the next hour or so, is to get on the radio and start calling guys I know. We have a net of people nationwide, and some of the guys on the East coast can talk to other Ham operators overseas. So, I'll find out what is happening in Kansas, Colorado, California, Washington, and Florida, all up and down the East coast."

"Great," Art remarked, "for you. But how do we find out?"

"Ask around. Watch for airplanes, helicopters and other service vehicles. If this thing is local, you'll know it probably within twenty-four hours. If it's not, you may never ever find out what caused it. But like I said, the why doesn't matter. All that matters is survival. But I plan to be long gone. Not to be callous to you guys, but I plan on saving myself. I think this thing is nationwide. Hell, maybe even world-wide. I think it will take over twenty years to rebuild, heck, maybe even fifty. So, unless I hear differently on the ham radio in a few hours, I'm outta here as fast as I can go."

Ray nodded, "Any advice of travel?"

"If you have a vehicle that will run, it will be faster, but you'll have hell maneuvering around all the stopped vehicles, plus, the downside of having a vehicle, even a bicycle, is that there will definitely be someone willing and ready to take it away from you by force. If you travel by foot, it will take you a lot longer, but you'll be able to move quietly and be less likely to be seen by those who might mean you harm. If you walk out, with nothing but what you can carry, your best bet is to stay off the roads and highways. Those will be dangerous to you, again, because people will want to take what you have. If you walk out, you can get into the woods and parallel the highway and stay relatively unseen. That reminds me, a pair of wire-cutters will come in very handy. I'd rather take longer and be safer, if you know what I mean."

"What if one does as you said, using shopping cart or two?" Eddie Poe asked.

"Well, that allows you more ability to carry your belongings, but it slows you down, and makes it impossible to cut through the woods, or just about anywhere off-road, unless it's a gravel or hard-packed road."

"Okay" Art nodded, "What else?"

"Travel at night if possible, stay away from people, get off the roads as much as possible, oh, and here is a piece of advice that could save your life many times over."

"Lay it on us." Eddie Poe nodded.

"In your travels, anyone you see, no matter what. . .you ask them for something, beg them, make them think you have nothing, and that you're just barely alive and hanging on."

"What's the purpose of that?" Ray asked.

"You want people to think you have less than they have so they will not consider hurting or killing you to get what they don't have. Act poor. Even if you just ate a pound of steak from a deer, and you're feeling full, if you see someone, ask them for something to eat. Always be the *gray man* . . . the man who blends in to the background and doesn't stand out, the invisible man that no one notices. If you are begging for scraps of food, no one will think to kill you for the pound of meat you are hiding."

James stopped talking and looked at his watch, "Guys, it's two thirty a m. The world is about to start waking up in a few hours, and I am going to head home, get on the radio and find out what's what. If it's bad, I will be packed up and on my way within two hours. Heed my advice guys, if you think this is more than local, then don't hesitate in bugging out. The cities will be miserable, dangerous shitholes within three to five days. Don't trust *anyone.* Be invisible. Let go of the past. All that shit is *gone.* Be smart. *Survive.*"

James paused and looked at his watch. None of the guys spoke. James dug out another cigarette and lit up.

"Boys, I want to wish you all good luck, but it's time for me to bid you all adieu. I've got to check the news, and then I'll be hitting the road, because I think this thing is fucked for good."

"Any possibility of sharing the news with us, so we'll know for sure whether to dig in and sit it out or get out for good?" Art asked.

James thought about it, and shook his head, "Well, I'm definitely not bringing back a bunch of people to my place because I'll have my bug out supplies in full view and I'll be heading out. Like I said, anyone with luck and a little planning, would be able ambush a man and take all his stuff."

Eddie Poe nodded, "Fair enough. We're on our own then."

James shrugged, "Actually, I guess I do have a way of helping you guys out."

Art stood up and stretched, "We'd definitely appreciate it," he looked back at the other guys, "leastways, I know I would. I am too old to go off half-cocked and I want to do this thing right if I do it, and I damn sure plan on surviving this mess."

Ray, Eddie Poe, and Nate all nodded in agreement.

"Okay," James said, "here's what I'll do." He pointed South, "I live about a mile and three quarters or so, south of this intersection, right on Preston. Well, that'll be my departure area anyway. Here's what I'll do." He checked his watch for the time. "Around five thirty or six a m, I'll be heading out. Don't try to follow me, you can't possibly keep up. For all you know, I have a vehicle, and it ain't a taxi cab, there's no room for riders, so don't even ask. You boys all live near here, right?"

They all nodded.

James continued, "Okay, so about five thirty or six, that will be just before sunup if you don't have a watch or clock that works, walk out here into the street, somewhere here on Preston Road, look down in that direction, and if I hear news from the Ham radio network saying that this thing is widespread and not local, which is going to be the worst possible news. . . then I will shoot off a flare, straight up in the air from an intersection further down there. Believe me, you'll definitely be able to see the damn thing. Anyway, you see that flare and that's my word to you that this thing is as fucked as it can get and it's your signal to get the hell out of the city as fast as you can do so. That's the ultimate bug-out bat signal.

There won't be a second flare, because one will be more than enough to draw attention to myself which means I'll be putting myself in harm's way just to warn you boys. Got it?"

They all nodded.

Art spoke, "Yes sir. We see the flare we get the hell out."

"Agreed." Ray said.

"Agreed." Eddie Poe said loudly.

Nate took a deep breath, as if he wasn't sure. He looked down at the ground. Of all the guys, he was obviously the one person having the hardest time coming to terms with their situation, "Agreed." He mumbled with a shrug of his shoulders.

He turned to walk away and then stopped and turned around, "Boys, I know I said some rough things, but until you know better, you treat what I said as gospel, and maybe, just maybe, you'll survive this thing. Maybe we'll all meet up again when things shake out. Remember, it's your God-given responsibility to survive. God didn't put you here on earth to be weak and to give up. He put you here to be strong, to survive, and to help others. You can't help others if you're dead. And I know I said that you should avoid other people and treat them as a danger to your own survival. The flip side to that is that there is a certain safety in numbers, but not huge numbers, so if there is someone you can help save, then it is your responsibility to do so. Like I've done here tonight, trying to help you as much as I can, maybe one of these days you can help others who need help. Just be cautious, that's all I'm saying."

They all nodded.

James gave them all a friendly salute, "Good luck boys, see you on the other side!"

He turned and strode off into the darkness.

For a few minutes, nobody spoke, and finally they began discussing the pros and cons of the advice he'd given.

"First time in my life I wish I was a smoker," Ray commented, "because those Bic lighters are going to be something you'd definitely want to have a couple of."

"I gave up smoking two months ago," Art responded, "right after I bought 3 cartons of cigs and one of those multi packs of Bic lighters. I bet there's ten of them in there."

"I got a carton of Kools and probably three or four lighters laying around the house." Eddie Poe added.

Ray asked Eddie if he wanted to team up and do a bug-out with him. "Two's better than one, like Art and Nate are doing."

Eddie nodded. "Fine with me."

"Guess I'm the only one who grew up not liking smoking," Nate said, "so I got no cigarettes, and no lighters."

"One thing I do have that I'm glad I didn't throw out last time I cleaned out the garage," Art said, "is a couple of fishing poles and a couple of tackle boxes full of fishing line, lures, sinkers, hooks and stuff."

"Damn, that's a treasure trove." Ray said.

"I got the one gun and two boxes of ammo." Ray said.

"What caliber?" Eddie Poe asked.

"Nine millimeter. It's a Glock. Just a basic gun. Two mags."

"Good, mine's a nine too. So between us we got three guns and about five hundred rounds of ammo, because I have ten boxes of ammo. Guy sold it to me had two Glocks and eight or nine boxes of ammo. So, we're set there."

"Hey boys," Art said, sliding off the hood of the car and standing up suddenly, "I've got an idea."

"Let's hear it." Ray said.

"Sounds like we all have several things that are going to be needed for survival, if this thing is as bad as James said it will be. If we see his flare signal, I have a proposition that we all ought to consider."

"Let's hear it." Eddie Poe nodded.

"We all head home right now, start packing up our bug-out supplies, take all day, do it right. Then come dark, tomorrow night, we meet right back here," he pointed at the strip center in the corner lot behind them. "See that space in between those trees and the backside of that building? We meet there, and we all take a look at what supplies we all have, and we do a little trading between us, that way we'll all be starting out in better shape than we are now. No forced trades, just a friendly swap meet." He held his hands out, palms up, "for instance, I don't need *ten* Bic lighters. Having extras will come in handy, but I'd hate to have a Bic lighter when the need for a gun arose and I didn't have one. See what I mean? I know I have two or even three fishing poles and several spools of fishing line, twenty or so hooks. . ."

Everyone nodded.

"I'm up for that." Ray agreed.

They all agreed and then split up to go home. It was four-thirty. They all agreed that if they saw the flare signal, they'd spend the day caching their supplies and then at dark, they'd meet back at the agreed upon rendezvous point and make their trades before setting out. Art and Nate said they were going to head towards the Turner Falls Oklahoma area, because Art had visited there several times with his wife over the years. He had stopped going when she'd passed away from cancer two years earlier, but he was confident that he could find them a great place to make a camp, back in the campgrounds area.

Ray and Eddie Poe had talked it over, and decided that they would head East, towards the piney woods of East Texas. Ray had been deer hunting with his father dozens of times when he was growing up, and he knew that the East Texas area was just as James had said it was, teeming with wildlife. The area would be easy to hide in too. Ray told Eddie that an additional reason to head East was that he was pretty sure that James was headed that direction too, and that setting up camp near James wouldn't be the worst idea. Eddie agreed.

Ray walked the half mile back to his apartment and spent thirty minutes locating a flashlight, and then finding every empty plastic water bottle he could find, he'd always had a habit of leaving almost empty water bottles around, and he came up with six of them. He filled them all with tap water, and he noticed on the sixth bottle that the water pressure was already getting low. Just as James had said, the water would stop running within the first day.

He found the old sleeping bag that he'd stuffed into the back of the closet and mentally thanked himself for having been too lazy to throw it out the last time he'd done spring cleaning.

He looked out the window and saw that it was getting close to dawn. He walked out of the apartment, went down the stairs and walked out to the street. There were still dozens of cars up and down the street, all still and quiet. There were hundreds of people milling about, talking in groups, and a dozen or so people were standing next to their cars in the apartment's parking lot, wondering why their car wouldn't start. He saw more than one person trying in vain to get a signal on their cell phone, holding them up in the air and squinting at the screen as if they were going to be lucky enough to catch some cell coverage.

Ray shook his head at them, and considered telling them it was useless, but decided he wasn't up to teaching a mini-class on survival as James had done for them. He doubted he'd be able to convince anyone of the EMP or CME anyway. He understood enough of the facts to convince himself, but not enough to talk about it authoritatively.

He walked past them, one of the women with a cell phone looking at him with a puzzled, beseeching face, no doubt hoping to lure him into helping her out. He shrugged and said his wasn't working either. He walked out into the middle of the intersection, and realized that it felt strange to stand at ease in the middle of the intersection and know that no vehicle was going to come near him.

He faced the South, and wondered if the other guys would actually show up for their rendezvous that night. He could tell that Nate was weak on the idea of leaving the city, and was pretty sure that the longer he was away from those who believed that he would allow more and more denial to creep back in. He was unlikely to show up tonight.

He heard a *pop* and looked up into the sky towards the South. The red trail of the flare raced straight up into the sky and then in a burst of orange exploded and lit up the sky.

He immediately wished that he could meet for five more minutes with James just to get more information about their situation. He began walking towards the next intersection where there were two large grocery stores on two of the corners, and a small boutique overpriced grocery store on another section of the shopping center. The shopping center filled all four corners of the intersection, but Ray wanted the store closest to him because they had the best shopping carts and he planned on grabbing two of them.

He realized that the information he suddenly craved from James, about the outside world was also a commodity that would forever be in short supply. He wondered if James had a way of taking his Ham radio equipment with him. He wished he could have talked to James privately, and convinced him to take on a partner in his bug-out plans. But, it was too late for that. He hoped that Eddie Poe would show up for their planned swap-rendezvous. If he was going to bug-out and live outdoors in dangerous times, it wouldn't hurt to have a big, younger, more physically fit travelling companion to pair up with. He had a feeling though, that all four of the guys together had about one hundredth of the knowledge that James had when it came to survival. Art seemed intelligent and he was of an age that he'd probably spent a great deal of his life outdoors, plus he had served time in the Army, so he was probably more qualified than himself, Eddie Poe, or Nate.

His own father had tried to teach him about camping and living outdoors, and when he was young, Ray had enjoyed it. But as he got older, he had started getting the attitude that what his father was trying to teach him was just *old-timey stuff that nobody cared about anymore*. At least, those were the words that he'd used when he had told his father that he was no longer interested in spending weekends in the woods in the deer season, in a cabin with no TV and no radio and nothing to do. His father had been pestering him for days about the upcoming weekend, and all Ray had wanted to do was go to a party and try to score with Nancy Morrison. He remembered now, with shame, the red-faced embarrassed look his father had given him, and how he'd probably thought that his own son was ashamed of him. The remembrance of the incident caused Ray's heart to sink a little bit. It would be pure Karma if something his father had wanted to teach him that weekend would be the very knowledge that Ray's ignorance of now would end up getting him killed. Plus, he'd gone to the party and had seen Nancy Morrison, with those incredible eyes of hers, kissing and making out with some asshole from the football team. The dude was the big man on campus that year, and now he worked at a Shell gas station. One of those self-serve stations where he just sat in the booth and doled out change and sold cigarettes and Twix bars.

Ray found a long train of shopping carts behind the grocery store. He looked around and saw that no one was paying any attention to him, the alleyway was empty. He pulled several carts out and began inspecting them. He wanted the newest and sturdiest. The store had both the new kind, all plastic and the old type, all metal. He had no idea which would be better for his purposes. He wondered if he should take one of each. He finally decided on the dark blue plastic ones. He figured if he ever had a reason, he could use a knife to cut through the plastic and modify its' shape, although he had no idea why he'd ever need to do that. He also figured that in the sun, the plastic would be too hot to touch like the metal one's would be. Plus, the dark blue plastic wouldn't reflect sun and give off a tell-tale glare during the daytime.

He inspected the wheels and picked over all the carts until he found two that looked almost brand new. If he was going to be travelling a couple hundred miles with them, he wanted the newest ones he could find. That gave him an idea, and he bent down to inspect the wheel assemblies. He pulled out a small leatherman tool and lined up eight carts and worked on them. After a few minutes he had eight extra sets of replacement wheels. He looked around for something to store them in and couldn't see a loose box or plastic sack anywhere. He walked over to the big green dumpster and lifted the lid and looked inside. He saw several plastic bags, so he levered himself up and over the lip of the container and dropped inside with all the trash. He scooped up four or five plastic bags that didn't have any holes or rips, and confiscated a small box, just for an additional storage container. When he picked up the box, he realized it was still sealed. Maybe it was something that an employee has tossed away by mistake, or maybe they'd thrown it in there to retrieve it later to steal or sell whatever was inside. He used his thumbnail to slice down the middle of the box parting the brown packing tape, and when he opened it, he saw a sea of white zip ties. There were probably a couple hundred of them, all fourteen inches long. Damn, he thought, this is a good find. Zip ties, as James had told them, were good for all sorts of things. He crawled back out of the dumpster, and realized that he now stunk like garbage, and there probably wouldn't be a way to shower when he got home. He realized that baths were about to become a luxurious memory. It would take some getting used to, but there was no way around it. Of course, he could bathe in lakes and creeks, but that was not going to be much to look forward to.

He pushed the two carts together where the rear cart was nestled into the front cart and began pushing them down the sidewalk, heading back towards the apartment. He took them both upstairs so that he could make some further modifications on them to make them easier to travel with. He found two old belts that didn't fit him any longer, and crudely strapped the carts together so that they made a train of two carts. He strapped the front of the rear cart to the back of the front cart, using the belts to connect the bottom shelf racks together.

As soon as he had them assembled he began loading them, placing the heavier items on the lower undercarriage rack, and then carefully packing in the other items into the upper baskets. It took several tries, but he finally got them loaded with everything he felt that he needed. He pushed them from one end of the living room to the other, making sure they rolled easily. They didn't roll well on the carpet, which told him that they'd be almost useless on anything other than pavement and hard-packed roads. Going off-road in any type of soft dirt would be next to impossible.

After he was sure of how he would load them, he unloaded them because he knew that it would be impossible to get them down the stairs while loaded. He looked out the window and saw that there were hundreds of people out in the streets and in the apartment's parking lot. He decided to take a nap, because when he went to the rendezvous tonight, he knew that he'd never again come back to the apartment. It might very well be the last time in a long time that he would sleep in a real bed. As soon as it got dark, he would take the carts downstairs, and then quickly load them, making trips up and down the stairs as quickly as possible. He knew that he would have to be quick about it, in order to reduce the chance that anyone pilfered anything from him. As soon as their rendezvous was over with, he expected that he and Eddie Poe would begin walking out of Dallas. He would have to convince Eddie that the East Texas piney woods area was their best choice for survival. He wondered how long it would take to get to their final destination. Probably ten days to three weeks, depending upon their success at making good time on the road. It seemed inconceivable that he was planning a hike that would take weeks, but that was the new world, he guessed. Eddie Poe may not even show up tonight, and if he did, he might not agree that East Texas was their best option.

Before he took his nap, he opened the blinds in the apartment and looked through a large U S atlas. There were maps of every state, and he studied the East Texas area. He saw Lake of the Pines, which was situated just North and East of Longview Texas. That seemed to him like the perfect place. He'd been fishing there once or twice with his father, and he remembered it as an out of the way place, hidden deep in the East Texas forest. There would be plenty of game, and fishing and since it was deep in the woods, there would be few people around. He calculated the distance from where he was sitting, which was Plano, Texas, and the distance was right at one hundred and fifty miles. Pushing heavy carts and dodging trouble, he knew they'd be lucky to make fifteen miles a day, so he figured on ten miles. That was a two week walk and he knew that his estimate was probably optimistic. He figured three weeks would be more likely. The two carts were ponderous and heavy. Plus, he realized, Eddie Poe would likely have a cart too, or a wagon of some sort, or at least a backpack. Hiking a hundred fifty miles would be a breeze, but lugging all their belongings was likely going to turn it into a nightmare trip.

The last thing Ray did before he lay down for a nap was to lock the front door, and then he checked the Glock. He knew that he would need to keep it loaded and at hand at all times now. That's the one thing that James had said over and over that had definitely sunk in. He'd probably said it two dozen times in the three hours that he'd talked to the guys, '*it's going to be like the old west out there from now on, strap your gun on, keep it loaded, and always, always be ready to pull it out and use it. Keep it in arm's reach at all times. Your life will depend upon it.*' Ray thought that James might be overdramatizing the danger factor, but he also realized that he'd be stupid not to heed the advice and find out the hard way that James was right.

He lay down and closed his eyes.

Ray woke up to see that it was beginning to get dark outside. One of the first things he noticed was the silence. No car sounds, no TV or radios, no constructions sounds from the new housing development from across the street. No electrical hum from any appliances and no sound from the air conditioner or fan. Total silence. The absence of sound eerily underscored the reality of what had happened.

He patted his pockets down to make sure that he wasn't forgetting anything, and when he felt his car keychain he pulled it out of his pocket and tossed it onto the counter. The car was worthless, and he doubted that he'd ever be back here to the apartment, so the keys were just added weight that he didn't need.

He looked out the window to see if there was any people at the bottom of the stairs where he planned to load the carts, and then he checked the Glock to make sure it was loaded. He also had a spare loaded magazine in his back pocket.

The landing was empty so he opened the door and quickly took the carts down the stairs, doing his best to avoid too much banging and clomping around, the last thing he needed was any neighbors being too nosy.

When he got them downstairs he quickly ran back up the stairs and grabbed his first load, and then made six more trips until he had the carts loaded and strapped down securely with belts and bungee cord tie downs. He looked up one last time at the stairs and the front door to the apartment, said a mental good-bye and turned and started pushing the cart-train North, up Preston Road. It was only half a mile to the meeting place, heck, he could see it from the window in his bedroom, but it still took twenty minutes to push the heavy carts that far. He mentally adjusted his time frame of the trip to the Lake of the Pines from what he'd thought would be a maximum of three weeks to five weeks. The very thought made him feel tired already, and he hadn't yet gone a mile. He wondered how he'd feel at the end of one hundred and fifty miles.

When he arrived at the bank it was full on dark. Art and Nate, and the dog, Buck were already waiting. They greeted him with a chorus of Hello's and Ray saw that they both also had shopping carts like he did, but they hadn't joined theirs together. While they waited for Eddie Poe to show up, Art looked over Ray's cart construction and they debated whether or not it was a good idea to turn two carts into one, or to keep them separate.

"If someone takes yours" Art reasoned, "in the middle of the night or something, you stand to lose everything. If someone takes one of ours, we lose half our stuff."

"True." Ray agreed.

"Plus," Nate added, "if Eddie Poe also has a cart, you'll have to turn it into a three-cart train, or one of you will be stuck pushing two carts while your partner pushes only one."

Ray nodded, "well, when he gets here and we see how much stuff he has, we'll figure it out. I'm hoping that whatever he has, we can just add it to this wagon train, and he and I will take turns, push a while, and then pull a while."

Ray showed them the three extra sets of eight wheels he'd taken from other carts and Art congratulated him on thinking ahead.

"If we see any more carts," he said as he turned to Nate, "we'll have to liberate some extra wheels, just like Ray did."

Nate nodded, "Or, maybe we can barter for a set right now."

They began listing off items they each had and digging through their supplies and pulling out items that each said they were interested in. As they were about twenty minutes into the process, Nate pointed South down Preston Road, "Here comes Eddie Poe!"

Ray and Art turned to see the tall black man walking towards them. He was dressed all in black, and was wearing two backpacks, one in front and one on his back. He also carried a walking staff like a cane. He came up to the group and greeted them and they all sat down and began talking about their plans. Art and Nate were heading North to Turner Falls, and when Ray told them that he felt that he and Eddie Poe should go to the Piney Woods in East Texas, Eddie Poe readily agreed.

"I ain't no outdoorsman, I'm a city boy born and bred," He explained, "but, I'm not afraid of anything, and I'll follow orders and do as I'm told. If you think East Texas is safe, then I'm all for it." He turned to Art, "You got the most camping and outdoors experience of everyone here, so, you tell me, is his plan of East Texas out in the middle of the woods next to that lake a good idea in your opinion?"

Ray knew that Art did indeed have the most outdoors experience of all of them, and he knew that he had the second most amount of camping experience. Both Nate and Eddie Poe were urban kids. Neither had even been camping out in the Boy Scouts during their young lives. This was undoubtedly going to be a difficult test for them.

"Well, Eddie, as an avid outdoorsman and a wise old fart, I will just say that it's an excellent idea, but I can actually improve on it for you boys!"

"Yeah?" Ray asked, definitely interested in anything that would make things easier, "how's that?"

"Well," Art leaned back against the wall of the bank where they were gathered, and lit up a cigarette, "years ago, when I was married, my wife, Millie, she dearly loved taking these weekend trips, weekend getaways she called them. And one of her favorite things to do was to find a B and B to stay in, instead of a hotel." Art saw Nate frowning and explained, "a B and B is a Bed and Breakfast." Seeing that there was still a puzzled look on the young man's face, he explained the difference between a hotel and a bed and breakfast.

"So, anyway, one year she wanted to go out to Shreveport to play the slot machines, and I agreed, and we also wanted to visit the little town of Marshall. That's about fifty, sixty miles east of Longview, and probably about thirty or forty past your idea of Lake of the Pines."

Ray nodded and allowed the older man to finish.

"So, she booked us into this quaint B and B called, Wagon-Wheel Ranch. It wasn't your usual bed and breakfast either."

"How so?" Eddie Poe asked.

"Well, because most bed and breakfast setups are in an old house, a converted firehouse, or school or something like that. This one though, was really unique. See, the owners had a couple hundred acres of woodland, and they had a main house that had bedrooms for rent, like a typical B and B, but they also had, sprinkled around throughout the woods, these log cabins, all set up like log cabins in the 1800's except for they all had a stove, bathrooms, kitchens and some modern comforts. But, the kicker is that they all had wood burning fireplaces, and wood stoves. Those old big, black, wood burning stoves, completely with working chimneys and a couple of cords of cut and stacked wood piled up next to each cabin. Our cabin was called a Field Hand Shack, or Cowboy Shack or something like that. Now, the cabin we stayed in had bunk beds, course we didn't touch the top bunks, but still, for a couple guys, you make it to one of those cabins, if they're empty, you'll have a pre-made camp, well off the beaten path, and no one around to see you, cause I'm telling you, these cabins are way off in the woods and nobody and nothing around you. The nearest cabin to ours was two miles away, and there was another one we saw that was a freaking full sized, real train caboose, sitting right there in the woods, had a pot-bellied stove in it too, and no one around for miles. I remember the owner telling me that hunting was not allowed on his property and neither was it allowed on the property next to his on either side, on account of it was a Federal woodland preserve. I woke up early one morning, made some coffee, took it out with me on the front porch, and there was probably ten deer grazing within fifty feet of me. They look up and me, didn't spook, and went right back on grazing, like it was no big deal!"

Ray's mouth dropped open, "Damn Art, that sounds like it would be paradise compared to what's going to be going down here in the city. Thanks for telling us about it! Can you point it out on the map for me?"

"Yeah, I can, but it won't be exact. You're going to have to search around and find it for yourself, just remember it's about five miles due west of Marshall. Plus, if you get there and the owner is protecting it you're going to have to move on. But the owners had their own house, plus they had ten or twelve other cabins scattered out in the woods. So, maybe you'll get lucky and get to it before anyone sees you or beats you to it."

"One question, Art." Eddie Poe asked.

"Sure, what?"

"How come, if it's so good, paradise, in your own words, why are you guys going there?"

"Fair question, Eddie," Art answered, "Because, where we're going, up to the Turner Falls area, it's probably seventy five to ninety miles of a shorter walk, and I'm getting old. Plus, I have been to Turner Falls dozens more times than East Texas, and there are some cabins up there too. Hopefully, we'll get there before anyone else gets to them and we'll stake them out for ourselves."

Eddie nodded.

"also, when me and Millie went there, to East Texas, and stayed in that cabin, it was probably twenty years ago. Heck, for all I know, they could be gone by now, so don't take my word on my memory that their still there. I'm just saying that if they are there, and empty, you'll have a ready-made base of operations all set up for you and you won't have to lift a finger to have a decent camp. Pretty sweet for you if it works out. Of course, both you boys are more than welcome to join us and head up to Oklahoma if that suits you."

Ray turned to Eddie Poe, "What do you say, partner? East Texas or Oklahoma? Cowboys or Indians?"

Eddie laughed, "they both sound good to me, but I think that going out to East Texas is the better idea, because it's just that much further away from the population centers. And I think it's really going to get hairy where all the people are. Turner Falls is about halfway between Dallas and Oklahoma city, so that puts it square in the path of two huge gobs of people. Whereas East Texas is way far away from Dallas, and Shreveport is not that much, so, I vote for the Cowboy shack."

"Done then," he stuck his hand out to shake with Eddie, "East Texas it is!"

The group then talked about all the items they had in their carts, listing everything as completely as they could from memory, and even taking some things out to show them. When they'd all four finished they packed everything back into their carts and pushed the carts against the exterior wall of the bank.

The group quieted as a pack of young black and Mexican kids skulked by, staring at them sullenly and Ray noticed that Eddie Poe reached his hand up under his shirt and never dropped eye contact from what looked like the leader of the group.

After they passed by, Eddie saw the looks he was getting from Nate, Ray and Art, "I didn't like the looks of that bunch. And yeah, I was putting my hand in my gun. I think our friend James was right too, with the next few days, this place will be like a war zone when everyone realizes that the world has gone to shit."

"Okay," Art spoke up, "I propose that we start the barter session of this meeting, and I want to start off with a bang." He turned to Eddie and Ray. "You guys have 3 guns between the two of you and we have no weapons other than a couple knives and a bow and arrow. The bow and arrow, I won't give up because it's for hunting game. As a self-defense weapon, it's a lot less effective than one of those Glocks you boys have."

Ray and Eddie gave each other a look.

Eddie spoke to Ray, "we have three Glocks, they're all nine millimeter. All fairly new. Five hundred plus rounds of ammo. Wouldn't hurt to trade for some useful stuff. We'd each have a gun, and they'd have a gun and a bow and arrow. That means all four of us would be armed."

Ray nodded, then shrugged, "Okay with me."

They ended up taking one gallon of bleach (Art had two gallons) to use in purifying water, plus a sauce pan to boil water in and cook with. Plus Art threw in one of the fishing rods, two hundred yards of fishing line and twenty fishhooks and sinkers. Then he pulled out the plastic baggie of Bic lighters and gave them five of them. Art and Ray both had packed two pounds of coffee each, so there was no need for either team to go without coffee.

Art also had three sleeping bags because when he and his wife had gone on a camping out kick years before, they each had a sleeping bag and

had bought a third one for their dog Buster that they'd taken along on

camping trips. He explained that Buck would use it.

"Don't know if it's the smell of Buster that Buck is adverse to, or if it's

just the idea of sleeping inside that thing, but he won't use it."

He ended up trading it to Ray and Eddie for two extra sets of wheels

for the grocery cart, and two steak knives.

After wrapping up their trading they talked about the future, smoked

cigarettes, and three times had to stare down groups of young men who

eyeballed them and their loaded shopping carts. Ray noted that every time

someone got within twenty feet of them, Eddie Poe's hand would go up

under his shirt for his gun. He was wary and on edge, and Ray realized that

that was a good thing. He knew he would have to develop that hard edge

too, for survival's sake.

They discussed ideas on how to travel and they all decided that James'

instructions to travel at night was a good idea. It would be cooler at night

and they'd be less likely to be seen. They also developed a plan whereby

they put one person on guard while the other slept as they made camp

every night, and the watch would be four hours on watch, and then four

hours of sleep. They'd only sleep eight hours when they could get off the road and hide well enough not to be seen, once every three or four days. Going too long without sleep would be dangerous.

It was mid-June, so the heat was already beginning in Dallas, and they knew that the trek to Oklahoma wasn't going to make that much of a difference from the weather in Dallas, but Art said that he thought that the trek through East Texas might be slightly cooler.

"The problem you boys will have out there in East Texas is varmints. Black bear may look cuddly and cute, but you stay away from them. You get near one of them and momma bear is around, you're gonna be bear dinner. Watch out for water moccasin's too. They're everywhere out there. Fox, mink, squirrels, cougar, puma, coyote, wild pigs, rabbit, raccoon, wolf, weasel . . . there's a lot of game out there, but be damned careful in those woods. Be especially careful of the snakes, Cottonmouth snakes, Coral snake, Copperheads, and timber Rattlers."

Eddie Poe shivered, "Wish you hadn't brought up snakes. Damn I hate snakes and spiders and scorpions."

"Well, you're going to see some of them for sure. Most likely you'll be seeing Cottonmouths in the Piney Woods like that. But watch out for those Timber Rattlers too."

"And between the four of us, no one has a snakebite kit!" Ray said.

"Yeah, that's true," Art replied, "but even if we did have it, it would be almost useless unless you'd had someone show you how to use it properly. Fact is though, most snakebites do not end in death, but it'll put you on your ass for weeks."

"Yeah," Ray said, "Of all the stuff we could all pull together, the first aid kits are what we're all lacking. Let's all hope that that doesn't come back to haunt us."

"Well," Art said, "in your travels, if you boys come across a pharmacy or hospital that hasn't been cleaned out, or isn't being guarded by armed men, you take as much stuff as you can. I know we'll do the same if the opportunity presents itself."

"Good idea." Ray nodded.

"Coffee too." Eddie Poe added, "any place we see, like roadside gas stations, if they're empty, if we can find coffee, that'd be a good thing to stockpile."

"Good idea." Art said, nodding at Nate, "we'll do that."

They talked for another hour, and Ray began to get the feeling that they were all wanting to put off their departure as long as possible. To put off the beginning of what might prove to be the last trip they ever made. To put off the final departure from what they'd all known as real civilized society. They all seemed reluctant to part with their new friends, even though they'd only known each other for less than a day. Ray realized that it would be highly unlikely that he'd ever see Art and Nate again. Ray thought about all the people he worked with, and random people that he saw every day, the people at the coffee shop, at the gas station, and the restaurants that he frequented. He'd more than likely never see any of these people again.

Finally, Art stood up and looked North, and turned to Nate, "Well, son, we better get a move on. It would be nice to get as far away from the madding crowds as we can before sunup."

Nate nodded and stood up and they positioned their carts facing North.

Ray and Eddie Poe both stood up too, and Eddie stretched.

All four men shook hands and spend a few minutes small talking and wishing each other well.

"Guys, you take it easy," Art cautioned them, "be safe, and stay well-hidden whenever possible, especially when you're holed up off the road when not travelling."

"Same to you Art." Ray replied, "Be careful, watch each other's backs!"

"Hey, guys," Nate spoke up, "I have an idea."

"Yeah?" Eddie asked.

"How about, in a year from now, if things are safe and it's at all possible, let's meet back up right here for another rendezvous?"

Eddie, Ray and Art all nodded, and it was agreed that a year from that date, if it was at all possible, they'd all meet up again at the same spot.

They shook hands all around again, and then they all hugged, and Eddie clapped the older man on the back and the two sets of partners set out on their journey. Art and Nate headed due North, and Ray and Eddie headed due South.

Eddie talked to Ray about security as they walked towards the George Bush toll road which was just about two miles South of their present location. That highway would take them due east and then turn South again about ten miles out where it would go five miles due south and then turn due East again. From there it was about twelve miles or so before it met with interstate 20, and it was then that their longest portion of their leg of a hundred and fifty miles travel due East towards Louisiana would begin. Of course, they wouldn't go all the way to Louisiana, but they both agreed that their easiest and least crowded travel would be on that highway. Finding the bed and breakfast cabins would be a whole new set of problems since they were, as Art had explained, hidden deep in the words. As they walked, he explained everything he could think of about the Glock pistols to Ray, and they both began wearing the guns in their waistbands for quick access.

#   #   #   #   #

It took two weeks and four days for Art and Nate to get to the Turner Falls, Oklahoma area. The route was one hundred and twenty five miles, and they made good time, except for days when they were slowed down by sore feet, twisted ankles, and hunger. Running out of their canned food after four days, they tried to carefully scrounge any and all roadside restaurants and gas stations they came across, but could see that they had been beaten by other hungry travelers at almost every stop. They ventured off the road almost two miles at one point, hiding their carts in some underbrush when they saw a farmhouse far off in the distance, and when they arrived, they found that the house had been ransacked and there was nothing there, but then Art had seen a tell-tale hump in the ground and discovered that it was what he thought it was, a storm shelter, or bomb shelter, something that Nate had never seen or even heard of. They forced the door open and found a huge stock of canned and jarred foods. They stayed there two days, gorging themselves on food, and taking all the extra supplies that they could carry, and it was this plunder that allowed them to use extra energy to hustle faster than they'd ever travelled and they'd finally stumbled upon the campgrounds that ranged throughout the area. They found some covered picnic tables and fire pits and water nearby, and set up camp at the furthest campsite from all the others that they could find. The entire area was still deserted, so it appeared as if Art's idea as a good place to bug out to and set up camp at had been a sound one.

#   #   #   #   #

Ray and Eddie found themselves struggling from the start. The George Bush Freeway had been easy enough to maneuver their carts upon, but once that freeway ended and they needed to turn South and take the I-635 highway towards the I-20 freeway, it turned into a mass of people. Three days after starting out, they found themselves on I-20 about fifty miles outside of Dallas. They had rarely stopped to rest for the entire three days since it was wide expanses of highway, and off to the sides it was non-stop shopping malls and retail outlets which were swarming with crowds of unruly mobs rampaging through the stores.

The highway was smooth, but even so, it was extremely rough on the small cart wheels, and on the third morning they switched out the wheels on the back cart. The wheels weren't completely shot, but they were already worn down enough that the rolling was rougher. They stored the old wheels, just in case they ever needed them again in an emergency.

When they turned due East on I-20 towards Louisiana, the crowds began to thin out considerably and as soon as they got to a wooded area just off the highway, they found a secluded spot to hide their cart-train and they covered everything up with branches and foliage and they stayed in place for two days, resting, eating, and rebuilding their energy stores in their bodies.

On the sixth day, they were a few miles from Longview, which put them about three-quarters of the way to their destination when they came across a group of four; two men and two women. Eddie had noticed them first, miles up the highway ahead of them, and after a couple more hours of walking, he told Ray that the group of four appeared to have stopped and were waiting for them to catch up to them.

He cautioned Ray, "I don't like the looks of that, four people waiting for us to catch up with them. Looks like it could be a trap."

They stopped and Ray pulled out the binoculars and they both spent a few minutes taking a look.

"Two men and two women."

"You want to stop and wait for them to move on, or what?" Eddie asked.

"You're the director of security for this trip, you tell me."

Eddie took the binoculars and looked again, taking his time and trying to absorb every detail that he could. "Looks like a big fat guy, a tall skinny guy, and two women, both somewhat average. The older man, fat guy, and one of the women look middle-aged and the younger guy, beanpole, and the other woman look younger. None look very threatening, and I can't see any weapons of any sort." He paused, "My take on it is to move on. I don't want any more delays. The faster we get up the highway and find those cabins, the happier I'll be. Let's roll."

They kept moving up the highway with Ray pushing the cart-train and Eddie at the front pulling the lead cart. Less than two hours later, they were fifty yards away from the group of four. Eddie spoke over his shoulder to Ray, "Keep your Glock handy, and be prepared to shoot, no questions asked if any of this bunch gets hinky. It's still too early to tell, but this could be a set up. Still don't see any weapons but that don't mean shit yet."

"Okay, I'm ready."

They made their final approach to the group, who were obviously stopped and waiting for them to catch up.

"Ahoy there!" The big man nodded at them and waved his hand for them to approach.

Eddie stepped back alongside Ray as the fat guy greeted them.

"Ahoy yourself!" Eddie grinned at them, while placing his hands on his hips.

Ray knew that Eddie was assuming that posture so that he could have quicker access to his gun if he needed it. Ray had never asked Eddie outright why he knew so much about guns, and felt racist for thinking so, but he felt that Eddie was no stranger to guns or some level of violence. He may not be a gang-banger, and he wasn't all tatted up, and he didn't speak the street patois of a thug, in fact he was very well spoken, but still, Ray felt a certain level of confidence and bravery that the man exuded. Maybe he was ex-military? Ray reminded himself to ask him soon, hopefully without offending the man.

Ray allowed the cart to come to a stop. The group of four had their own cart, but theirs was a warehouse flatbed cart with large ten inch rubberized wheels. The cart was piled about four feet high supplies which was covered with a heavy tarp. They must have had a ton of stuff under there Ray thought. The younger guy had a large two-wheeler hand truck that was also covered in an Army green tarp and both the hand truck and the flatbed cart had everything lashed down by cargo strap ratcheted tie-downs and elastic bungee cords with hooked ends.

Their kit looked very well put-together. Strictly top-notch stuff compared to Ray and Eddie's grocery-cart convoy. Ray looked them over carefully, as he knew that Eddie was also doing, and could see no visible weapons, and no bulges in their clothing that would indicate that they were carrying concealed.

The fat man introduced himself and his three friends. Ray thought the man appeared to be a blustery, self-important blowhard who affected an attitude of superiority. He'd introduced himself as 'Chuck' and had made sure that Ray and Eddie knew that he was the leader of their group of four, by virtue of being the owner of a manufacturing company that the other three worked for. Ray wasn't the least bit impressed, and by the way Eddie rolled his eyes when he heard the fat man talking, he could tell that Eddie was even less impressed.

He introduced his friend as Nolen, naming him as the Vice President of their manufacturing company.

Ray wondered why the guy was so intent upon making his corporate identity know, as if it still mattered, but he figured the guy was just one of those blowhards that would also see themselves as better than others because of position, money, and status. Ray guessed the man hadn't fully grasped the idea that things had forever changed.

Chuck introduced the dumpy-looking woman his wife, her name was Vanessa. Ray thought that she looked about as humorless as a dirt clod, and then Chuck introduced the other woman as Kelly. She was younger than Chuck and Vanessa by about twenty years, and she was as plain as a paper bag , and she had a downcast look about her. She was probably in her forties, but looked eighty in her face. She seemed nervous, mousy and kept her eyes on the ground. Ray noticed that the girl never made eye contact with any of them, and she never uttered a sound.

Ray and Eddie introduced themselves and the group pulled over to the side of the road where there was one of those roadside rest stops, the kind that had two small buildings that housed rest rooms, and a water fountain which didn't work, and a small sidewalk path leading from the parking lot to the restrooms, with a small circular area in the middle of the path that contained decorative rocks with a flagpole centered in the middle. The American flag was still flying with the Texas flag waving beneath it.

The rest stop had four concrete park benches all covered by latticed pergolas and they decided to hold up there for the night. The rest stop also featured a two barbeque grills, which was a feature that Ray had never seen in a rest stop before. He just wished that they had some meat to cook in them, but he figured meat, especially barbecue was something that was now relegated to luxury status. Just looking at the grills made his stomach rumble.

They sat around talking about what had happened and why, and Ray and Eddie were surprised when Nolen mentioned that they had a portable ham radio set up and enough batteries to run it for a while. They mentioned that they'd been able to get news from as far away as West Virginia to the East and from Denver to the West and Corpus Christi to the South and North as far up as Minneapolis. The news was bleak, in that it seemed as if the entire country was without power. Nolen said that they'd constantly asked everyone they spoke to for hard news regarding what had happened, what had set off the EMP, but there were no factual answers. It was all just guesses, conjecture and some outright nutty conspiracy-theories involving illuminati and aliens. The simple fact was what James had told them days earlier, that they may never really know the truth, and chasing it was a waste of time. Time better spent working on surviving.

Eddie seemed annoyed by the fact that Chuck, who Ray was now thinking of as 'fat guy' would never let anyone speak without interrupting them and blustering over them with his own never-ending stream of blowhard opinions and the longer he talked the louder his volume rose. He was clearly a man in love with himself. The younger guy, Nolen, acted superior, as if he wanted to be seen as the smartest guy in the room at all times. Ray saw them as blowhard and junior-blowhard. The wife, Vanessa, wore a nasty look of hatred on her face at all times. Ray secretly named her bitch-face, and the girl, Carla, seemed like she was barely there. She was all but invisible.

Chuck and Nolen set up their two tents and the two women went into separate tents and Ray and Eddie pumped the two men for information but didn't get much of anything useful. The blowhard, Chuck, seemed more interested in bragging about his company that had made him a millionaire, and the kid, Nolen, seemed intent upon letting them know that he was an IT expert.

Ray said he had to go take a piss, and he walked back behind the rest stop bathrooms to tend to his call of nature because the inside of the buildings stunk so badly. Eddie followed him and also took a nature break.

When they finished Eddie shook his head back towards the highway.

"Those two are clueless aren't they?"

Ray nodded in agreement, "Yeah, I guess they think that money and all that supposed IT knowledge will buy them something out here in the new Wild West."

"Fat boy sure is an egotistical blowhard isn't he? He acts like he's the world's foremost expert on every subject under the sun. I swear, the next time he mentions his fucking bank account, I might just punch him in the throat."

Ray laughed, "and IT-boy thinks he is still on top of the world like the computer nerds *used to be*. He's got quite a shock coming."

"Yeah, I think his qualifications are bogus. Anyone who knows anything about computers will know that a widespread EMP event would literally wipe his entire industry off the face of the earth."

"Well, I look at them and can't help but think that there's something creepy with those two dudes."

"Yeah, and that wife, what a piece of work she is," Eddie said, "she looks like she hates the world. What a bitch-face she is!"

"That other one too, there's something strange going on there, for sure."

They walked back to the picnic tables and could see that Chuck and Nolen had several items spread out on a blanket that covered the table top.

"Boys," Chuck said as they approached, "we thought we might do a little bartering session, if you care to join in?"

Ray expected Eddie to say something about the 'boy' but Eddie just grinned at him and sat down across from him. Ray sat down next to Eddie.

They had a layout of items on the blanket, including the portable ham radio, one large knife from a kitchen, a can opener, a large wad of hundred dollar bills, two Rolex watches and a couple of men's rings, a box of condoms and, absurdly enough, two kindles.

The fat man, Chuck, spread his hands over the items, "Up for some barter, boys? Now, that there Ham radio is not for sale or barter, but I would rent you out a block of time on it!"

Eddie laughed in his face. "Fat boy, what you have here isn't worth jack shit."

Chuck's face reddened and his friend Nolen came to his defense, "Mister, you're looking at almost fifty thousand dollars' worth of items here."

"What are you *boys* looking for, barter-wise?" Eddie asked.

Fat man answered, "we noticed you guys have a couple of guns. We'd like to trade for one," then he nodded, "plus ammo, of course."

Ray laughed at the absurdity of their offer and Eddie answered for them,

"Not a chance in hell." He snorted derisively, "in fact, you could offer everything on this table for one fucking bullet, and I'd turn you down flat. No way, no how."

"Well," the fat man said, "we have something else I bet you won't turn down. Something you might find a bit more valuable," he waved his hand over the blanket, "than these paltry items."

"Yeah, what's that?" Ray asked, thinking that any moment now, one of these weird guys was going to pull out a weapon and try to rob them. He kept asking himself *what would James do in this situation?*

The fat man and skinny boy put their heads together and whispered. Ray didn't know why he kept thinking of the younger of the two men as a 'boy' or more precisely 'skinny-boy' because he appeared to be in his late twenties. He had that millennial-douche-bag look about him, as if he expected to be treated special because he was young and knew about computers, and Ray wanted slap him and let him know that the reign of the nerds was finished, but he figured that he'd come across someone else, sooner or later who would straighten him out. The older man seemed as if he should be able to answer to the names of fat-boy, or blow-hard, and he seemed to have an incredible excess of ego. He had already mentioned, three times no less, that he owned both a Corvette and a Hummer, so Ray automatically assumed that the fat man suffered from micro-penis syndrome. After all, a Corvette and a Hummer? How much more overcompensation could there be? He tried to act young, what with the ridiculous do-rag on his head, but the effect it had was to make him look like a ridiculous white-man trying to appear street and hip. In the Dallas ghetto, he would be ripped apart in minutes, like a pack of hyena's on a crippled deer.

But, they didn't pull out any weapons at all. They were too timid, Ray realized, to attempt anything so bold. Instead, Nolen got up and walked back to the tents and opened a flap, and bent down and said something to the woman inside. Then he walked back alone to the bargaining table.

"Well?" Eddie asked them.

The fat man held up a finger as if to shush Eddie, and Ray thought that Eddie was close to grabbing that finger and breaking it.

Eddie turned and looked at Ray, "These two dudes are idiots, we should go make camp somewhere else."

Ray nodded, but said, "Let's hear them out."

As soon as he spoke, the other woman, Kelly, came out of the tent and stood at the end of the table.

Eddie and Ray looked at Chuck and Nolen as if to say, *what?*

The fat man wiggled his eyebrows up and down, "That gentleman, is our *piece de resistance.*" he said, mangling the French pronunciation.

"What the fuck are you talking about?" Eddie asked him.

Nolen explained, "Vanessa is his wife," he said, nodding at the fat man, "but she is," he nodded at the woman, Kelly, ". . .she is a free agent, so to speak. *If you get my drift.*"

Eddie looked at Ray and Ray shrugged.

The fat man spoke up again, "she is available to you, for an hour, *each*, and all we ask in return is that we get one gun and at least fifty rounds of ammo. You want more time with her, we can negotiate further. We will even supply the condoms for your pleasure."

Eddie looked at him as if he were insane, "you're bargaining for her to be used as a prostitute, seriously?"

The man nodded, proud of himself, "and remember boys, I did say one hour *each*."

Ray looked at the woman, she kept her eyes glued to the ground, "You agree to this bullshit?"

She never raised her eyes, but nodded, keeping her eyes on the ground.

"You should walk away from this fucking creep." Eddie urged her.

"Hey, we take care of her!" Nolen protested vehemently.

"Fuck you, *boy*, you're just a lowlife fucking pimp." Eddie stood up and leaned over the table. Nolen shrank back and looked frightened.

"No deal." Ray said, sick to his stomach at the thought of dealing with these two.

"Well, now," the fat man said, "the deal won't get any better. My wife in there," he nodded towards the tent, "she's not available for any amount of money or goods, and this one here, she is clean, disease-free, and she'll do whatever you want, long as it doesn't mark her up any. Gotta keep my main *product* in good shape for future customers, *if you know what I mean.*" He said leeringly.

"Go to hell, fat man!" Eddie spat at him.

The younger man, Nolen, bristled at hearing his friend called fat man, and Eddie glared at him. "You want to say something to me, beanpole?"

"No reason to be rude mister, we're businessmen, not thugs. I'm a vice president and he's a CEO and we have been in business for almost fourteen years-"

Eddie laughed at him, "Fuck you, and fuck your piss ant business.

Your business, your titles, and your bank account are all gone. You need to understand that. You are a fucking nobody, and if I had my way, I'd just as soon pull out this Glock" he patted at the bulge at his waistline, "and put a round through your forehead right now!"

Nolen went pale, "Mister, you touch me and you'll be in jail for-"

"As a matter of fact," Eddie pulled out the Glock and placed the end of the barrel a few inches in front of the man's face, "If you say one more fucking word to me, I might just go ahead and blow your fucking head off! Get it?"

The man nodded, and the fat man next to him started to say something, and Eddie swung the end of the barrel towards his forehead, "You too, fat man. If I hear one more blowhard word out of your mouth, I'll put a pullet down your gullet. Let's see how much you talk then!"

Both men leaned towards each other.

"Now, you boys just wrap up all your goodies here, and get back in your tents and leave us the fuck alone. We're leaving, first thing in the morning, and if I see either of you following us, or if anyone touches our belongings tonight, I'll put several extra holes in your face."

The two men wordlessly scrambled to wrap up their barter items into the blanket and then put the blanket back under the tarp on the flatbed cart. Ray wished he could see what kinds of supplies they'd cached under the tarp, but he'd also be content to get away from them as soon as possible.

The two men disappeared into a tent, and few minutes later, the wife came out of the tent and went into the tent where the other woman, Kelly had returned to.

Eddie turned to Ray and gave him a WTF look, and then they both set about getting their own camp set up. They put a tarp over a low-hanging branch, and then dug out their sleeping bags to cushion the ground to make it more comfortable to sleep on. It was still too warm out to sleep inside the sleeping bags.

Exhausted after the day's events, Ray fell asleep immediately. He tossed and turned most of the night and woke up with Eddie shaking his by the shoulders.

"Get up, come on Ray, wake up! Hurry up and get out here!" he whispered, and then scrambled back out of their makeshift tent.

Heart racing, Ray sat up and pulled on his shoes and his shirt and then got to his hands and knees and crawled out into the brush and then ran towards the parking lot area.

He found Eddie standing there, hands on his hips, looking South down the highway.

"What? Eddie, what happened?"

Eddie pointed South, and far off in the distance Ray could see their four friends, just disappearing over the horizon, heading back towards Dallas.

Ray shrugged, "So what? We wanted nothing to do with them, right?"

Eddie turned towards him and pointed back towards the rest stop.

Ray turned, "what, Eddie?"

Eddie spoke, "See anything missing? Those motherfuckers stole our carts, and everything we had!"

Ray's eyes widened as he looked for the area where they'd parked their cart-caravan, and saw nothing.

Ray turned and looked at Eddie, unable to speak.

Eddie help out a piece of lined notebook paper that had been crumpled into a ball, "they were kind enough to leave us a note too."

Ray took the piece of paper and unfolded it and read the message:

Sometimes you eat the bear, and sometimes the bear eats you. LOL

Hopefully, you BOYS will have learned your lesson.

Fuck You.

Ray looked back up at Eddie.

"What the fuck are we going to do, Eddie?"

"I'll tell you what we're going to do," Eddie said through clenched teeth. He grabbed the piece of paper from Ray and held it up in between them, "we're going to after those motherfuckers, we can travel *a hell of a lot faster* than that fat ass and all that plunder, and *four fucking carts* full of supplies," he turned around and started walking South, "and when we catch those cocksuckers, I am personally going to wipe my ass with this," he help up the note, "ands then I'm going to make fat man and skinny boy each eat half of it. Then we'll take back our supplies, and I might just take all of theirs to boot. Come on, let's hustle. We'll catch them by nightfall."

Ray started to argue, but then he was already falling behind, so he began trotting to catch up with Eddie. He didn't know how long they could keep up the pace, but he didn't doubt Eddie one moment when he said they'd catch them by nightfall.

This should be interesting, he thought.

#   #   #   #   #

They had caught up to within several hundred yards of them by dusk and then Eddie suggested that they stay back until full dark. "They'll make a campfire, and we'll have no problem finding them in the dark. We'll surprise them real good, believe me. They're too stupid, too cocky, and arrogant to even think about being followed."

"Yeah, you're probably right about that," Ray agreed, "We've been following them all day, and they've never once looked back to see if we were coming after them for our stuff. Pretty stupid, if you ask me."

"They're beyond stupid." Eddie seethed.

Ray had never seen Eddie so upset, but he had a point. Without their supplies returned, they were up shit creek. True, they still had both of their Glocks, but the ammo, other than what was in each mag in their guns, was in their cart. Less than thirty rounds between the two of them wasn't nearly enough. Even if that's all they could salvage, it was worth it. Plus they still had pots, pans, canned food, knives, ammo, water and hundreds of useful items, including their binoculars. The loss would not only be devastating, it could be life threatening.

They made their way up the highway, and sure enough, when they got closer to the area in the edge of the woods just off the highway, they could see a campfire going. Completely open to view by anyone passing on the highway, that campfire was like a shining beacon of stupidity.

They crept closer, "Fools" Eddie muttered.

"What's our plan?" Ray asked.

"We go in on the right side there, where the trees are most dense. We wait until they are both in their tents, catch them by surprise. Easy fucking peasy."

Ray nodded.

They moved off the road two within about fifty yards of the two couples. They were sitting around the campfire, eating from heated up canned vegetables.

They could barely hear their voices, but not well enough to hear what they were talking about. The voices were just a low murmur, and every now and then fat man would laugh. Ray whispered to Eddie, "You ever in your life hear an egotistical blowhard like this guy? It's unbelievable."

Eddie shook his head, "You think the asshole would eventually run out of ways to tell you how great he is. Dumb cocksucker."

Ray laughed, "Hey, Eddie, you're not going to kill him, are you? I'm not sure I'm up for that kind of shit."

Eddie sat back for a moment and looked at Ray, "You do realize of course, that their stealing our shit like they did, could have killed us?"

Ray nodded, "I know, and I want to hurt them, but murder? I'm just not sure about that."

Eddie shrugged, "Okay, I'll tell you what, I promise not to kill that fat-ass motherfucker. That suit you?"

Ray nodded.

They watched for another hour, hearing the fat man's annoying voice droning on and on, uninterrupted until finally, the two women got up and left the campfire and went into one of the tents together.

Eddie looked at Ray and shrugged, "maybe the women are lezzing out together?"

Ray shook his head, "I don't think so. At least I didn't get that kind of vibe from them. Could be wrong I guess."

A few minutes later fat man and skinny-boy went into the other tent.

"How can that pipsqueak kid stand to listen to that annoying blowhard so long without wanting to cut his throat?" Eddie asked.

"Good question."

They waited for another hour, giving the couples time to go to sleep, but they never saw anyone change tents. Finally, Eddie nodded and they began creeping towards the tents.

As they came closer to the tents, they began hearing sounds. Sex sounds. Eddie whispered to Ray, "maybe they changed tents when we didn't see them. Sounds like someone is definitely having sex."

Ray responded, "Probably beanpole and mute girl. I can't feature anyone having sex with fat boy, or that dead-eyed soulless bitch-face of a wife either."

Eddie nodded, "Yeah, plus the blowhard fat-man isn't talking, so that pretty much guarantees that he is asleep."

Ray grinned, "okay, let's hit the tent on the right first. I think if we'd have trouble with any of them, it would be skinny-boy. The women don't worry me, and fat man can't get up enough steam to come fast at me, or work up enough steam to make any sort of a fight of it."

The crawled forward on hands and knees and stopped at the front flaps of the tent and paused. They could still hear whimperings of sex, and light grunting. Eddie nodded and they both rose to their feet and each grabbed a handful of the tent fabric flap liner. Ray nodded and they both jerked the fabric open and stepped inside and they both stopped dead in their tracks, appalled at what they were looking at.

Mute girl was sitting up, tied with rope at her wrists and ankles, and she had a flimsy top on and some white cotton undies. There was a cloth bunched up and stuffed into her mouth. Tears were streaming down her face. Vanessa, the wife, was sitting next to here with a lit cigarette, and the smell of burning flesh permeated the inside of the tent. There were circular cigarette burns all over Kelly's stomach, the tops of her legs, and her breasts.

The wife, Vanessa, *bitch face*, glared at them and then spoke in a low mean voice, "get out of here, you nigger!"

Ray blinked, and looked at Eddie, who simply stepped over the bound girl, drew his arm back and punched bitch face as hard as he could in the mouth. She dropped backwards to the ground, knocked out cold. Blood spurted from her mouth and nose. Ray figured that she'd have a broken nose, and would probably lose most of her front teeth. The punch was that hard.

They looked at the girl, Kelly, mute girl, and Ray wanted to ask her if she was okay, but it seemed like an absurd question. He knelt down to take the cloth out of her mouth, but Eddie grabbed him by the arm stopping him. Eddie nodded towards the other tent and whispered, "Let's get them taken care of before we tend to her."

Ray nodded and they crept out of the tent and made their way over to the other tent, and just like minutes before, they each grabbed a flap of the fabric on each side.

They could hear whimpering sounds again, and Ray wondered if they were about to see the same scene they'd just witnessed with the women.

Eddie nodded and they rushed in. Once again they were stopped dead in their tracks, stunned by the scene they witnessed. Both men were completely naked, and Beanpole was thrusting into fat man from behind and grunting *Chuckie, Chuckie*, with every thrust. Meanwhile, Chuckie was biting down on a stuffed animal, that looked to Ray like a terrier pup. Neither man was aware that they were being watched until Eddie pulled his Glock and raised it up and fired off a round through the top of the tent into the sky.

The deafening roar of the gunshot made the two men yelp and they came apart and scrambled under the cover together, their arms wrapped around each other.

Ray blinked his eyes, because the muzzle flash had momentarily blinded him, and his ears rang. A small tendril of smoke rose from the end of the barrel of the Glock.

Eddie laughed, "You boys having you some good old Deliverance-style fun?"

Beanpole, obviously too young to get the reference yelled back at him,

"Fuck you, asshole, get out of here, this is a private tent!"

"You sass me one more time, *boy*," Eddie said as he aimed the Glock at Beanpole's face, "and this here tent will be your very own burial shroud."

Ray nodded at Beanpole to shut up. The last thing he wanted was for Eddie to shoot these guys, even though they had attempted to rip them off.

"Come on, Eddie, let's just get our stuff and go. Let's just leave these losers behind."

"I got a better idea." Eddie replied.

"What's that?"

"I'm going to teach them a lesson. A lesson about stealing."

"Let's just get the fuck out of here. They won't be stupid enough to follow us."

"Well, they were stupid enough to steal from us in the first place. We have to at least hobble them so that they can't catch up with us again and try to get revenge. I'm not going through this again. Not with this bunch. Besides which, they cost us a day's travel time. That has to be accounted for."

Ray said nothing.

"Go to the other tent, get those women out there by the fire."

Ray nodded, and then let himself out of the tent. He went to the other tent and instructed the women to get to their feet. He held the Glock pointed at them the whole time.

By the time Ray had the two women out to the campfire, Eddie had marched fat man and Beanpole out to join them. He hadn't allowed either man to get dressed.

"Sit down, ladies" Eddie commanded.

The two women sat down and Eddie pointed his Glock towards fat man and Beanpole,

You two boys just stand there, hands at your sides. Don't be trying to hide your junk. You were caught red-handed in the act. Don't try to be all shy now. I see those hands covering up those tiny puds, I'll put a bullet through them. Understood?"

Both men nodded and left their arms dangling at their sides.

Eddie took out the note that they'd left at their campsite. He threw it on the ground, rubbed it into the dirt with his shoe, and then tore it in half and took half and gave it to the fat man, and then gave the other half to Beanpole and told them both that they had thirty seconds to eat and swallow it or he'd cut one of their fingers off for failure.

They both began chewing. A few seconds later they both opened their mouths to proves that they'd swallowed.

"Lady," Eddie said, "did you know that your hubby and his boy-toy were giving it too each other behind your back?"

"I could care less about Shrimp-dick and douche-bag boy." She spat angrily.

Eddie laughed.

"That certainly is one teeny-tiny dick isn't it?" Eddie said.

"Bag of blubber can't get it up anyways, so who cares?" she replied.

"Come on, Eddie, let's just get the hell out of here. We got our stuff."

Eddie nodded, "Yeah, we got our stuff, but we still need one thing. *Justice*. We need to mete out some punishment that will guarantee that this bunch won't dare try to exact any revenge."

"Let's just split. They have no weapons. We see them again, we'll shoot them for sure."

"Oh yeah, that's true, we definitely will do that."

"You said we wouldn't kill them." Ray reminded him.

The two men tensed up considerably at that, and then the fat man spoke,

"You listen to me, sir. I am a very wealthy businessman, and I swear to you, before this is over with, I'll hire the best private investigator in the country to hunt you both down. You'll spend the rest of your lives in jail. You can count on it. I have the money to make your lives miserable, you sorry punks."

Eddie walked over to fat man as he was making his threat and when he stopped talking, Eddie reared back and punched the man in the face as hard as he could. Then he stood him up and punched him several more times. The man's face was a bloody mess when he finally stopped.

"I'm tired of hearing your blowhard mouth you fat son-of-a-bitch. Now, what I want you to do is to get some exercise."

"Sum wha?" the fat man was having talking through his bloodied mouth.

"Some exercise! You're too damn fat!"

"Fuh ooh ah whoa"

"Fuck me? Is that what you say?"

"Ywah, fuh ooh!"

Eddie held the gun up to fat man and nodded, and he walked over to bitch-face and held the gun to her head, "Turn to face your boy-toy, and start doing some toe-touchies, right now, or I'll blow a hole in her skull, and then I'll start working on boy-toy, from the bottom up."

Ray gulped, "Just do it, man, just humor him and we'll be on our way."

The fat man turned sideways to them and raised his hands over his head as he'd been taught in junior high school, which was probably the last time he'd ever done any exercise, and began slowly bending down to stretch his fingers towards his toes.

"Do twenty of them, blowhard, I'll have wifey count them off!" Eddie commanded.

The fat man grunted and strained and began his exercise set and Eddie looked down at the man's wife, bitch-face, and saw that her face was cold and emotionless. But she counted off the exercise iterations.

When the fat man got to eighteen, Eddie moved his arm that was holding the gun against the woman's head towards the fat man. He took careful aim and then squeezed off a shot. The gunshot boomed across the clearing, startling them all, and when the muzzle-flash and smoke had cleared, the fat man began howling in pain, and Ray could see that Eddie had shot the man through the fleshy part of his ass-cheek. Blood was running down the back of his leg, and he was grabbing his upper thigh with both hands. It was obviously very painful. Bitch-face looked pale.

Eddie turned to Kelly, "You have anything to say?"

She shook her head silently.

Ray waved towards the fat man and Beanpole and then pointed at Bitch Face, "They were renting you out like a piece of meat and you have nothing to say about that?"

She shook her head.

Eddie put the gun in front of her, "You take this, I'll allow it. You want to, I give you permission. Go ahead, put a round through that bitches skull. You know she deserves it. Better yet, put a round through her stomach. That's a painful way to die. Takes a long time too."

Ray gasped, "No, Eddie, we're taking this too far! You said you wouldn't kill them!"

Eddie smiled, "And I haven't killed anyone. Fat man there had a round go through his ass. Not fatal. Just a flesh wound. If she decides to kill this bitch, then it won't be me going back on my word, no siree."

Ray started to argue, but before he could get a word out, the woman grabbed the gun out of Eddie's hand and pointed it at bitch-face and pulled the trigger. The gun roared and woman fell backwards as blood sprayed out of the back of her head. Her body twitched several times and then lay still.

Eddie looked over at the two men, "That was one angry woman. Your wife should have known that sooner or later the tables would turn. Some people never learn, huh?"

The gun roared again and they all jumped, thinking that the woman had shot at them, but they were stunned to see that she had put the barrel of the Glock under her own chin and had pulled the trigger. She slumped to the ground in a heap.

Eddie bent down and picked up the gun. He wiped the blood from the gun onto the woman's clothes and then walked back across to the opposite side of the campfire.

Fat man was still holding his leg and groaning in pain and looking at his wife.

Eddie turned to Beanpole, "What do you have to say, skinny-boy? You got anything to say? You want to issue anymore threats?"

Beanpole nodded, "Not a threat, but a promise."

"Yeah, what's that?"

"When this country gets back on-line, and it will, you can count on it. I will be able to hunt you down quickly and easily, and I'll see to it that you spend a lot of time in jail."

Eddie looked back over at Ray, he sounds like he means business."

"You can count on it mister."

Eddie laughed, and then walked over to the tall kid and got right in his face, "Oh, I believe you Beanpole, and I'm *plenty scared*, so I guess I better do something to slow you down." He waved the Glock in Beanpole's face and then pointed it down at the ground and pulled the trigger, sending the round through Beanpole's foot. The tall man collapsed into the dirt, grabbed his foot and began screaming in agony.

Eddie turned to Ray, "Don't worry, he won't die from that. I am a man of my word. Besides that, he swore he'd chase us down, and they've already stolen our supplies once. We don't need them in travelling shape to come after us like that again. Now come on, let's get the gear and get out of Dodge, *again.*"

#   #   #   #   #

Two hours later they were trudging North up the highway again, and this time they were pushing the two men's flatbed cart and the hand truck. They'd switched out their two shopping carts knowing that the flatbed cart rolled easier, and they'd gone through all of their own carts and the flat bed cart that fat man and Beanpole had been using, and they'd kept everything useful they'd found, and left the lesser value items behind. They were now up two tents, and three heavy-duty tarps, the portable Ham radio, and shit load of batteries and water and ground coffee. The flatbed cart had been a treasure trove of decent items.

They'd also come across a small travel suitcase stuffed with cash. Two million in cash, in one hundred dollar bills. With a glint in his eyes, forcing fat man and beanpole to watch, Eddie had dumped the packets of cash into the camp fire and they'd watched it burn as fat man and Beanpole both cried. They still didn't realize that the cash was worthless.

Before the crossed a rise in the highway, they both looked back and could see a small orange dot of fire that represented the two million dollar campfire.

Two days later, just as they were about to turn off the highway to head northeast to begin the search for the bed and breakfast cabins, they were accosted by five men, Cajuns, who had been travelling from New Orleans.

As they drew within about fifty yards, Eddie spoke over his shoulder to Ray,

"Pull your weapon and keep it at the low ready position, these guys are definitely wanting to cause trouble."

Ray stopped pushing the cart, and pulled the Glock and help it in the low ready position. Eddie stepped back with him and kept his Glock in the same position.

"We'll stand right here, and as they pass by we'll encourage them to keep walking and not stop. If we have to shoot, you shoot the one on the far right and then shoot your way in towards the man in the middle. I'll start on the left side and work to the right. That way if any of them break out to run, they'll be running across our line of fire. Don't talk to them, just stare. If they twitch, start shooting. Empty the mag if you have to. This for real."

"How do you know they're dangerous?" Ray asked.

"Look at them. They're filthy, and mean-looking, and I don't think any of them has a gun, because they're all wearing knives in an open fashion, and they all have their hands on the hilt of their knives. If they had guns, they'd be unconcerned about getting close enough to use the knives. They'll be wanting to get into knife-throwing distance. Do NOT talk. Let me do all the talking."

The men drew nearer, and when they were within knife-throwing distance, Eddie raised his Glock and aimed it in their general direction and called out to them, "Howdy boys, from the great fucking State of Texas. Just keeping walking on past. There's nothing here worth asking for, and nothing definitely worth dying for if you're foolish enough to try and take it."

The lead man grinned at Eddie as if he might try to attempt an attack and Eddie warned him off as he walked past them, "That's right, keep walking boys, *stay calm and stay alive*, yeah that's the ticket. *Stay calm and stay alive*. Looking at your guts spilling out on the ground is not how you want to spend your evening."

The men filed past them, and Ray and Eddie turned as they filed past, keeping their Glocks aimed at the bunch. It was a very tense few minutes, and Ray could feel the sweat pouring off his forehead. Finally, as the group was a hundred yards past them, Eddie urged him to go ahead and start pushing the cart, and they both began pushing and putting more and more distance between them, and Eddie turned around every few minutes to ensure that the group wasn't coming back up on them.

They spent a tense night in the woods, each talking turns standing guard in case the ragged bunch came back for them. The next day they passed the sign for the bed and breakfast and Eddie took the sign down and tossed it deep into the woods so that other travelers wouldn't see it and decide to look for the cabins.

They pushed and pulled the carts, they were harder to move now, because they were on dirt and gravel roads. It was backbreaking labor, but they believed that they were going in exactly the directions that Art had given them weeks ago.

After a day and a half of floundering around in the woods, they came across the Ranch Hands cabin and it was exactly as Art had described it. It was empty, and they managed to get the door open and find that there was some canned food, and coffee and other items in the pantry. The wood-burning stove was in excellent condition and there was a bunk bed and a second bedroom with another bed, a queen sized bed. The kitchen featured a second wood burning stove and there were two rocking chairs on the wide porch, and there was a couch in the living room with three other easy chairs. It was a paradise.

They unloaded their carts and brought firewood inside, and finally, around nine pm in the evening, they finally had time to collapse into the rocking chairs on the front porch. They lit cigarettes and relaxed.

Saying nothing, they just relaxed and looked out into the dark woods. The stars were out, and with no city light pollution from anywhere round, the stars looked as if they were two feet over their heads.

Ray thought about their trip, and he thought about Art and Nate and James. The predictions that James had made, that had initially shocked Ray, had been entirely true. Whatever had happened, that thing that had stripped away their electricity, had also stripped away their civilization. Men had begun acting like animals. What shocked Ray the most though, was the speed with which that thin veneer of civilization had dropped away. People had begun acting completely uncivilized within days.

They talked softly through the night, about Art, Nate, Buck and James and they promised themselves that they would definitely try to get back to Dallas for the rendezvous the next year. They decided that if they could, they'd try to convince Art and Nate to come back here with them.

They talked until the early morning hours, and were surprised when the early morning light began filtering through the trees and a light fog rolled in. Then they began seeing shapes materializing in the woods, and Eddie shushed him, thinking that they were about to be attacked by the Cajun gang, or someone else. Bu then the next thing they noticed was that the shapes were a herd of deer, walking through the woods and feeding on grass. There were probably about forty deer or more.

Eddie turned to Ray and smiled, "Breakfast delivered to our doorstop in the mornings? It doesn't get much better than that, huh?"

The End

The truth about CME and EMP

CME – Coronal Mass Ejection

Our earth has a roughly 10-15 percent chance of experiencing an enormous mega solar flare erupting from the sun in the 20 years. Such an event would cause trillions of dollars' worth of damage and could take several decades to recover from.

Some scientists say that such an extreme event is considered to be rare, while others say that it is inevitable. That it's not of matter of if, but when it will occur. The last disruptive solar storm was the Carrington Event, occurred in 1859 and was the most powerful such event in recorded human history.

Our sun goes through a 10 to 11 year cycle of increased and decreased activity. While it's at a solar maximum, the sun's surface is dotted with sunspots and enormous magnetic whirlwinds erupting from the surface. Sometimes these flares burst outwards, spewing a mass of charged particles out into space. The Carrington Event was observed by astronomer Richard Carrington as he watched an enormous solar flare erupt from the sun's surface, emitting particles streaming towards the Earth at more than 4 million miles per hour.

When these particles hit the Earth's atmosphere, they generated light known as auroras. Auroras which are typically seen at the most northerly and southerly parts of the planet, but with the Carrington Event the auroras reached as far as Cuba, Hawaii, and northern Chile. People in New York City watched the heavens light up and were able to read newspaper print at night due to the lights that were so bright.

With today's electrically dependent world, a solar storm would have catastrophic consequences. Auroras damage electrical power grids and can disrupt GPS satellites and completely black out radio communications on

Earth. During a geomagnetic storm in 1989, Canada's Quebec power grid collapsed within 90 seconds, leaving millions without power for up to nine hours.

The potential damage in the U.S. of a Carrington-type solar storm might be between $1 trillion and $2 trillion in the first year alone, with full recovery taking an estimated four to 10 years.

EMP - Electro Magnetic Pulse

A few years ago the US Senate Committee on Homeland Security and Governmental Affairs assembled a number of experts to discuss a critical threat to the homeland and our way of life: electromagnetic pulse (EMP). Even though the issue of EMP has worried our government for years, little has been done to safeguard against it or do any planning whatsoever for it. The science behind EMP is simple and terrifying. An EMP event can occur either naturally (through solar flares, or Coronal Mass Ejection) or artificially, as the result of a high-altitude nuclear explosion (for instance, by terrorists or an enemy state. The dense energy particles from such an explosion cascade down to Earth, interacting and overheating with the planet's magnetic field and destroying the electronic systems below. The resulting waves could fry millions of transformers in the electrical grid as they travel along power lines, ultimately bringing down the nation's power system. The power lines themselves would be fried, as would every microchip in every electrical or computer device. We would be instantly plunged, in the matter of a second, into a pre-industrial world. There would be no simple fix, such as replacing the chips that are not in the computers, cars, and other devices, because all of the devices, plugged in or not, would be instantly rendered useless. No electricity, no computers, no cell phones, no anything. The repair for such an event could last for decades as every mile of telephone cable, and electrical cable and every microchip in every device would have to be replaced.

The possibility of man-made, or terroristic EMP events has grown with the technological sophistication of America's adversaries. Both Russia and China already have the capability. Both countries have carried out experiments relating to the generation of EMP in recent years.

Iran and North Korea may not be far behind them in their quest. Iran is known to have simulated a nuclear EMP attack a few years ago using missiles fired from a freighter. It is believed that North Korea has acquired plans to build an EMP warhead and in 2013 a North Korean freighter made it to the Gulf of Mexico with two nuclear capable missiles in its cargo hold. How frightening is that?

In addition, both countries have orbited satellites that have the ability to evade US early warning radars, and if they were carrying nuclear warheads, they are at the ideal altitude to generate an EMP across the entire continental US, rendering us completely vulnerable to their attack.

Scientists agree that such an attack would have almost completely devastating consequences. A nuclear warhead detonated 20 miles off the ground anywhere over the eastern seaboard would collapse the entire eastern grid, which generates 75 percent of our country's electricity. The recovery time from a nationwide EMP attack might be anywhere from three to thirty years, maybe more. During that time, tens of millions of Americans would likely die from starvation and/or societal collapse, and some experts say that the deaths could be as many as a hundred million.

At this point though, it is possible to classify a man-made attack as unlikely. By contrast, a naturally occurring EMP event is, such as a CME like the Carrington event is, as some experts bluntly say, practically inevitable.

PART FOUR

E R O L

Excessive Rule of Law

Abuse under Color of Law

The knock at the door startled Freddy Douglas and he jerked

awake on the couch and looked towards the door. His heart was racing

because he had been in a tired, deep sleep from what had been a twelve

hour day at the construction site. He glanced at his watch, and saw that it

was eleven-thirty pm. He'd come home at eight o'clock, and had collapsed

onto the couch without even making any dinner. Who the heck would be

knocking, *banging loudly* now, on his door at this hour at night?

He stumbled sleepily across the living room, and looked through

the peep hole on his apartments door and his heart immediately began

racing at the sight of a trio of balaclava masked cops with M4's slung over

their shoulders, and outfitted in black paramilitary-looking uniforms.

Freddy looked behind him, towards his Glock on the coffee table. If this

bunch were a band of armed robbers, he would be lucky to survive any assault with one handgun and one full mag of ammo. He had three more handguns in a closet, but they were locked in a small box safe and they were unloaded. Most of his ammo was in another locked box, it even if he hurried, it would take him several minutes to unlock each box and load the guns. By that time these three *whatevers* on the other side of the door could be in here and have him cuffed. But for what? He'd done nothing wrong. He had a license to carry a handgun and it was current, plus, this was his home. He knew that he also had an AR in the closet, and it was locked and loaded, as was the shotgun leaning next to it.

The question is, did he want to open the door with a firearm in his hands and get shot accidentally? Because whatever they wanted from him, whatever reason they were here for, they'd obviously made a mistake.

All of these thoughts raced through his mind in the few seconds between the knocks, which had quickly turned into ear-splitting pounding. He made a decision. He'd open the door, like any law-abiding citizen, and show that he was no threat. Whatever these law enforcement officials wanted, they were simply at the wrong house. A mistake had been made somewhere.

Freddy yelled out, "Coming! Hold on a minute!" and then he went to the Glock, picked it up, and hid it behind the couch cushion. He walked back to the door where the angry cop on the other side was still pounding with his fist.

Freddy opened the door and immediately had the business end of black-barreled M4 pressed into his forehead. His knees went rubbery. Were these guys cops or robbers?

The man holding the gun moved forwards forcing Freddy to walk backwards into the living room and the other two Stormtrooper looking men barged into the apartment past on either side of him. The man with the gun screamed at Freddy to *'get on the floor! Now, or I'll blow your fucking head off!'*

Freddy dropped to the carpet and the man reached down and roughly grabbed his arms and twisted them behind him and then Freddy felt the metal cuffs slapped around his wrists, and then he heard the ratcheting as they were closed tight and he felt the cold metal biting into a circle around his wrists.

The man ordered his to get to his knees, and Freddy did so, but it was difficult to do while his hands were cuffed behind his back. When he got to his knees, the man screamed at him to stand up and as soon as Freddy straightened up, the man put a hand on Freddy's chest and shoved him backwards so that he fell backwards onto the couch into a sitting position.

The other two men wearing tearing through the apartment, obviously searching for something. Was this a drug raid gone bad? Maybe they had a wrong address?

Freddy spoke for the first time, "What the fuck is this all about?"

His watcher pulled off his Balaclava and tucked it in between his black uniform shirt and the bulletproof vest that he was wearing. Then he reached into the other side and pulled out a paper. He flicked it with his hand to open it and looked at Freddy.

"you are Freddy Douglas? Sole occupant of this residence at 3414 Tulane Drive. . . "

Freddy nodded at him

"This is a search warrant from Department of Homeland Security working in conjunction with local law enforcement. This is a legal search and seizure of weapons."

"Why would you need to search my apartment for weapons, I've done nothing wrong!"

"Well, buddy, if you've done nothing wrong then why would you object to us having a look around?"

"Because I don't like having my rights violated?"

The cop smirked and held up the warrant, and rustled it "but this legal warrant *gives* us the right. So, we're not violating anything."

"What's the reason for the warrant?"

The cop looked at the paper and read, "Occupant is believed to own excessive amounts of firearms and ammunition in violation of DHS Order number *two-niner-niner-six-eight-zero-four*, and D T S Order number four-one-zero-six, that's the Domestic Terrorist Suspect Order, and this agency is hereby tasked with *immediate removal* of said firearms, ammunitions, and all other items claimable under this statute, meaning any and all devices that could be used, converted and repurposed as weapons, from these premises no later than this date . . ."

"That's bullshit. I never heard of such a statute. There's no legal grounds for this!"

The cop shook his head and rattled the warrant in his hand, "This says differently, sir."

"I have a legal right to own firearms, hell, I have a legal carry permit!"

"Is that true?" the cop asked.

"Yes, I have a legal CHL license, and it is up to date, and I have never been arrested or convicted of a misdemeanor or felony. My record is clean.

Spotless!"

"Where is your CHL license, sir? I'd like to see it."

"It's in there, in the bedroom, in my wallet on the nightstand next to my bed."

The cop yelled over his shoulder at this buddy, who was searching the drawers in his dresser in the bedroom, and told him to find the wallet and bring it into the living room.

The man appeared with the wallet, handed it to the main cop, and then turned and went back into the bedroom.

The cop flipped open the wallet, and seeing the plastic window with the driver's license, he slid it out, and behind it, was the CHL, which was almost indistinguishable from the driver's license. He looked it over carefully, comparing it with the driver's license.

"See, I told you I'm legal!" Freddy challenged the cop.

The cop nodded, "Unfortunately sir, I have to confiscate this." He said as he slipped the CHL into his shirt pocket, "this Concealed Handgun License has been duly revoked by the licensing authority of the State of Texas in conjunction with the DHS and you are now in violation of the Domestic Terrorist Act of 2016 and are hereby ordered to surrender any and all firearms and ammunition to the proper authorities, *that would be us*, and I hereby urge you to   comply with this directive and give us the locations of all guns and ammunition and other weapons on these premises, and that includes knives, bats, batons, pepper spray, stun guns, explosives and any explosives materials, timers, fuses, grenades, expandable batons, swords, Koga batons, come-alongs, brass knuckles, ceramic knuckles, and any other items that could conceivably be used as a weapon."

The two cops that had been in the bedroom came out with the AR and the shotgun,

"These are the long guns listed on the form, and there's two lock boxes that seem to be locked, probably has the other handguns and ammo in them."

The main cop checked the list. Should be five handguns and the AR and the shotgun. He looked at Freddy, "You want to cooperate and give us the combo to the two gun safes?"

"Freddy glared at him, "This whole thing is unconstitutional, so no, fuck you. I'll see you in court, you jack-booted son-of-a-bitch."

The man nodded, "Okay then, you're officially under arrest, looks like we'll be going downtown." He turned to the other two cops, "break open the safes. We'll just have to do it the hard way."

They nodded and one of them slid a small slim bar that looked like a miniature crow bar and they disappeared back into the bedroom and then into the walk in closet. Freddy heard some banging, and then a crunch, and then the two cops came back out with the tow boxes, the lids had been ripped open, and they sat them down on the coffee table.

The main cop, cop number one, looked down at the open boxes, "one Smith and Wesson, one Sig Sauer, and one Kimber, I know those two dudes cost a pretty penny" he looked at the second box, "and about seven hundred and fifty rounds of nine mil ammo. Just missing one more gun, and that would be," he consulted the warrant in his hand, "a Glock 43, nine mil, single stack, purchased last year in April. So, Freddy, *where's the Glock?*"

Freddy glared at him, "Up your mother's ass where I left it last night! She likes it rough!"

The cop laughed and turned to the other two cops, "This guy's a funny boy. Too bad he was too stupid enough to know that you never try attack a cop! You see how he swung at me?"

The two cops grinned and nodded, "Sure did, and you had no choice but to pop him one in the face to prevent yourself from getting hurt!"

Cop number one nodded, and then leaned forwards and grabbed Freddy by his shoulder with one hand, lifting him up off the couch, and then cocked his other arm back and slammed his fist into Freddy's face, knocking him back down on to the couch. Freddy's head swam in pain and he felt as if he might pass out. The pain was excruciating. His lip started swelling immediately and some blood trickled down from his nose. His forehead tingled with numbness.

When he fell back against the couch from the punch, the back couch cushion fell down exposing the Glock.

Cop number one picked up the Glock, checked it to make sure it was clear and then they gathered up all the guns and toted them down to the Black and White SUV and then put Freddy into the back seat. Within twenty minutes they were at the station where he was booked and fingerprinted, read his rights and then placed into an interrogation room.

He sat for an hour, steaming in anger, until cop number one, his name was R. Clooney, came back into the room to interview him.

"I am not talking to you, asshole, I want to call an attorney!" Freddy started out.

Clooney laughed, "I'm sorry, but that's just not possible."

"What are you talking about, *not possible?*"

"I'm saying, sir, that you are not allowed an attorney. You're being held under the terrorist act of 2016. That means you don't get an attorney. You get nothing."

"That's ridiculous. This is the United fucking States of America. I damn sure have a right to an attorney!"

Clooney shook his head, "Not under the revised Patriot Act of 2016. Foreign and domestic *terrorists* are not considered *true citizens* because of the fact that *they are terrorists* you see? Why should the U S allow *terrorists* to have legal representation?"

"I'm no terrorist. I'm a law-abiding U S citizen. I've never been arrested, much less *convicted* of any misdemeanor or felony. How can I be considered a fucking terrorist?"

"You had excessive firearms in your possession. You attacked a federal agent, and you were uncooperative with our search. Those things alone make you a de facto domestic terrorist, no trial required, as per the Department of Homeland Security statute number eight-niner-niner-six-two-three-four-one B."

"This is bullshit! I demand to be allowed to talk to an attorney. I want to be released now, and I want my concealed handgun license returned to me, *now,* along with all of my guns and ammo. You guys better start cooperating with *me,* because I fully intend to file a civil rights case over this! This is total bullshit!"

The man shook his head and looked down at a manila file folder he had in front of him on the table. He opened it, "You belong to a web site called Texas Guns, is that correct? It's billed as *a forum for gun enthusiasts and second amendment activists in Texas*, is that correct?"

"What the hell business is that of yours?"

"Your screen name is GlockDawg34, is that correct?"

"Who gives a shit? It's a free country. It's illegal to get online and talk about your hobbies nowadays, is that it? You cops have something against freedom?"

"Actually, it's agent."

"Okay, *Agent*."

"And yes, it is illegal to get online and talk, especially when that talk is regarding amassing a huge cache of weapons, and hiding them strategically so that they can be used to overthrow the government."

"I have no clue what the hell you're talking about, and I don't think you do either."

Agent Clooney read from the paper in front of him, "Three months ago, you had a conversation with three other forum members, one SigSargeant, and another man, who goes by the screen name of RogerRuger, and also a woman that uses the screen name of BettyBlaster. You discussed ways to hide firearms and ammo and at one point the three of you began instant messaging each other, presumably to be unseen and make plans for stockpiling weapons."

"That's the biggest load of shit I've ever heard in my life!"

"Where is the guns cache hidden? How many more people are in your group?"

"Agent, this is ridiculous. There is NO group, and no guns cache. It was just a couple of people I was bullshitting with on a guns forum, which by the way, is perfectly legal." He paused and looked around the room. There was no one way mirror on one wall where other cops were watching and listening, but there was a video camera mounted in an upper corner. He looked up at the camera and raised his hands, "If I'm not under arrest, then I plan on getting up and walking out of here right now. If you attempt to stop me, I'll just add illegal detention to the lawsuit that I plan on filing against you."

Agent Clooney slid a piece of paper across the desk to him, "You can leave, but first, you'll sign this."

"You want to explain what the hell it is that I'm signing?"

"It's a statement saying that you will provide us with the name of every person you know who owns a firearm, and we want every shred of information you can give us about them. Names, addresses, phone numbers, number and types of guns they own, everything. Once you do that, your duty to us is absolved and you can go back to your life, and everything will be hunky-dory."

"Fuck that and fuck you, agent, I'll sign it, but I'm not going to rat out my friends, and I'm signing it under protest just so I can get the hell out of here." he said the last words loudly as he looked up at the video camera. He looked back down, took the pen, and signed the bottom of the document. He then walked to door, and turned the knob, half expecting it to be locked, but it turned easily and he opened the door. He looked back in at the Agent, "You will be hearing from my attorney and I expect my CHL and my guns and ammo to be returned, and damned fast too."

The Agent smirked at him and Freddy walked out.

He called a cab and when he arrived home he was still shaking with anger.

He immediately drank a beer to calm down, and then got online and logged onto the gun forum web site.

He immediately started a new thread and was sure it would be viewed a lot, because he'd been a member on the site for years, and had posted thousands of posts, and was in fact, a senior member. He also knew that it would be read by most of the people who were visiting the site, because in the title of the thread he mentioned the word arrest. That was a subject guaranteed to make visitors to the site read the post.

Within two hours he was stunned to read that he not the only person in Texas that had been arrested that day just for owning a gun, but that there were at least forty or fifty others that had experienced the same treatment!

They'd all experienced the same type of treatment too. Classified as a 'domestic terrorist' for owning more than one gun, and they'd all had pressure applied to them to give up any other hidden guns, and most had been questioned about 'terrorist plots' being hatched through on-line meetings such as on that very gun web site.

They'd all been pressured, just as Freddy had been, to give up the names and addresses of their on-line cohorts and terrorist accomplices, which of course was impossible to do since they all only knew each other by screen names and city locations.

The overriding consensus was that the government, or at least the State of Texas, was instituting a 'gun-grab' and that they were doing it in as heavy-handed a way as possible. All guns of any sort MUST be registered or the owner will be charged with 3rd degree felony for each and every violation including a fine of up to $250k for every violation.

Freddy explained that he had been coerced into signing a piece of paper just so that he could leave and that he had signed it without reading it. He got an avalanche of immediate replies chastising him for signing it, and several other people said that they'd done the same, that they'd signed it just to escape the confinement. No one knew what it meant, because to a person, no one had bothered to read it.

At almost six am, he'd calmed down enough that he felt like he could get some sleep, so he went to bed. It was a Saturday morning, so it wasn't a work day.

He woke up at three in the afternoon, and the apartment was stuffy and hot. He went to turn on the AC, and noticed that the electricity was out throughout the entire apartment.

He checked the circuit breaker boxes, and found that none of the breakers were tripped.

He checked his cell phone, and saw that it was working, so he dialed the electric company and waited on hold for twenty minutes until he finally got a live person. He explained to the girl that his electric was out, and that he'd just paid his bill, so there shouldn't be a problem.

She checked his account and verified that he was current and that he should have power. He asked if there was any other apartments in the complex that were also having problems and she verified that there were no trouble tickets being issued for that area and that no one else had reported any other power outages for the complex.

Finally, he asked for a manager and after about a ten minute wait he was talking to a supervisor. He was beginning to think that his cell phone would soon run out of charge.

The supervisor did some checking and finally came back on the line with an answer for him. "I see the problem, sir"

"Okay, what is it?" Freddy was relieved that they were finally getting to the bottom of the problem.

"You've been flagged and we've had to discontinue your service."

"Flagged? What the hell is that?"

"Honestly sir, I don't know. I've never seen this before. It must be something new."

"Well, my payment has been received, why won't you turn my service on?"

"Well, sir, I can't. There is a government directive here, I'll read it to you, 'this domicile is currently restricted from receiving utility services at this point, and to continue indefinitely under this directive, as per DHS order number six-oh-four-nine-three-two-seven. Any person or persons interfering with this directive will be in defiance of DHS security restrictions and will be found guilty in violation of state security violations resulting in no less than ten years in U S Federal prison and a fine of not less than two hundred and fifty thousand dollars." He paused.

"Sir, I don't know what this DHS order is, I've never heard of it, and I've been a supervisor here for eight years, but I promise I'll go look into it for y-"

"No need," Freddy said, "it's a Department of Homeland Security thing."

"What?"

"Never mind." Freddy said as he hung up the phone.

Angry, Freddy paced the living room, alternating between despair, and wanting to scream out loud. He finally had an idea, and he walked to the apartment managers office and caught Angelina just as she was about to walk out the door.

"I'm sorry, Freddy." She told him, "but I got a visit from two guys earlier today. They were dressed in suits, had DHS badges and everything, "they explained that we, the apartments, were forbidden to allow you to rent another apartment, or to use an extension cord to get electricity from another apartment. They even went to the other apartments in your building block and warned all of them that allowing you to stay with them or use their electricity or other utilities was a federal crime! There's nothing we can do, our hands are tied. But, if it makes you feel any better, I will say this, I don't believe that you're a terrorist."

"Jesus!" Freddy hung his head, "well, thanks for telling me, I appreciate it."

He stood up to leave and was at the door when Angelina stopped him.

"Oh and by the way, Freddy?"

"Yes?"

"When this is all resolved?"

"Yes?"

She looked down at her desktop and nervously fiddled with a pen, "On the first, that's uhm, next Monday, we're going to have to insist that you vacate the premises, on account of the corporate ownership of the company that owns Excelsior Properties throughout the U S, have a very strict anti-gun policy. We can't rent to persons who own guns any longer. Background checks of all residents are being conducted by the DHS and they're going to send us a list of all gun owners. We have to evict them all. I'm so sorry! They also told us that everyone who is evicted on gun charges will be placed on a list, meaning that any other apartment complex in the country will not accept you. Maybe you could buy a house?"

Freddy stared at her and then closed the door and walked back to his dark apartment. She was an idiot if she thought he could just up and go buy a house if he was living in their dumpy apartments anyway.

He took his cell phone and charger and walked down the street to a coffee shop and plugged in to recharge. After an hour, he called his boss and explained to him what had happened. His boss explained that he wasn't able to take Freddy in as a lodger, and then he explained that his brother was a mayor in a small town in West Texas, and that he'd been on the phone with him all morning. Apparently, all the states were enacting draconian laws and measures to confiscate all guns. They were going to make life miserable for everyone that had guns, and then they'd start going after non-gun owners to rat out their friends and neighbors that had guns. They were being told at the city government level, that the federal government was hell bent on grabbing every gun, legally owned or not, from every citizen.

He also told Freddy that he had received an email that morning, he was in the habit of checking his work email daily, and that he'd received a message from DHS stating that all employees that were known to own guns were to be summarily suspended without pay until they received a form 6665 to bring back to work before being reinstated. The form was a DHS form that stated that the DHS was convinced that the bearer of the form was no longer in possession of or had any ownership of, or access to any firearms. Then he gave him the capper. He explained that if any person changed jobs from this point forward, they were considered unemployable until they could produce the form. Therefore, before Freddy was allowed to come back to work, he had to produce the form. He also explained that any employee that planned on seeking legal advice save their time and money, because it was a federal DHS order and no court would have the right to rule on it. No attorney would even be allowed to take the case. Basically, you complied or they'd eventually round you up and throw you in prison.

Freddy thanked him, and then put his phone back on the charger and waited for it to fully charge. He then sat for an hour, thinking about his situation until he realized that he had no other choices to make.

An hour and a half later he was back at the Police station, which was buzzing with an unusual amount of activity. Freddy asked for Agent Clooney, and was taken back to the same interrogation room. A few minutes later, the agent arrived.

"Well, Freddy, imagine seeing you here, back so soon!"

Freddy gave him the finger, and spoke, "give me the damned paper, I'll tell you what I know."

THE END

The truth about gun control efforts and gun confiscations

Measures taken to disarm law-abiding firearm owners in the wake of Katrina's devastation in New Orleans should show clearly why gun owners guard their rights to bear arms.

The glaring failures of local law enforcement to contain the instability in the aftermath of Katrina brought into stark clarity the importance of our right to keep and bear arms in order to defend oneself, loved ones, and community citizens. Stories of looting and violence in New Orleans were abundant. A police chief described post-Katrina New Orleans saying that *it was like Mogadishu.*

Several days after the storm passed, New Orleans officials ordered the confiscation of lawfully-owned firearms from city residents. In September, 2005 the New York Times described the scene, stating, "Local police officers began confiscating weapons from civilians in preparation for a forced evacuation of the last holdouts still living here… Police officers and federal law enforcement agents scoured the city carrying assault rifles seeking residents who have holed up to avoid forcible eviction."

New Orleans Superintendent P. Edwin Compass made clear, "No one will be able to be armed," and, "Guns will be taken. Only law enforcement will be allowed to have guns." At the time, NRA Executive Vice-President Wayne LaPierre noted the nature of the seizures, stating, "In many cases, it was from their homes at gunpoint. There were no receipts given or anything else at a time when there was no 911 response and these citizens were out there on their own protecting their families."

City authorities were selective with their own order, simply applying the order against the most vulnerable citizens. The Times noted that the order "apparently does not apply to the hundreds of security guards whom businesses and some wealthy individuals have hired to protect their property… Mr. Compass said that he was aware of the private guards but that the police had no plans to make them give up their weapons."

Gun rights and gun ownership in Nazi Germany

Few citizens owned, or were allowed to own firearms in Germany in the 1930s and 1940s. The Weimar Republic had strict gun control laws. When the Third Reich gained power, some aspects of gun regulation were loosened, such as *allowing ownership for Nazi party members and the military*. The laws were harshened in other ways. Nazi laws *disarmed unreliable persons*, especially Jews, but relaxed restrictions for ordinary (wealthy) Germans. The policies were later expanded to include the confiscation of arms in occupied countries.

American Democrats are going all in on gun control.

President Obama has expressed interest in issuing executive actions intended to curb gun violence by expanding background checks on people buying firearms online or at gun shows.

The effort underlines the Democratic Party's decision to keep gun control as an issue it believes will be way to sway voters from undecided or weak Republican voters.

Gun control has divided Democrats in the past, and Obama barely touched the issue in his first term. The Brady Campaign to Prevent Gun Violence gave him an "F" in 2009, calling his record an "abject failure."

The Democrats hope the gun control issue will help with Hillary Clinton's election as president and their party winning back control of the Senate. The Democratic party that Republicans are blocking common-sense reforms that would reduce the number of mass killings in the country.

The common-sense citizen realizes that guns do not, and cannot, kill on their own, it is the human holding the gun that is causing the problem.

Political strategists believe a seemingly ever-escalating spate of mass shootings in recent years has shifted the politics of the issue.

Gun control in the past has pitted urban and rural Democrats against one another.

Many Democrats saw the 1994 assault weapon ban as a major reason why they lost control of Congress to Republicans that year.

When Bill Clinton's vice president, Al Gore, lost the White House to Republican George W. Bush in 2000, some saw gun control as playing a role in several states.

Democratic presidential front-runner Hilary Clinton has voiced support for the new background check rules before Obama, saying she intends to go further than the president on gun control.

Hillary Clinton is making a big issue of guns. The president jumping on board increases the size of the audience for the message.

The December 2012 killings of 20 school children and six adults in Newtown, Conn., spurred Congress to take up the issue of gun control, and to impose tougher background checks on gun sales but it failed to move forward in the Senate in part because of objections from Senate Democrats.

The MYTH of the Gun Show Loophole

After every mass shooting, the anti-gun activists rush to tell people exactly how to stop mass shootings in the future. Anti-gun proponents demand strict gun control. Gun rights and second amendment advocates dig in their heels and explain why laws can't stop evil people from doing evil things, especially when current laws aren't even enforced.

The debate between the two sides eventually comes around to the so-called gun show loophole. The gun show loophole is a *myth*. It simply does not exist. There is not one single loophole in federal law that specifically exempts gun show transactions from any other laws normally applied to gun sales. Not one.

If you purchase a firearm from a federal firearms licensee (FFL) regardless of the location of the transaction — a gun store, a gun show, a gun dealer's car trunk, etc. — that FFL must confirm that you are legally allowed to purchase that gun. That means the FFL must either run a background check on you via the federal NICS database, or confirm that you have passed a background check by examining your state-issued concealed carry permit or your government-issued purchase permit. There are zero exceptions to this federal requirement. If an individual purchases a gun across state lines — from an individual or FFL which resides in a different state than the buyer — the buyer must undergo a background check, and the sale must be processed by an FFL in the buyer's home state.

The only thing that does exist is a federal exemption for sales between two private citizens, non-FFL residents of the same state, regardless of whether that transaction happens at a gun show or not. The identity of the parties involved in the transaction, *not the venue of the sale*, is what matters under federal law. This federal exemption makes perfect sense: there's no federal nexus for a purely private transaction between two private individuals who reside in the same state. Many states, including Oregon, Colorado, and Illinois, have enacted universal background checks in order to eliminate the exemption for same-state private firearms transactions.

Federal universal background checks may or may not be a wise idea — the U.S. Senate in 2013 explicitly refused to enact them — but referring to the federal exemption for private, same-state sales as a gun show loophole is completely wrong, and one hundred percent factually inaccurate.

Your government thanks you for your cooperation

Anita Olsen flipped the light switch up and down several times, and getting no light in the bathroom, she called out for her husband, who was still snoring in bed "Jack!"

"Yes, honey?"

"I think a circuit breaker has tripped. The light in the bathroom is not working!"

He groaned and rolled out of bed and padded slowly over to the bathroom, and tried the light switch. Nothing.

"I'll go down to the garage and check it."

She sat down at her makeup station and turned on a make-up mirror that had a circle of lights around the mirror, and was battery operated. She began applying her makeup. She had several clients on her agenda for the day, and one late afternoon court hearing for her star client, a man that had been arrested on a charge of terrorism, but the state was floundering with it, because there was no evidence to speak of, just some low-level government rats who were fabricating entire conversations that they claimed had happened. They were desperate to put him in jail, but they were spinning their wheels. Anita expected the judge to see the prosecution's case as a total farce and cut her client loose by the end of the day.

"It's not a circuit breaker, honey," Jack said as he came up the stairs and back into the bedroom, "It's the whole house."

"Well then you need to call the utility company and report an outage."

"I'll do that right away honey."

Anita finished dressing and was going out the door to go to the office. Jack was on the phone with the electric company.

She started the car in the garage and then she pressed the automatic garage door opener, which did nothing, because the electric was off. She went back inside to get Jack and he was still on hold with the utility provider.

She held the phone for him and waited on hold while he unhooked the door from the electrical pulley apparatus, and then he lifted the garage door for her and she drove in to work.

When she arrived at her office she already had a client waiting in her office for her. She asked her paralegal secretary who the man was, and she shrugged and admitted that she didn't know.

"Well, hells bells Erica, you have to get some sort of info from a client. I need to know who I'll be talking to, what his crime is, I mean, what the hell girl, do your job!"

"Well, he's not a client, and he flashed a badge and wouldn't take no for an answer, so I let him in."

"Oh, for Christs' sakes." Anita huffed at her, "I'll take care of it. Just tell my next appointment that I'm running a few minutes behind. And then get over to Starbucks and get me a double."

Erica nodded and was happy to be walking away from her demanding boss when Anita called out to her, "Erica?"

"Yes, Ms. Olsen?"

"What kind of badge did he flash? City cop, or what?"

"Oh, he is DHS." She paused, "That's Department of Ho-"

"I know what it means, Erica!" Anita snapped at her.

Erica left the office on her coffee expedition and Anita walked into her office and didn't even glance at the man. When she finally settled in at her desk, she looked up at him, as is she was surprised to see him there.

The man smiled. He wasn't intimidated by power games. He'd seen them all too often and he wasn't the least bit impressed. He was immune. He leaned back in the chair and crossed a leg over his knee.

"Miss Olsen."

"Yes, as you are?"

"Jake Wayne, Department of Homeland Security." He pulled his badge out tossed it carelessly across the desk and it skidded to a stop in front of her.

Anita frowned, and picked it up and scrutinized it. She then made a show of jotting down the badge number.

Jake smiled, "Double check it if you want, I'll wait. Go ahead, and call. Check out my bona-fideys."

Anita frowned. She wasn't used to being treated like this, and most federal agents were a lot more intimidating than this guy. He seemed like he could care less. Something was stinky here. She watched his face as she called his bluff and picked up the phone to dial it. He grinned and turned his back to her and walked over to her ego wall and began checking out her diplomas and pictures.

She spent about three minutes on the phone, and found out that this man was no imposter, and furthermore, no one she talked to would tell her what he was doing in her office.

"Okay," she shrugged at him, "so, what do you want? Barging in here without an appointment, or a warrant . . ."

"He shrugged back at her, "I don't do *appointments* and I have no warrant because there's no evidence in here that I need to search for."

"Well then," Anita said icily, "perhaps you can *enlighten* me, mister DHS badge-man, as to why I'd want to sit here and waste my two-hundred dollar an hour time *chit-chatting* with you?"

"Because I'm about to free up some of your *oh so valuable time* by clearing some of your schedule."

"How *exactly*," Anita said as she made an obvious glance at her watch, "are you going to do that?"

"Well, I'm going to lighten your work load by taking a heavy case off of your plate. The J D Carrey trial?"

Anita frowned. J D Carrey was her highest-profile case. J D Carrey had *supposedly* set off a bomb near a government facility and while there was evidence pro and con for both his guilt and innocence, Anita was determined to get him a not-guilty verdict. She felt that he was, in fact, guilty, but that was academic. He job was to somehow get him a not guilty verdict, and she planned on doing just that.

The case was high-profile enough that it was considered a career-maker. If she got him off, she would join the ranks of great trial lawyers such as F Lee Baily and Johnnie Cochran, Gloria Allred, and Robert Shapiro. Not exactly Clarence Darrow territory, but he was in a class all his own. There was no way she would allow herself to lose this case.

The media and the government was making him out to be the second-coming of Timothy McVeigh, which, when she thought about it, he probably was, but again, her job, her career, her lifestyle, hinged upon getting him a not-guilty verdict. In her mind too, she felt that he'd be rendered impotent, terrorist-wise after his life-changing brush with the law. He would be watched very closely for the remainder of his life. If she got him a not-guilty verdict, or for that matter, anything less than a death sentence, she'd be saving his life and possibly many other lives because he would be rendered useless as a viable terrorist. At least that's what she told herself in order to avoid any feelings of guilt for representing him.

As a defense lawyer though, she had long ago erased all doubts about her profession and had learned to approach the guilt/innocence equation with an intellectual perspective. There were millions of people out there who had gotten away with every conceivable type of crime and had never repeated their sins and were now respectable citizens. So, why should her clients be afforded any less of a chance for rehabilitation?

"And why would you have any way of doing that Mister Wayne? It's my client, and we're heading to trial. If you have any legitimate standing in the case, which you don't then I suggest that you take it before a judge. But, as far as I'm concerned, you have no business poking your nose into my case. Check with Judge Pitt if you think differently."

"First of all," the agent smiled, "It's *Agent* Wayne, and secondly, you will be dropping your representation of mister Carrey. He is going to be represented by a general practitioner by the name of Roscoe Washington. He is a family friend of Mr. Carrey's. He typically handles divorces and simple bankruptcy's and the like, so he has time to devote to the case."

"A general practitioner? That's absurd! Why on earth would I hand over my case to some klutz with no criminal defense experience?"

"Because we've asked you to, that's why."

"And I've declined your ridiculous offer," she laughed, "now, if you don't mind, I hate to be rude, but I have a lot of work to do, so, *go away.*"

Agent Wayne stood and appeared about ready to leave the office, but then spoke,

"So, did you have any problems getting dressed for work in the dark this morning?"

Anita's jaw dropped as she looked up at him. He grinned at her.

"How do you know about that? Are you people spying on me?"

He shook his head, "No, we don't spy, that's another government agency you're confusing us with."

"But-"

"Just as we're *not* the same agency that will be freezing your bank accounts, cancelling all your credit cards, and issuing a taxpayers' audit summons very soon. We're also *not* the agency that will have your Mercedes GLA250 SUV towed into a lockdown car-pound until the title is cleared which could take months. Also, we're *not* the same agency that will issue a warning to your homeowners association that your house, uhm, *estate*, is in violation of several city codes which will trigger a title transfer to some sort of officious red-tape agency whose name escapes me now, and of course, we're also *not* the same agency that will shred your credit report to the point of no return." He paused, "No, *we* don't do things like that, however I know from experience that these things happen. You know, ridiculous government screw-ups, red-tape catastrophes, and just plain old *clusterfucks* that can make a person's so miserable as to be almost unlivable. Then there's also hackers who somehow get access codes o people's bank accounts and strip them clean. We're working on those things because they're so vicious. They can really screw up your life. Unfortunately we can't catch them all. Weird huh? But then again, I check my bank account every day. *You should do the same.*"

Anita felt her fury rising.

Agent Wayne nodded towards the laptop that Anita had open in front of her, as if he was daring her to do as he'd instructed.

Anita quickly logged into her bank web site and followed the links to check her balance.

Her eyes widened when she saw the comment *Balance unavailable due to DHS banking regulation security act # 8675309. Please contact this institution for further information.*

"You can't do this! This is coercion, harassment, and all sorts of illegal and-"

"But," Agent Wayne said firmly, "we have, we did, and you have, shall we say, extremely limited options available to you."

"I'll be filing a case in Federal Court within the next hour-"

"You can attempt to file all the suits you want, Mrs. Olsen, but the fact is, this is a DHS driven initiative and there's not a judge in this country right now who will even be allowed to hear the case. Mainly because your law license is being pulled at this very hour. Your best option is to capitulate and admit that you're outgunned, overpowered, and way out of your depth in this matter. Sorry, but *we live in a political world.* Give up the case or begin building a new life."

Anita put her elbows on her desk and put her face in her hands and sighed. She knew the power of the DHS, and with the full backing of the government allied against her, she was pretty much powerless.

She nodded her head.

Agent Wayne walked to her office door to let himself out.

"I had a feeling you'd see it our way. Your government thanks you for your cooperation."

The End

The truth about Tyranny or Abuse by Color of Law

In U S law, the term **color of law** denotes the appearance of legal right, or the pretense or appearance of right; therefore, an action done under **color of law** colors bends the law to the circumstance, yet said apparently legal action contravenes actual law. **Under color of authority** is a legal phrase used in the US which indicates that a person is claiming or implying the acts he or she is committing are related to and legitimized by his or her role as an agent of governmental power, especially if the acts are unlawful.

Color of law refers to an *appearance* of legal power to act but which may operate in violation of law. For example, when a law enforcement officer acts with the color of law as his authority to arrest someone, if such an arrest is made without probable cause the arrest may actually be in violation of law. The law enforcement officer may be in violation of law and could even be denying a citizen their constitutional rights. If police or law enforcement act outside their lawful authority and violate civil rights of citizens, the FBI is usually tasked with investigating their actions.

I must see your papers comrades. You must have your papers.

"Daddy, when are we gonna get there? I want to ride on the airplane!"

"Lizzie Galecki! If I have to tell you one more time to be still I'm going to take away that candy!"

"Chill out, Kaley, they're just anxious to get the vacation started." John cautioned his wife.

"Well, the sooner we get to Miami the better," Kaley told her husband, "I'm ready to hit the beach and get some warm sun on my skin."

"Mommy, Lizzie stuck her tongue out at you!"

"Jimmy, you just ignore her." John told his son.

The girl taunted her brother, "Tattletale!"

Kaley sighed at her two children, and looked over at her husband who was grinning. He put his right hand down in the seat between them and she put her hand in his.

"There's the exit for the airport entrance, better start pulling over now to get in the right lane." Kaley told him as she squeezed his hand. This was the first vacation they'd taken in three years, a long overdue vacation and they were all anxious.

He nodded, "Check out that sign up there"

"Where?"

He took his hand out of hers and pointed out the windshield towards the right.

She saw the billboard he was referring to and read the message aloud.

Notice your neighbors! If you see something, **say something!** *The next terrorist may be living next to you now!* **DHS Hotline 555-9035-768** – There may be a reward in it for YOU! - **This message is sponsored by Patriots Against Terrorism, Call now, be a good citizen for your country!**

"Wow, he shook his head. They're wanting us to spy on our neighbors?"

Kaley scoffed, "Typical government bullshit. Heck we never even *see* our neighbors!"

"Yeah," John said, "and I saw something on the internet the other day, one of those Public Service Announcements, you know, the ones the government makes the media put out every so many hours of programming time? Anyway, it said that one of the tip-offs for recognizing a possible domestic terrorist is that you rarely ever see them. So, by the Department of Homeland definition, we should be calling the snitch-line and tipping them off to our secretive neighbors. Maybe we'd get a nice reward out of it." He laughed.

She shivered, "Don't even joke about that type of crap. We're not turning anyone in. Heck, for that matter, if we never see our neighbors, then they probably never see us either, and therefore they might be turning *us* in as a suspicious couple."

They sat patiently in the line of cars waiting to go through the toll gates that led into the airport area, and after almost an hour their tempers were rising, along with the heat in the car, even though they had the AC going full blast. The car was about to overheat and when they finally pulled into the toll both line the orange and white-striped wooden gate lowered, forcing them to stop. John took a ticket that spit out of the metal parking ticket dispenser box and them waited for the barricade arm to rise.

After five minutes, John began laying on the horn, trying to get the attention of the toll taker two lanes over. The man, who was wearing a black uniform and an orange and blue safety vest gave them a dirty look and waved to them to hold on.

After another minute, the man approached their car with two other men in similar uniforms. John looked at the patch on the upper left breast of the men's uniforms. *Department of Homeland Security – Travel Division.*

The three men approached the car on the driver's side.

John held up the parking ticket, "Can you guys lift the gate, we don't want to be late for our flight."

The man leaned down and looked into the car, past John towards Kaley, and them looked at the kids in the back seat.

"Sir, could you just put the car in park and shut off the engine?"

John gave the man a confused look, "What's the problem. I have the paring pass, and like I said, we need to hurry up, we don't want to miss our flight. This is our vacation."

The man straightened up and nodded, and one of the other men stepped into the toll booth cube and pressed a button and ten feet in front of the wooden barrier bar a line of spikes rose up from a section of the roadway directly in from of them. Driving over them would puncture all four tires. Ten feet behind them, another section of similar spikes popped up out of the roadway. They were effectively locked in to the area. Even if the barrier bar was raised now they'd be unable to travel twenty feet without getting four flat tires.

The officer leaned back down towards the driver's side window, "Sir, please step outside the vehicle and present your travel papers so that we can inspect them."

John blinked, and then looked at his wife. Kaley was pale and shaking, "What is this all about John?"

John shrugged, "Some sort of bullshit government travel restrictions probably."

"Exit the vehicle, *now*, sir!" The officer said in a loud firm voice, as he placed his hand on the butt of his service weapon.

"Jesus fucking Christ!" John swore loudly, "what a fucking hassle!"

The second and third officers in the trio had now taken up their positions, officer number two was now positioned just outside Kaley's passenger side window, and the third officer was standing just behind the man who was giving the orders.

"Sir, do not become belligerent and uncooperative" the officer warned sternly, "That would be a mistake on your part. We don't need trouble, we just need to examine your travel papers, and any other documents you're carrying."

John stepped out of the car, and held his hands up, "Travel papers? What the hell are you talking about?"

"Your airline tickets showing your destination and travel dates, sir"

John rolled his eyes, "Are you serious? What the fuck business is it of yours where we're going on vacation?"

"Sir, do NOT get belligerent with me."

"I'm not being belligerent sir, I am just wondering why we have to be hassled before we enter the airport. We already have to go through the TSA checks before we board the plane, so I just want to know what this bullshit is before we even get onto the airport grounds?"

"Sir, I'm not going to warn you again" the man leaned in close to John's face. John could feel the menacing waves of hostility radiating from the man.

"One more use of foul language, sir, and you're considered to be uncooperative and antagonistic and you can be arrested for attempted violence upon a government employee, attempted trespass into a secure facility, and failure to produce travel documents that are now required when traveling across state borders. Several of these offences place you in violation of the domestic terrorist act 2017, USDHSDPOT." He paused, "Now sir, I'll ask you one more time, produce your travel documents now, or yourself and every member of your family will be placed under arrest and detained until we can determine what your intentions are."

John sighed, this was completely ridiculous. Air travel had become more and more restrictive since 9/11 but this was completely insane, but he knew better than to argue with three men with guns.

"Kaley, get out plane tickets out and give them to this gentleman please!"

Kaley produced their tickets and officer number one examined them closely.

John kept checking his watch. After twenty minutes, it was clear that they would be missing their flight and they'd have to reschedule.

Finally, officer number one pulled out his phone and began taking pictures of their documents, and the cars behind them had given up on honking at the delay, and they all began streaming through the other toll portals. John couldn't imagine what it was about a family of four that raised suspicions of any sort. They were about as harmless as anyone could possibly be.

After the officer had finished taking pictures of their plane tickets he herded them together and began taking pictures of them; posing them together and then taking pictures of each and every one of them individually.

It was when the officer began taking pictures of his children that John nearly lost it. Kaley had to physically hold his arm and whisper in his ear to calm him down, telling him that they couldn't afford to be arrested, and that they could complain to other authorities later if they decided to.

Officer number one finally told them that they could leave, but he also explained that the airline tickets would be *re-processed* before they were allowed to board another flight. John asked what *re-processing* meant and the officer explained to him that there was a new law in effect that added a U S Transportation *surcharge* to all persons travelling past state lines. In effect, every time any individual crossed a state line it would cost fifty dollars, per person, per state. The officer explained that the re-processing fee would be charged for every person in their family, which was four, and the charge would be for every state that they flew over. Flying from Texas to Florida required crossing four states borders, so the extra fees would be two hundred dollars each way, so this new transportation policy would cost them an additional four hundred dollars. But, officer number one cheerfully explained, that money goes towards *the fight against terrorism*.

John nodded and got the family into the car and they drove on in to the airport proper and made their way towards the ticket counter to go about re-arranging their trip. The entire time, he was thinking about the novel he'd read in high school, nineteen-eighty-four, by George Orwell. He realized that the government's utilization of the constant, threatening spectre of terrorism and it's cousin, domestic-terrorism was about as pervasively chilling as nineteen-eighty-four's concept of *thoughtcrime*. It was the new bogey-man and the government used it as a club to beat the backs and heads of its' citizens to bend them to its' rule.

He knew the old saying though, *Render unto Caesar the things that are Caesar's* . . . and he knew that one man alone could never fight back, and he was living in a land of sheep who would go along to get along. He paid the extra fees and sat down to wait with his family for the next flight.

Across the waiting area he saw an upright circular column that contained wrap around advertising messages, three different messages, depending upon what view you were looking at determined the message you viewed. The message he could see was perfectly positioned for everyone in the waiting area to see. The advertisement was another Public Service Announcement and it pictured a large photo of the current president, with the text message over his head reading *Follow the leader* and the message under his chest reading *don't let the terrorists win!*

John looked at the picture. The propaganda was an obvious, over the top bit of excessive jingoism that wasn't fooling anybody.

John watched as a couple of teens gathered around the picture and began mocking it relentlessly. Good for them. Normally he hated young urban punks, but these kids seemed fearless. He watched as they all gathered in front of it, shielding the picture from his view. Two of the four kids looked around nervously and they all bunched together closely. John figured they were figuring a way to steal the picture, but they scattered suddenly.

John looked at the picture. The kids had altered it. The president now sported a Hitler mustache. He smiled for the first time in hours. Maybe there was hope after all.

The End

Plastic or Paper?

Caroline Schumer pushed her cart towards the checkout station and waited while the grocery checker scanned all the items in her cart. While the girl did that, Caroline opened her phone and checked her email messages and then checked her Facebook updates. When the girl finished all the items in her cart and then asked Caroline, *plastic or paper*, Caroline told her paper (because she was after all, environmentally conscious) and then she was told to scan her loyalty card, and then her credit card, which she did.

The girl frowned and asked her to zip the credit card through the machine again, because she said she was getting a *weird message*. Caroline slid the card again, and the girl shook her head. Caroline tried it a third time, but the result was the same. *Declined.*

Now it was Caroline who frowned. She wondered if Doug had changed something earlier in the day on that Visa card that had caused them to go over their limit, although that was highly unlikely, seeing as how there were only about two hundred dollars in charges on the card, and the limit was five thousand.

She shrugged, thinking it was nothing more than a credit card company glitch, and pulled out a different card. This one was a Mastercard, but it got the same result. Now she was beginning to get worried. Two bad cards in a row was a strange problem. They always paid off their balances every month. In fact they had been doing that for the past ten years. They *never* carried a balance on either card. She asked the girl if it was possible that their terminal was down? The girl stepped over and asked the other checkers if they were having any problems, and the girls both shook their heads no.

Exasperated, she pulled a third card out and swiped it in the terminal, and it declined almost instantly. Now she knew something strange was happening. She asked the girl to call the manager over and when she was waiting for him to arrive, she called her husband who assured her that he hadn't put anything on any of the cards that day with the exception of coffee that morning at Starbucks. She hung up and dialed the number to the credit card company for the first card and was told that her card was operational and that she had almost five thousand in open credit available. She then spoke with the second card company and was assured that her card was useable and that the open credit limit was almost eight thousand. The third card company was the same, telling her that the card was ready to use with a little over nine thousand in available credit.

The grocery store manager, and man named Frank Goodman arrived and took her aside to explain what was happening.

"It's the new governmental policies that are causing this," he explained, "not your credit cards."

"What kind of governmental policies would be regulating purchases at a grocery store?"

"Well," he explained, step over here and I'll see if I can explain it, he said as he led her over towards a vacant area next to the customer service area.

"The government, along with several other government agencies, most notably the Department of Homeland Security, is as I'm sure you're aware, making this big push towards eradicating terrorism and especially domestic terrorists. Part of the new President's big Peace Plan to Ensure a Safe America. You've seen the billboards and heard all the politicians harping about it I'm sure."

Caroline nodded, "but what does all that have to do with buying groceries?"

He leaned towards her and half-whispered, "If you ask me, nothing. But, the government says differently and here's how they are explaining it." He paused.

"I mean, if my cards are a problem, I can walk right over there to that ATM in the lobby and get cash out and pay that way."

He shook his head. "No, that's the worst thing you can do. We're no longer able to accept cash for any purchases of more than forty dollars. They're keeping tabs on *all* cash purchases too."

"So what is this all about?" Caroline asked.

He chuckled, and shook his head, "Believe it or not, it's about terrorism. See, the government believes that these people who are called preppers, or survivalists, are stocking up on supplies. Groceries, guns, ammo, medical supplies, and all types of items that would help one survive in case of some sort of calamity, or crisis, or what those types call a *shit hits the fan* scenario. Like a hurricane, such as Katrina, or a massive earthquake, or the economic collapse of the country or some sort of political purge, or a nuclear strike . . . basically anything that would shut down society in any meaningful way for an extended period of time. These people, survivalists, preppers, or paranoids, whatever you want to call them, are smart enough to stockpile food, water, medicine, and survival essentials because they all think that something big and bad and devastating could happen, or will happen soon, and they want to be ready."

"Okay," Caroline said, "but I still don't get the connection."

"Bear with me. I'll make it clear." He paused, "you see, the government, paranoid as they are in their own right, they want people dependent upon them if anything like that was to actually happen. They want the power, and the power rests upon the people being dependent upon them, and not being self-sufficient. So, they have, years ago, begun classifying these preppers and survivalists as *potential domestic terrorists*. Because if the shit *does* hit the fan, these preppers and survivalists will be the most likely groups to have the ability to take over the power that the government now has. That scares the government." He paused again. "You following?"

Caroline nodded, "Yeah, I guess, but I still don't understand how the groceries fits into the government's ideas of who is and isn't a terrorist or potential domestic terrorist."

"Well, it's like this. Some government group, probably the Department of Homeland Security or some group under their authority got together and decided how much groceries a person, or family needs on a twice-monthly basis. If they determine that someone is buying more than that, they will cause the transaction to be cancelled. The interruption software is automatically patched into our system. We had no say so about it at all. It was just done and we were informed that it was to stay in place or else. National security and all. Then they decided that there are certain types of foods that trip the software alerts. Foods such as rice, quinoa, flour, sugar, things like that which had a log shelf life. In other words, items that would make long term survivability easier. Especially toilet paper, bottled water, and matches, and Bic lighters and Advil, batteries, and first aid kits. All those things are highly regulated now."

"So you're saying that the government, our own fucking government doesn't want us to be self-reliant in case of emergencies?"

He nodded, "I'm not saying it's right, but that's exactly what it means. Oh, and another thing, if you're Mormon, you are already on their watch list!"

"Mormons? What does that have to do with anything?"

"Because, Mormons have always been taught, as a matter of principle, to stockpile food, water, and supplies for emergencies. Many Morons will routinely have anywhere from three months to three years' worth of food and supplies stockpiled."

"So, Mr. Goodman, what caused them to flag me?" Caroline asked as she pointed to her grocery cart."

He glanced into her cart, "See you got a box of rice, some band-aids and Advil, toilet paper, and a case of bottled water. That'd be my guess. You're obviously not Mormon."

"No," she shook her head, "I'm not."

"Well, I'm sorry, but you got flagged, and all you can do is put some of it back and let us try to re-ring you up and see if it flies."

She nodded, "But what is to stop me from buying here, and then going across the street to your competitor and finishing buying what I just took out of my cart here? Or going store to store to store spending less than forty bucks cash each time?"

He was already shaking his head, "they got you that way too. You see, there's no grocery store out there now who will allow you to make any purchases whatsoever without that store's loyalty card. It is forbidden. Can't do it. So, you're being tracked, real time. No store will sell you anything without that loyalty card, and those cards now are just as powerful as giving out your social security number. Granted, you could do the ten stores one after one scenario you can up with, spending less than forty bucks every time, and there will be people who attempt that. But with even the cash purchases, all stores now must, by law, swipe your loyalty card to enable tracking you. Also, don't know if you've heard it or not, but the government has directed the banking industry to stop producing all one hundred dollar bills. Early next year they'll make everyone turn them in for smaller currencies, and if you wait too long they'll be worthless, because they'll forbid businesses and individuals from using, or even owning them."

Caroline was stunned. This is crazy!.

"You haven't even heard the worst part of it. Every store now must begin using the lane spotters. Lane spotters are cameras set up in the leading edges of the shelves and in the ceilings, and what they do is they wirelessly access your loyalty card, and or your driver's license as you walk through the store. *Automatically*. U S grocery stores are now about to become the most highly efficient spying machines on the planet. So, even if you were able to pay by cash, and not swipe your loyalty card, it is being swiped while it is in your pocket."

"I guess I can always leave it at home. That would certainly throw them off!" Caroline laughed.

Goodman shook his head, "Afraid not. The government is patching in facial recognition software into all the scanning protocols in the stores. We might as well face it, we are outmanned, outgunned, and we can't even begin to outwit the technology they can use against us."

Caroline shook her head, "Jeez, I guess we can expect some of those hard-core preppers and survivalists types to be rooting around in the dumpsters back behind the stores huh? I'm sure they'll come up with some ways to outwit the government."

"Goodman nodded, "You'd think so, but there are new city regulations being put in place in all cities nationwide, too require locks on all dumpsters, and cameras facing them at all times, just so that they can catch the preppers, survivalists, and that bunch that calls themselves freegans. Those are people who live on free food that has been dumped out by grocery stores and restaurants. Freeganism is eventually going to be classified just like the preppers and survivalists as a group that is termed as domestic terrorists."

Caroline talked with the store manager for another half hour and then he helped her sort out her cart, and sure enough, when she removed several of the tagged items, she was able to pay for her groceries and leave.

Two weeks later when she checked her mail she found that she'd been mailed a new loyalty card from the grocery store, and the instructions noted that the old card was no longer valid. The new card, the advertising proudly proclaimed was geared specifically to her. The card even had a space on the lower right hand corner that had her thumbprint. Where the grocery store had obtained her thumbprint was a mystery to her that creeped her out, and upon reading further she was stunned to learn that when paying for groceries, she need only to wave the card within fourteen inches of the card terminal, and then press her thumb on the glass, and the card would transmit her info to her bank account or credit card account, and the purchase amount would be automatically deducted.

She felt strangely violated when she read that part. Of course it was labeled as a convenience factor, but she equated it to being raped and then being told that it was a convenience because now she could have a baby.

Caroline walked to her pantry and looked inside and mentally calculated how long she could last on the food she had. Her pantry was fairly large and well stocked, and she was not overweight and had learned to eat small meals.

In the long run, she guessed that that made her a de facto terrorist.

The End

The Iron Heel of Soft Tyranny

Lance Statham cleared his throat into the mic at the dais to get the attention of the employees in the room, and as he did the chit-chat in the room quieted.

"Good morning everybody!"

A chorus of replies rose up from the hundreds of persons gathered in the room.

"Welcome to the Fischer Devices 2017 new year corporate conference! Let's talk about how we are going to have a happy, healthy and profitable year!"

The room erupted in cheers and clapping.

After the noise died down, Lance began his speech. The almost three hundred persons assembled were all management from the company's eighty-five offices nationwide.

"The main purpose of this meeting is to go over some changes that will be taking place this year, changes that will hopefully, increase the profitability to our bottom line. These changes will be enacted at the store and employee level, and they will add profitability to our bottom line by providing us with some attractive tax incentives. Reduced taxes are obviously an attractive way for companies to retain more profits, so we are going to embrace these changes will the same full vigor and enthusiasm that we use for sales to new customers."

He paused and the audience clapped.

"Because of the products we sell, communications devices of every sort, we know that some of our customers have the ability and desire to use them for purposes not intended, and there are some customers that even while using the devices in the way that they are intended, are still using them for less-than-legal purposes. Since 9/11 the security of every company in the United States has been under attack by evil persons whose every waking moment and whose deepest desires are to disrupt and harm our people and our way of life. Now, while we are not in the business of war, or security, or law enforcement, we at Fischer Devices take seriously the unspoken pact we have with all God-fearing, true American patriots, and I sincerely hope and pray that every Fischer employee is a true American who wants to exemplify the true American spirit that this country was founded upon!"

The room broke out in raucous cheers.

"Every employee, each and every one of you should be dedicated to caring for your fellow employees, the company itself, and for the greatest country on earth, our country, the United States of America!"

More cheers erupted.

"There are going to be some changes made, and when you managers get back to your stores tomorrow, we will immediately implement these changes. Before I go over these changes in detail, I will say that this new initiative is going to be called, *Stars and Stripes and Fischer Devices 2017!*"

A round of applause resounded through the room.

"The aegis of this new program, *Stars and Stripes and Fischer Devices 2017*, is that we, Fischer Devices, is going to be proactive in Making America Great Again, and Safe Again. That's the new slogan too, *America: Great Again, and Safe Again!*"

This time the applause started and he stepped back and applauded along with the crowd as a banner with the new slogan unfurled on the wall behind him.

After almost two minutes of non-stop applause, he stepped back to the podium.

"How will we be doing this you're probably asking yourself now?

Well, here's how," he paused and took a sip from a bottled water on the podium, "All U S companies consisting of more than fifty employees are now partnering with a collection of agencies including but not limited to, OSHA, the IRS, Department of Homeland Security, NSA and several other agencies to help *Make America Safe Again* through a concentrated effort to reduce workplace violence, domestic terrorism and conspiracy and also, probable planned conspiracy and also what the agencies are calling *Planning of Imminent Conspiracy*, or *PIC*, and *Profiled Actionable Conspirator Theoretical*, or *PACT*."

He paused, "Obviously this is new to most of us, but we all know that since nine-eleven, the terrorists have been on an unending quest to harm our country, our way of life, and our very lives. We also know that workplace violence has gotten far out of control with disgruntled and violent workers acting dangerously towards co-workers because of hidden mental issues. We also know that there is no way we can peer into the future to see what a person will do, however, these agencies have banded together and are asking the American people to Help Make America Safe Again! Let's hear it for making America Safe Again!" he cheered and pumped his fist into the air and the employees assembled in the room dutifully aped his cheer.

"So, how does it work, you may be asking? How do we *Make*

America Safe Again? He yelled out the slogan again and pumped his fist in the air again, and once again, the employees screamed out the cheer.

A few of the managers in the room had puzzled looks on their faces, but they cheered anyway, knowing that they had better not appear as if they weren't going along.

"Okay, well, here is how it works. We have these new forms," he waved a piece of paper in the air, "and every manager will have a stack of them on his or her desk, and they will also be available on the internal company web site. The forms allow the employee to fill out the form anonymously and submit it to their manager, you guys and gals, and you will then send the form *not* to human resources, but to a *new* department that we have already formed and staffed. This group will be known as the *Group of Eight*, because there are eight of them in the company, one person in each district, and in turn, the *Group of Eight* will determine the severity of the offense and then submit the forms, along with their suggested punishment to the *Triad of Three* who will approve of that punishment, or suggest a lighter or heavier punishment for the offender.

Once the punishment has been approved, you managers will make a copy of what will be called The Action Report Page, or *TARP*, and once that's been sent to the HR department you will be free to dispense the punishment. You will not be required to wait for HR's approval for these punishments, once you file the TARP with HR, basically just emailing it to them, then you're done with them at that point. Now, these punishments are not only legal, but they are *required by law*. Now I'm not going to stand up here and quote actual law statutes and legal mumbo-jumbo to you, you'll just have to take my word on it, this is legal, and will be enforced, and as a matter of fact, if there is anyone in here right now who has a question about this, I heartily encourage you to raise your hand and make yourself known and we will erase your fears." He paused and looked out at his audience.

"*Anyone?*" he asked as he looked around. No one dared raised their hand.

He continued, "The punishments will range from a minimum of loss of vacation days with a three day loss being a minimum, or a loss salary, with a one day loss being a minimum. Also, a punishment could be loss of seniority standings in the company with a six month loss being a minimum, loss of break times and lunch hours, loss of parking privileges, loss of commissions for commissioned sales persons, loss of cafeteria access for those working in the larger offices, and there are thirty of forty more listed in the handouts we'll be giving you at the end of the meeting." He paused again to take a sip of water from his water bottle.

"Now, here's the fun part!" he grinned, "I sincerely hope, no, let me correct myself, I completely *expect* that most, if not all of you managers will be able to get creative and put your thinking caps on your noggins and email the *Group of Eight* some of your own suggestions for punishments. Does that sound like fun? Heck yeah it does because we're going to," he pumped his fist and screamed the slogan, *Make America Safe Again!*"

The assembled managers gave the yell in response, showing that they were on board.

"Does it sound scary, coming up with creative punishments for your co-workers and even knowing that some of these punishments, maybe even your own, could be used against you? NO! and do you know why it is NOT scary?" he yelled to the crowd, "Because, by doing it, we're doing what?"

The crowd answered his yell with their own, '*Making America Safe Again!*'

He nodded enthusiastically, "There you go, now you're getting with the program!"

"Now, chances are, as managers, we will not be needing policing as nearly as much as the rank and file, so I don't want anyone in here being nervous. Now, if you're doing something wrong, if you're thinking bad thoughts, then yes, you should be getting nervous!" he laughed and the audience, picking up the cue, laughed along with him, and the result sounded like over-laughing. People laughing too hard at a joke that wasn't amusing.

"So, we've talked about the punishments, now let's talk about the crime. The crime is what we all fear. Terrorism. Foreign or *home-grown*. I shouldn't have to say this, and it's bad to imagine, but imagine it we must. Your neighbors and best friends and co-workers can kill you just as easily as Jihad suicide bombers!. In fact, the FBI and Homeland Security tell us that we are *a thousand times more likely* to die in the workplace by *violence from people we know* than from any foreign terrorist! Think about that! When you get back to your offices, look at the people around you. Study them. Listen to them. *Profile them! 'it's for your own protection. We are trying to protect you from terrorists and other external and internal threats. Domestic terrorists have been wreaking havoc throughout our country and there is some evidence that foreign governments are supporting and funding them. "* He paused and pushed his black-rimmed glasses up his nose with his forefinger.

"Now I know that *profiling* has gotten a bad rap in the past few years, and law enforcement personnel all over the country have been trained to stop profiling, but guess what ladies and gentlemen? *We are not law enforcement!* If we want to profile in the private sector, we are free to do so! In fact, our law enforcement brethren in the aforementioned agencies who have put together this program for us to follow, and follow it we will you must have no doubts about that, . . . have told us that we are free to profile all we want."

"Therefore, we will *watch* our co-workers and employees. We will *take notes* when we hear *certain words* or *phrases* being uttered in the workplace. We will pay special attention when we hear an employee talk about guns, we will fill out the TARP sheets when we get the gut feeling that an employee is a pepper, a survivalist, someone who buys far too many groceries because they're stockpiling foods, we will note when we see men, or women, wearing the tactical pants with all the pockets, or who wears camouflage patterns. Who needs all those pockets? Who needs camouflage in an office environment? We will notice and take note of employees who sport bumper stickers touting second amendment rights, or product endorsements such as Glock and Ruger and Smith and Wesson. We will look closely at tattoos on our co-workers and engage them in discussions about what they represent. If we have anti-Americans among us they will be rooted out. Why? Because we want our workplace to be safe? And because we want to *what?*"

The crowd roared, '*Make America Safe Again!*'

"That's right. And you know what, people? We WILL *Make America Safe Again!*"

He paused again, and allowed the attendees to yell and make some noise to show their support and then he picked up the narrative again.

"I want you managers to understand something about this new initiative. This is not punitive. This new safety initiative helps us become a more profitable company for several reasons; number one, the company's insurance carrier will be receiving safety reports from us quarterly, and the absence of safety violations will raise our score, and also, the number of genuine TARP sheets that are generated will actually lower our insurance costs. Now that doesn't mean that I want you to falsify bogus TARP reports. If I ever see, or even suspect that a TARP report on an employee has been generated in a fictitious manner, you will be summarily fired on the spot, and you could face criminal prosecution for insurance fraud! But, I do want every manager to try to find a minimum of three events per week to come from your store personnel. What does that mean? It means that you'll need to listen to your employees, and you'll need to impress upon them the need to *listen to each other!* Let's face it, there are many people out there who have disturbing thoughts and ideas and if they start talking about them in the workplace, we need to know about it to protect ourselves and to also protect *you!*"

"We can't tell what someone is thinking, *however*, you can tell *what kind of person they are*, and by listening, and looking very carefully, you can probably *predict* that they might be considering violence or what I would call *un-American attitudes and action-potential*. These are the ones that you will want to write up TARP reports on.

"Now, a person who consistently displays anti-American sentiments, or shows aggression-expressions, or ventures anti-establishment opinions, or shows displeasure regarding American foreign policies, or expresses thoughts or opinions about a freer, less regulated society, these types are most often characterized as those most-likely to erupt into violence in the workplace and, or, against government agencies or personnel. These are the types that need to be carefully weeded out of our company, and in a general sense, out of our society totally."

"Another reason that this new initiative will help us become a more profitable company, is that, in addition to lowering our insurance rates, the IRS will be receiving reports from DHS and other agencies regarding our reporting procedures. If we hit our numbers, in other words, the number of TARP reports that we generate and the total number of personnel that we cull from the company as perceived possible violent offenders, is as high as the agencies think we should produce, we will receive generous tax abatements! That, obviously, adds profits to our bottom line! So, we can not only become a safer company, but at the same time we become safer we will become more profitable! That, ladies and gentlemen in the business world, is known as a win-win! All because we want to what?" He leaned forwards and cupped his hand behind his ear to egg the audience on to a louder cheer.

The crowd roared, '*Make America Safe Again!*'

He nodded, "Yes, that's right!"

He took another long drink of water, and waited patiently as one of his minions, an admin secretary of some sort walked over to him and pointed out something on a piece of paper and whispered into his ear,

He strode back to the podium and continued, "So, to recap what we've learned to day . . . we will *watch* and *listen* to our employees . . . we will *urge* our employees to *watch and listen to each other* . . . and we will *document* activities, moods, personalities, lifestyles and opinions and *perceived opinions* and *perceived possible actions* as often as possible. In other words, do you *think* that this person has the capacity for violence and un-American thoughts and actions, and if so you *will* take action so that that *threat* is removed and we will be a safer work place and a safer society. Remember, there are lots of bad people out there, and unfortunately we can't help but to have some of them in our workplaces among us and it is our *job* to *remove* them! Keep in mind that it is incumbent upon every manager to be diligent enough to report at least 3 behavioral or lifestyle or subversive activities or thought patterns per week, and not doing so will result in the manager being written up for their own *refusal to adhere to company policy*. Don't make anything up, no fictions allowed, but you should be perceptive enough to find these situations and people on your own, and if you don't, or can't, then that's a failure upon me for hiring the wrong person, and *I am not a failure!* Do not make me look foolish! I respect our government and our country enough to take this very seriously and as one of our valued employees I know that you will too! So, let's end this meeting with what our new mission is. So let me hear it loud and proud, what are we going to do?" he cupped his hand behind his ear again and leaned forward.

The crowd roared, *'Make America Safe Again!'*

One manager, Winston, in the back of the crowd looked around, wondering if anyone was looking at him being one of the few who neglected to cheer the ridiculous slogan. A man standing next to him gave him a look and winked at him. He leaned close in to Winston and whispered,

"Did we just get sent back in time to 1943 in Nazi Germany?" he chuckled.

Winston grinned, "Maybe we did. Sounds like we just lost a butt-load of rights, you know, free thought and all that?"

He nodded, "No kidding. You think our fearless leader there is one of those rabid Republicans?"

"No doubt."

The man whispered, "Friend of mine was saying that he felt that if the Republicans really had their way we'd all be losers. Coporatocracy he called it. Everything's okay as long as it's done in the name of profit. All sorts of human rights violations. Back to the sweat shops, or as the Republicans called them, *the good old days*."

Winston nodded, "Yeah well, we haven't really lost *all* of our rights, but if you want to know what rights you *do* have, you just need to check with your employer."

The man nodded, "Well, I don't have any rotten fruit to throw at this lunatic, so I'm leaving."

The man walked away and Winston looked back towards the front of the room.

Their CEO stepped out from behind the podium and walked to the edge of the stage to be closer to the crowd as it cheered. He raised both hands up into the air as if he were reaching for the clouds, hands open as if he was beseeching the heavens for rain, and the crowd responded.

The crowd roared again, loud enough to rattle the walls *'Make America Safe Again!'*

Winston looked at the company president and for a moment he pictured Hitler standing before the masses in Germany as he was being given the Heil Hitler salute.

Winston shook his head and turned and walked out of the meeting.

THE END

American corporations could care less about helping America succeed, despite their rhetoric to the contrary. Big business these days consists mostly of corporations staffed with rabid Republicans these days, and their overriding mission is to generate profit and nothing else. They're not interested in quality merchandise or creating jobs, or enhancing the lifestyle of the average American. Truth is, that most American companies have nothing but greed in their hearts and would sell out their employees and the planet itself, and indeed, their own souls if it would guarantee more bottom-line profit. Not only do most big corporations (along with many small and mid-size businesses) not care about the employees whatsoever, but if they could do completely without them, they would gladly do so. The typical business owner begins his business understanding that employees are vital and the company needs them to sell the product and allow the company to function, but the higher up the ladder the upper management and ownership rises, the more they look down upon the workers and the very people who are putting all of that profit into their pockets. They begin to act condescendingly at their employees, and then movie into a stage where they act as if they can barely tolerate them, and eventually they start actively disliking them and treating them with disdain and contempt, and then in the final stages of a company, the ownership and management will begin finding overt ways to mistreat them, in mental, physical, and then financial ways. This is why businesses thoroughly detest the unions, because they hate having their bluff called, and being forced to treat employees fairly.

Nowadays companies exist now exist solely for profit. When government policies, regulations and laws stand in the way of their profit making efforts, they simply find ways to purchase political goodwill in the form of favors through campaign donations. When employee's salaries or environmental issues of the planet stand in the way, they'll eliminate them because those issues inhibit growth. This system of oppression is why Americans have recently begun fighting back.

Congress is no help because it is so corrupted that they voted down creating over a quarter million jobs for teachers and first responders just so that they could protect millionaires from a paltry .05% tax increase.

America is being corrupted to a point of no return now by a corporatocracy where the 1% power elite dictates the policy for the remaining 99%.

Americans need to remove the corporate relationship from government through direct action and the voting booth. We must bring brave new leaders from within the workers movement. When the people lead, our leaders will have no other choice but to follow what the people truly dictate.

PART FIVE

Side Effects May Include . . .

Michael Bayer sat in the coffee shop drinking his first cup of coffee

for the day, and was updating the quarterly reports on his laptop. He had

two hours before the team meeting, and he knew that if he went in to the

office before the meeting started he'd get sidetracked on a hundred other

items, and he needed the final numbers for his presentation. It was

unseasonably warm for early spring in Fort Worth Texas, and the

temperature was predicted to hit almost ninety for the day.

After working for about forty-five minutes he began having problems

concentrating on his work, partially because he was feeling a bit under the

weather, probably because he had tossed and turned from about three a m

until his alarm went off at six a.m. He knew that it was probably stress,

because of this meeting and his presentation, but the company's' entire first

quarter had been stressful. Plus, he noticed that the woman sitting two

tables away was coughing almost every thirty seconds and it was irritating

the heck out of him. He considering walking over to her with an offer of a throat lozenge, which he had in his briefcase because his throat had been ticklish two days ago, but he figured if he did that she might cause a scene over his presumptiveness and he was not the type to remain unfazed by other people's rudeness or anger or ill-manners. He always got mumbly and embarrassed, turned red, apologized, and then felt shamed whenever anyone was passive-aggressive towards him, so he tried to shut her out of his mind and ignore her constant hacking. Maybe she wasn't sick, maybe she was a heavy smoker.

An hour later he was finished with the numbers and was beginning to construct the simple Power Point presentation to use to show the numbers. It would be extremely simple, just cut and paste onto slides, no fancy artwork, the numbers were what he wanted to show, not fancy presentation and artwork. He began to notice that the coughing was louder now, he could actually hear the woman over the music in his ears from the ear buds. Her coughing was actually louder than the music! He looked over at her and pulled out the ear buds. Her coughing was extreme and almost violent, as if she was about to cough up a lung. Then he realized that there were five or six other people in the coffee shop who were coughing just as loudly and violently as she was. He looked around and started counting the people coughing. There were probably forty persons in the coffee shop, and at least seventeen of them were coughing, loudly, violently, and their exhortations were making all of them bend over and their faces were reddened with the effort they were expending.

He wondered if there was some sort of flu going around. Whatever it was, the incessant hacking and coughing was loud and obnoxious and somewhat creepy. He decided that he didn't need whatever germs it was they were spreading around, and he began gathering up his laptop, mouse, cell phone and briefcase and headed for the door. As he got to the door and was leaving, he saw one of the customers clutch his stomach, and bend over and vomit all over the floor under his table. Then a woman did the same. Michael was glad that he was getting out of there. The last thing he wanted was to get sick. He couldn't afford it. This next quarter needed to be a big one and he needed as much of that quarterly bonus as he could scratch out, and being out sick wouldn't work for him, not even one missed day. In fact, he planned to work on his days off for the entire quarter, just to max out the bonus.

When he arrived at work and set up his presentation in the conference room he was surprised to see that several people were running late for the meeting. He had a strict rule about meetings, and it had been months since anyone had been late or a no-show. His people were reliable, prompt and attentive in his meetings, and this was a very important meeting.

He sat at the head of the conference table with eleven of the managers, and checked his watch every few minutes, and when the other fourteen managers were well over twenty minutes late, he picked up the phone and dialed the company receptionist.

"Levea? Has any of the other managers called in to say that they're running late because of traffic, or anything like that?"

"No sir, but I have a list of several that have called in sick, Ii was just about to bring the list in to you, there's so many-"

"A *list*? How many have called in?"

"Thirteen sir, and there have been six secretary's that came in this morning and have already gone home sick. I think there's some sort of flu or something that's going around."

"Okay, well, let me know if any of the others call in, this is an important meeting and we need to get started."

"Actually sir, I was just about to call you. I am not feeling well either," she paused and coughed, "and I'm going to go to the emergency room. If this is the flu, I want to go get a shot now and get it taken care of. I have called the temp service and they're sending someone over. Sorry, sir!"

Michael placed the phone back on the base and looked up at the managers gathered around the table,

"Apparently there's some sort of flu going around and some of the others have called in sick. So, we need to go ahead and get started."

One of the managers raised his hand, "Sir, actually, I'm going to have to leave too, I just got a text from my daughter's elementary school," he held up his cell phone and wagged it, "apparently this flu is so bad that they're closing the school for the day, and I have no way of getting a baby-sitter to go pick her up on such short notice, so I have to go get her and take her home and take care of her today. If she's okay tomorrow, I'll be in, and if not I'll try to line up a sitter." He nodded and stood up.

Michael sighed and waved him out of the room.

Just what he needed was a flu outbreak that seemed centered on his office.

As soon as he had the thought, one of the female managers pushed her chair back from the conference table and bent over at the waist and vomited on to the floor underneath the conference table.

Within two weeks, over fifty thousand people in the greater Dallas-Fort Worth area had been admitted to hospitals for the flu which was now officially being called an epidemic.

Within ninety days almost six million people worldwide had

succumbed to the mysterious illness and the CDC in Atlanta, and the WHO

had both issued dire predictions for mass casualties world-wide resulting

from the virus. Several African countries were off-limits to everyone except

medical personnel. The President issued a nationwide travel ban on U S

citizens for international travel, and all incoming flights from outside the U

S were forbidden. Parents were being urged to keep children indoors, and

Public Service Announcements were being run on TV and radio hourly,

encouraging companies to allow employees whenever possible to work

from home.

The virus was dubbed WEXXX 2019 and internet memes instantly

tagged it as World Ender and the conspiracy theorists began postulating

that whatever it was had been the brainchild of the Illuminati or the CIA, or

some sort of terrorist action, and some had even suggested that it was some

sort of eugenics experiment that had spiraled out of control.

The truth is though, that no one really knew what it was.

THE END

A quick look at Pandemics

542 AD: Mediterranean epidemic kills between 25-50% of the population of the Roman Empire. Emperor Justinian contracts the disease but survives.

1334-1347: Black Death devastates Europe, spread partly by Crusaders from Constantinople. Three-quarters of the population are killed.

1563: Bubonic plague in London. One-half to one-third of population die.

1665: The Great Plague of London. 20% of the population (100,000) die.

1729-30: Worldwide influenza pandemic. The first officially recorded 'pandemic' (an epidemic of worldwide proportions) in history. Originating in Russia, it spread to Europe and the United States.

1781: Worldwide influenza pandemic. Cited as among the worst in history, there were tens of millions of cases in Europe, North America, Spanish America and the West Indies.

1817-23: First global cholera pandemic. This highly virulent outbreak spread from India across all of Asia.

1829-51: Second cholera pandemic. Spread from Bengal, India to Europe, Japan and the United States. 33,000 deaths were recorded in one 24-hour period in Cairo and Alexander alone.

1852-59: Third cholera pandemic. Multiple sporadic eruptions of the disease killed thousands across the world.

1857-59: Worldwide influenza pandemic.

1863-79: Fourth cholera pandemic.

1881-96: Fifth cholera pandemic.

1889-90: 'Russian flu' pandemic. An estimated 250,000 die in Europe, three times that worldwide.

1899-1923: Sixth cholera pandemic.

1918: 'Spanish flu' pandemic. 20m-40m die worldwide, more than were killed in the first world war. The worst pandemic in history.

1957-1958: 'Asian flu' epidemic. Affects 10-35% of the world population, though with proportionally low mortality rates (100,000 killed).

1961-1970: Seventh cholera pandemic. Some argue that this pandemic is ongoing. In 1991, there were nearly 4,000 deaths in 16 countries in the Americas.

1968-69: 'Hong Kong' flu pandemic. Kills 700,000 worldwide.

About this book

This book is obviously a book of fiction scenarios regarding possible events. I do not claim to be a scientist, but rather a storyteller.

While I sincerely hope that none of these five scenarios ever plays out, my hope is that I have entertained you and caused you to *think* about precautions that could be, and I believe, should be taken in order to reduce your risk and increase your safety if one of these life-altering events should ever happen. There is plenty of information available on the internet about SHTF (Shit Hits the Fan) and TEOTWAWKI (The End Of The World As We Know It) scenarios, and WROL (Without Rule of Law), EROL (Excessive Rule of Law) and Color Of Law (Abuse of Law), as well as prepper and survivalist web sites and forums to seek out for information and guidance.

ABOUT THE AUTHOR

Doyle Sinclair lives in Plano Texas and is the author of three previous novels, and one non-fiction title. If you wish to contact the author about aby of his titles, he welcomes your feedback and comments and may be reached at **dwstxs1969@yahoo.com**.

All titles are available on Amazon in print and in e-format for Kindle and most other e-readers.

Blue-Eyed Son; Take a trip in the 60's and experience the adventures of a group of freewheeling hippies as they trek from San Francisco to Dallas, to Woodstock in 1969, and then back to the Northwest States. A coming-of-age story told through the eyes of David St. John as he grows from a young man in 1969 to a mature adult forty years later.

Over the Horizon; In 1937 Amelia Earhart and her navigator Fred Noonan attempted a circumnavigation flight around the globe and went missing in the Pacific Ocean. The story begins as Amelia and Fred are plunging towards the sea as their aircraft has run out of fuel. The last time they were heard from before they disappeared forever. Over the Horizon picks up where reality left off, with their last distress calls for help, and the story begins as they attempt to stay alive on an uninhabited island with no food, and only each other to cling to for their lives.

Deliver Unto Me The Innocents – A junior high school in the small East Texas town of Cottonwood, Texas is the scene of a brutal mass shooting by a crazed teen-ager. A mysterious hero arrives on the scene and manages to save hundreds of children's lives. Local police investigate, but are unable to find the reluctant hero. He is not who he seems to be. The local law enforcement officers and detectives all begin experiencing PTSD after having witnessed the brutality of the crime scene, and their investigation soon is hampered by their own inabilities to deal with the stresses they endured because of the event. Adding to stress and depression that hundreds of families city-wide are fighting after the mass killing, a young blonde pre-teen girl is abducted and the detectives must hunt for the kidnapper while dealing with their own mental issues.

MAPPS – Masterful And Profitable Powerwords for Sales - This sales manual gives sales pros a n adrenaline shot or power needed to help close sales and learn the fastest, most powerful way to interact with customers. Call it Jedi Mind Master Sales tricks, or the Akido martial arts of sales techniques, just use it and watch your sales closing percentages rise dramatically. Easy to use, and easy to understand.

www.ingramcontent.com/pod-product-compliance
Lightning Source LLC
Chambersburg PA
CBHW061308170626
46817CB00001B/96